saved *by the* salsa

a SULLIVAN'S CREEK *novel*

BARBARA BARRETT

Previously published by the Wild Rose Press

First Champagne Rose Edition, 2014

Republished January 2024 by Barbara Barrett

Paperback ISBN: 978-1-948532-70-9

Sullivan's Creek Series, Book One

Published in the United States of America

CHAPTER 1

"Coming, Lacey?" Senior architect Scott Dalton rushed ahead of Lacey Rogers into the soggy farmland while she still negotiated the gate. Good looks and charm might be oozing through the man, but patience definitely was not his strong suit.

"Any idea why we're here?" she asked, joining him.

The head of Mackenzie and Associates Architectural and Engineering, Cameron Mackenzie, had summoned both of them with little notice to leave their headquarters in Des Moines and ride with him out to the countryside west of town to view this property. So far, he'd been very close-mouthed about why he wanted them here.

Scott blew out a puff of air and cocked his head. "Client's a big shot from out of town. Don't know who. Guess the project's a residential development of some sort."

"Oh." Not much to go on. She thought he'd be better informed, since he was the firm's golden boy. Or was he holding back? Keep the new kid guessing?

"You were probably invited along on this wild goose chase since you've been earning a rep in single family homes."

This hotshot knew about her? She smiled to herself, and couldn't resist asking, "And your part?"

He drew a hand through his gorgeous black mane and rubbed the back of his neck. "I presume it's something major, which is why I've been brought in."

Ouch! She wasn't qualified to take on the big clients by herself yet? Probably true, but it still stung. At twenty-six, although she'd been with the firm only two years, she'd done well.

"Are you sure you want to go tramping around out there?" Lacey asked. "It looks pretty treacherous after last night's storm." She thanked her lucky stars she'd stashed a pair of jeans and hiking boots in her office. The sloppy field would have made short work of the suede shoes she'd been wearing earlier. Scott, on the other hand, appeared to have been caught off guard in the wardrobe department. Dressed in tan slacks, white shirt and designer loafers, which probably cost at least half her weekly paycheck, the muck would get him for sure. At least he'd had the sense to leave his navy blazer in the car.

Her question netted her a smoldering glower. She took a step back. "Uh …"

Then, as if a switch had been flipped, the glare decompressed into a warm, chocolate brown gaze. "If you don't think you're up to personally surveying the property, you can always stay here on the sidelines." His honeyed tone didn't disguise the taunt.

His attitude bordered on the insolent, reminding her of the sophomoric posturing of high school boys who challenged each other to ridiculous feats of stupidity just to prove their manhood. Best dispel any misconceptions he might be harboring about her not being up to the task right now. "I'm definitely ready. But I'm in hiking boots, you're wearing what appear to be expensive loafers. I was concerned about your ruining them."

He glanced down, most likely the first time he'd noticed his footwear, and grimaced. "Good point." He seemed to briefly consider his options, which boiled down to stay or go, then shrugged. "What the heck? They're only shoes. Let's go."

"I'd like to check out these site maps first. A little research never hurts."

"Waste of time. This is a site inspection, not a test."

"Don't you want to know what to anticipate?"

"I'm more a spontaneous kind of guy." He pivoted and set off.

"We won't have any reference points if we don't use these maps," she called to his fast-disappearing back.

He swiveled around, his dare-you-to-kiss-me lips fixed in a tolerant expression. "It's a field, Lacey, not a jungle. Fence, dirt, road, north, south. Not much more to take in."

"There's a lot more."

He tilted his head. "You must be under the impression we're here to actually gather information."

"But … but—" She had to stop gaping at the patch of dark hair where he'd unbuttoned his shirt. It was hindering her ability to form full words.

Sighing as if it pained him to discuss the subject further, he returned, placed a hand on her shoulder and gently twisted her toward the field.

Her shoulder burned from the contact.

"Somewhere back in Site Inspection 101 they probably laid out a laundry list of conditions to check. When the time comes to execute such list, if ever, I'm sure you'll shine. But not today."

"Why not?" *Get a grip! He's acting like you're an intern rather than a colleague. Don't let him get to you like that.*

"The boss is treating this property like his new toy. A cat with a cornered mouse. He likes to play at conquest before he comes in for the kill."

She moved away from the hand searing its way into her shoulder. "They never taught about bosses with new toys back in *Site Inspection 101.*"

He rolled his eyes, as if the effort to explain was costing too much energy. "He wants to show it off first. Get reactions from various people, in this case, us, while he's adjusting to the enormity of the project."

"He's afraid of new ventures?"

"On the contrary. Cameron Mackenzie lives to push the envelope."

She glanced at the maps and other documents she'd hauled along, debating if she could put off studying them until later. "If he's so anxious for our opinions, why isn't he out here with us?"

"Said he had a call to make and he'd join us as soon as he's finished. He's a master at keeping himself clean."

"That's why he's the boss and we're the foot soldiers."

His mouth crinkled into a wry smile. "Foot soldiers, huh? Good one. You've learned the first rule of the jungle. Keep a sense of humor."

Those twinkling, coffee brown eyes made her throat go dry. "Thanks for the vote of confidence."

He offered a mock salute. As he did, a strand of dark, wavy hair spilled over one eye. Her fingers itched to put it back in place, but not while this project, whatever it was, was underway. She needed to invest her energies staying one step ahead of him. At least keeping up.

"Take all the time you need with those maps, but this *foot soldier* can't wait."

So much for chitchat. He was off. Definitely didn't want any more to do with her than necessary. Arrogant know-it-all.

She returned to her papers. This could be her big chance to break away from the firm's pack of junior architects. Show everyone, particularly one Scott Dalton, that she could handle bigger projects. But which way? By relying on her research or modifying her usual fact-gathering tactics to fly with this eagle?

Out of the corner of her eye, she caught sight of Scott flailing his arms. Had he stumbled across something already?

"Getting messy." He shouted. "Nearly slipped. Stay over there on the side."

Right, Scott, like you'd be willing to share whatever you learn out there with me. Although well aware of his reputation, both as a top gun architect and a ladies' man, she wasn't sure about his sense of fair play. Not ready to bank on it, especially since her presence on this junket clearly irked him.

Why had she really been invited along on this expedition? Senior architects were usually loners. Surely not as Scott's assistant? She'd proven herself enough to warrant a larger role. But if her assignment turned out to be Girl Friday, could she go along with it? Probably could learn a few things from the guy, but not from the sidelines.

In for a penny … "Messy or not, I want to see as much as I can."

All six-foot-something of him stomped around, shaking mud off his shoes. When he stopped, his back to her, he raised a hand to shade the April morning sun from his eyes and his white shirt stretched tight over broad, buff shoulders. *Wow!* She had to remind herself she wasn't there to scout out the Dalton landscape.

Now or never. She gritted her teeth and plunged into the field, stepping gingerly through the morass. "How's it going?" she asked with studied nonchalance as she approached him.

Scott kept going, not waiting for her to catch up. Apparently it was now a race.

Moisture-kissed grass skimmed along the tops of her boots, but the ground was still firm. Encouraged, she sped up but kept her eyes planted on the ground, watching her step, just in case.

"Lacey!" Scott's voice sounded different than the last few times he'd prodded her. More anxious? She lifted her eyes to see what was bothering him only to discover…no Scott. Must have found the drop-off she'd seen on the maps.

She headed the direction of his voice, picking her way cautiously. Where had he gone? Surely she would have seen him climbing the other side by now?

"Lacey!" There it was again, his voice was now tinged with a note of panic.

Then she spotted him. At least the upper third of him, the rest was lodged under a huge, felled tree trunk about a hundred feet down the hill. Bits of mud and dead leaves peppered his gorgeous head of hair.

"Scott!"

The man needed help immediately, before the rest of him slipped under the trunk. What could she do?

"Don't come any farther. Find Cam." His breathing sounded labored.

No sign yet of their boss. Not enough time to summon him and get back to help Scott before he completely disappeared. Up to her to rescue the Great Dalton.

Thanks to the hiking boots, she managed to get halfway down the incline without mishap. Then her luck changed. She stepped on a wet, leafy branch which, like a slalom, sent her sailing down the rest of the hill directly toward the submerged architect.

"Oh! Oh, no!" That was all she could get out before she, too, made contact with the tree trunk and slipped under.

She landed with a thud, flat up against Scott.

"What the …"

The impact of her landing pushed him farther under the tree. She was almost completely under herself, except for her head and shoulders. One arm was free, but the other lodged against Scott, immobile. His face rested in her chest.

A sea of black mud fringed with green grass and weeds churned around them. The redolent smell was so overpowering it made her want to faint. She attempted to crawl out, but she couldn't move her legs, which, along with Scott's body, were wedged tight against the tree trunk. The bark cut into the backs of her legs through her slacks.

Lacey tried to grasp something with her free hand and pull herself out, but all she could reach were wet leaves and more mud. "Oh, Scott, I'm so sorry."

"Thought … you were … getting Cam."

"No time. Had to help you myself," she said to a wayward branch draped over the side of the tree.

She felt, rather than witnessed, his reaction as he shouted into her shirt. "Now we're both stuck."

The branch flipped out of the way before she could secure a grip. "Maybe not. If I can worm my way out of here."

"Push up with your feet."

She tried his suggestion.

"Ow! You mauled my shin!"

"Sorry!"

"Can that idea."

Had to find another way. "Okay. Let's try this. Are you able to move your arms?"

"A few inches, maybe," he replied. "Why?"

"Are you able to boost me up? Even a little? Then I can reach one of the branches."

Silence. Was he considering her idea or had he passed out from lack of air? "Scott?" Her voice cracked.

"What?"

"Thank goodness. I thought you'd lost consciousness."

"If only."

"So? Can you give me a boost?"

Again silence. "You don't seem to appreciate the geography down here," he said finally.

What was he getting at? All she was asking for was a little lift.

"Through no fault of its own, my hand is fast becoming intimately familiar with your rear end."

That wasn't a branch pinching her backside? Realization shot liquid heat through her lower portions. "Oh."

"Well?"

If they didn't proceed, the physical torture of their confinement would only increase. Did she dare allow his hand any closer to her private areas? She took a deep breath, which initiated a coughing fit from Scott. "Go ahead. We've got to get out of here."

She had to rethink her decision when a shock wave from the increased pressure of his hand on her derriere rolled through her body. Her insides ignited while she quivered with an excitement having nothing to do with impending liberation.

"Lacey? Did it work?" His voice grew even hoarser as his face became buried in her bare abdomen, where her shirt had pulled up.

Still couldn't reach the branch, and her boots now dug into what must be his thighs. "Just a little higher. I'm close but not there."

He breathed a one-word response into her stomach. Why couldn't he shut up? Every time he said something, his hot breath tickled and tantalized in tandem.

SCOTT DIDN'T KNOW how much longer he could keep his libido intact with Lacey's body sprawled over him. Parts of his own body had already rebelled and shown up ready for business.

Every time he tried to speak, he inhaled the scent of lilacs.

Who'd have thought this little blonde fluff ball could turn him on like this? Like he hadn't been with a woman in months. His body had never reacted so swiftly to one of his other lady friends. Just what he needed. Another female thinking she'd corralled him. Hell. That's exactly what she had done, though if she'd tried, she never could have intentionally pulled off a stunt like this.

"Scott, is that your cell phone I feel?"

"No."

"Darn! I thought maybe we could call Cam, if he ever … oh—"

She'd finally caught on.

"I, uh—"

"Don't squirm. Don't even move."

"Got it."

Great. Now she knew the state his body was in. Last thing he wanted her to figure out. Would she panic or take advantage of the situation?

Though various ideas flitted through his brain, none of them were escape plans. They were stuck here a while, literally, until Cam got bored and came looking for them. Then there'd be another kind of hell to pay. Cam would think he'd deliberately snared the junior architect into this prison. For once, he regretted his reputation as the office lothario.

Why hadn't he thought to change before making this trek? Even the novice had known enough to wear hiking boots. If he hadn't been wearing these new tasseled loafers, he might have stood a better chance of negotiating this hill. Instead, a couple steps on the slick ground and he'd sailed pell-mell down the side and right under this monster of a tree. Talk about your slippery slopes. Should have known better.

Where was his cell phone? Of course. He'd stuck it in his slacks pocket just before sailing out into the soggy field. "On second thought, I do have my cell on me," he told her abdomen.

"Great! Can you reach it?"

"Depends. Can you roll to the side so I can get to my back pants pocket?"

"I thought I wasn't to move."

"That was before I remembered about my phone."

No immediate reply. "Worth a try," she said finally.

The next thing he knew, she was rocking her pelvis in an attempt to dismount. "Not what I meant!" he screeched.

"Doesn't feel like I made much progress."

You made progress, all right. But not with the task at hand. She'd succeeded in finding yet a new way to torment him. "No luck," he gasped in between the deep breaths he forced himself to take.

Think of other things. Like this project, whatever it was. But he had zilch to go on since he'd accomplished exactly nothing since they'd arrived. Had she been more productive? She didn't have him worried. She was barely beyond neophyte status. But Cam's inviting her along today had him a tad concerned. Was he off his game, and this was Cam's way of propping him up? Was this why he hadn't been named principal yet?

What a ridiculous notion. He was the firm's superstar. Coated in mud and debris at the moment, but still Numero Uno.

"What on earth?" Cam's voice. Finally.

"Watch your step, Mr. Mackenzie," Lacey warned. "Slippery hillside. Did us in."

"Both of you?" He sounded incredulous. But Scott preferred incredulous to incensed or mocking.

"Crazy, huh?" Lacey said.

Bless her naïveté. She didn't have the slightest idea by speaking first she was deflecting Cam's wrath.

"Had to see it to believe it," Cam said. "How'd you both land there? There's hardly any space beneath the trunk."

None anymore.

Scott took a stab at explaining the two-phase catastrophe. Finished, he prepared for the laughing and guffaws. He could picture Cam describing their predicament at the next meeting of the senior staff.

"Whew! Almost fell down myself." Cam's voice grew nearer, apparently he'd made it down the hill without incident. "Besides bringing in a crane, any ideas how I get you out?" The man barely cleared five-eight and was twenty pounds overweight.

Yet again, Lacey beat him to the punch. "Do you see anything you can anchor yourself to so you can pull us out without slipping?"

Cam didn't respond immediately. Probably looking around the site.

"If I had a crowbar, I might be able to pry the tree away from you, let gravity send it farther down the hill."

More silence.

"Mr. Mackenzie, are you still there?" Lacey called out.

"Yeah. Trying to dislodge a limb."

Scott expected a tree part to jab him any minute, but instead, Lacey's body was dragged out and over him. Though relieved to have her freed up, getting her there cost him. He was sweating profusely by the time Cam returned to him.

"Easier than I thought," Cam said breathlessly. "All it took … was getting a grip under her arms … and heaving."

"She's okay?"

"Yeah, she's fine. Forgot what a little thing she is. Though a hernia may still be in my future."

"Can you give me a hand now?"

"You hurt?"

"Just my dignity."

"Then grab hold of this limb. Use it to worm your way up until I can get a better grip on you."

"I'm in enough dirt and organic matter down here to feel like the worm itself."

After several frustrating minutes and gouging of hands on the rough bark, Scott finally dragged himself free. He collapsed on the side of the hill, panting, trying to catch his breath. Five feet away, Lacey also stretched out. Other than her muddy and grass-stained jeans, she didn't look worse for wear, thank God. Foolish woman, thinking she could rescue him.

He hadn't fared as well. What he could see of the back of his slacks was dark brown with drying mud and other yuck, but bloodstains colored both sleeves of his previously white shirt.

Cam knelt next to him. "Better?"

"I can breathe again. Nothing appears to be broken, although my ego took a bruising."

Cam's mouth twitched, fighting back a smile. "I'm sure you'll heal." He turned to Lacey. "How are you doing, young lady? Probably not what you had in mind for this little outing."

Lacey came to her knees cautiously. "A little wobbly." As she ran her fingers through an errant strand of hair covering her face, she managed to smear more mud across it.

Both men exchanged looks. "Your cue," Scott told Cam. "My handkerchief's in my jacket back in the car."

Cam obliged, wiping away the smudge covering one of Lacey's cheeks.

"Huh, oh, thanks, Mr. Mackenzie."

"Considering the circumstances, how about you start calling me Cam?"

She offered a shy smile. "Okay, thanks … Cam."

Cam sat back on his haunches and looked from one to the other. "Okay, heroics over. You both survived. Send your cleaning bills to the firm for reimbursement." Pregnant pause. "What do you think of the place?" he said like a teenage boy showing off his first car.

CHAPTER 2

Did Cam really want to know what he thought of this property? Scott wasn't sure. Was his role today that of Yes Man or did his boss want his honest, professional opinion?

Before he could formulate a response, Lacey cut in. "It's charming." She surveyed the area around them, eyes gleaming. "Great possibilities."

Great possibilities? What possibilities had she identified from her position under the infamous tree trunk?

Cam warmed to the subject and offered her an expectant smile. "Tell me more." Despite the mushy conditions, he settled himself on the ground next to Lacey, ankles crossed over his knees.

Scott held his tongue. Not particularly crazy about the attention Cam was paying her.

Lacey hesitated, appearing to gather her thoughts. "Well, like I said, it has great possibilities—"

Cam leaned closer. "Yes? Like?"

"Uh, for one thing, the lay of the land. Gently rolling, with maybe a few exceptions." She patted the ground. "But not flat and boring either."

"Uh-huh. You agree, Scott?" Cam asked without looking at him.

Scott examined his fingernails, seeking the appropriate response. He wasn't one to hedge when bad news had to be delivered, but with Cam's enthusiasm for the place becoming more obvious, it would have to be dispensed in small doses. "One thing's for sure. This is a lot of land, Cam. Enough for a small town."

Cam slapped his thigh. "Brilliant thought." He held up his hands as if framing a sign. "Mackenzie Junction or Cameron City or—"

"Whoa, hold on. That town-building part was an idle comment. A little Dalton humor."

"Don't sell yourself short, man," Cam replied. "I like how you think. A few urban elements couldn't hurt."

"We're architects, not developers, Cam. Naming this place is your client's task." Scott swatted away a clump of matted grass stuck to his pants leg. "Which brings us to the question of the hour: who is our client anyhow? And what are we building?"

Lacey apparently was just as curious. She'd been fingering her hair, flicking out pieces of grass and dirt, but stilled at his question.

Instead of responding, Cam turned his attention to a clod of loose dirt in front of him, appearing not to have heard Scott's question.

"Cam? Who is our client? What's the scoop?" Scott asked again.

Cam rose. "I have some other business to attend to once we're back in town. Let's reconvene first thing tomorrow morning and talk over where we go from here."

Scott rolled his eyes. This was not going well. Not well at all. He wanted to be named principal by the time he was thirty, now a mere six months away. His next assignment had to clinch the deal. But there was no way he was going to compete for it with Miss Great Possibilities. The very thought was insulting, although a tiny doubt digging its way into his brain since they'd arrived refused to go away. Had he lost his spark and didn't know it?

His cohort prattled on, while his blood pressure continued to rise. "For our meeting tomorrow morning? It would help if we knew a little about what the client has in mind."

Scott wanted to know too.

Cam returned to kicking the dirt in front of him, avoiding eye contact with both. "Thought I'd give you a chance to sleep on your impressions before going into more detail. But since you both seem so anxious to hear about it now—"

"Tell us what you have in mind," Scott said. A boom was about to be lowered, and the sooner he knew which way to duck, the better.

Cam appeared to consider Scott's demand, then exhaled at length. "Okay, why not?" He pulled at the collar of his sport shirt, then eyed them both. "Our client wants to build a retirement compound for baby boomers. Hasn't specified anything else, other than it be green and environmentally sustainable. Our job is to come up with a world-class design concept prior to getting master planners involved. Since he's reasonably well known—and I use the pronoun to mean either a man or a woman, because I'm not to reveal even the client's gender—and has ties to the community, he wants to remain anonymous. Probably a bit over the top, but I want this project for the firm. We're receiving a hefty fee in return for catering to our client's eccentricity."

Scott couldn't restrain himself. "*Eccentricity*? Cam, this simply isn't done. There's too much at stake with a project this size not to know more about who we're dealing with."

"Point taken, Scott. But I've done my due diligence. Everything's legit. Since this is my call, you'll just have to go along with me."

Scott shook his head. Sounded suspicious, but once Cam dug in his heels, Scott knew better than to challenge his boss until Cam admitted his own folly. "Okay, I've said my piece. But keep an open eye, Cam."

"Always do. I've tentatively named our work Project Arabella."

"Project Arabella?" Scott had once dated a woman named Arabella. Ended poorly, which didn't bode well for this new assignment.

"It needed an innocuous title. So I picked my late mother's name. It's gonna be so big, we don't want anyone to pick up on it too soon, or suppliers and subcontractors will immediately jack up their prices. Which is why I remained behind in the car."

How big of you.

"Lacey, you're fast making a name for yourself designing single-family residences," Cam continued. "And Scott, you could charm the flute player into the cobra's nest. We need your people skills. I thought

I'd double our chances of gaining his business by bringing you both in on the deal."

"Double our chances?" Scott smelled a rat. "Since when do we put so many resources into one project?"

"Since the fees to be realized from it are way beyond anything we've done to date."

"We're going to give him two choices?" Lacey's naiveté appeared to know no bounds.

Scott was pretty sure he knew the answer to her question but wanted Cam to confirm his suspicion.

Cam cleared his throat. "Uh, not exactly."

"Not exactly?" Scott pursued, knowing what was coming, like he couldn't tear his eyes from an impending disaster.

"The client may be a bit eccentric, but he's still expecting us to pitch our best shot, not a shopping list of ideas."

Scott pounced. "So, it is a competition!"

"Sort of."

Scott's vision blurred. Better judgment told him to cool it, wait for an opportunity when they were alone to talk his boss out of this insane idea, but the anger roiling inside him like a disturbed rattler couldn't leave it alone. "Dammit! I shouldn't have to prove myself at this point in my career. Especially when the contest involves a relative newcomer."

Cam reached over and touched Scott's sleeve. "Calm down, Scott. What's gotten into you?"

"Clue in this *relative newcomer* too," Lacey added.

Now she was demanding equal footing? The last shred of Scott's good sense evaporated. "Stay out of this, Lacey. For a beginner, you should be grateful just to be here."

Her eyes narrowed, her expression hardened. Jumping to her feet, she planted herself less than a foot from Scott and fisted her hands. "Beginner! I've got some pretty great projects on my resume, you … you … prima donna!"

He once again inhaled the faint scent of lilacs before his male ego took over. "Prima donna? You're just jealous because I get the high-profile jobs and you have to settle for—"

Cam edged between them. "Scott, Lacey, let's not get carried away. The idea was to have the best from both of you to choose from, not to have you at each other's throats."

Scott glared back at his boss. "Competitions are not collaborations. When the prize is this big, they're outright warfare."

Cam offered a fatuous smile. "Not my intent. C'mon you two, get your egos in check. Act like grownups and shake hands. I've got to get back to town."

"If she's so fired up to make her name on this job, let her have it." Scott regretted the statement immediately, but the words had already escaped.

Lacey eyed him like she wasn't sure what he was up to but suspected his motives. "I don't take hand-me-downs, even if I do want the challenge. I'm out of it too, Cam."

"Just a damned minute, you two!" Their boss drew himself up to his full height, his previously placating expression gone. "You don't make those decisions. I do. Just because I gave you a little inside information on this deal, neither of you is in a position to decide how we're going to tackle it."

Scott rose too. The three of them formed a triangle, each with hands on hips. No one spoke, heavy, irritated breathing was the only sound.

Finally, Cam broke the stand-off. "Okay, kiddies. Here's what I'm going to do. You don't want to compete against each other? Fine. You are now a team. Pool your best ideas and come up with one plan between you."

Cam kicked a clump of mud out of his way and stomped off to the car. Twenty feet away, he did a quick one-eighty. "Bus is leaving, folks. Who's going back with me?"

Scott shook his head at Lacey in frustration. "Great, just great. See what you did?" He was as much to blame, if not more, for this turn of events, but he couldn't get past his resentment of the woman.

"Me?" Her blue eyes sizzled like glowing sapphires. "You're the one who doesn't play well with others. You backed me into a corner and I came out swinging."

Had to hand it to her. She hadn't capitulated, not even knowing she was standing up to the firm's wonder boy. He brushed dried mud from his sleeves."

"You're bleeding. Did I do that?" Her tone suddenly morphed from warrior princess to concerned partner.

Should let her think she was responsible for whatever cuts and abrasions he'd sustained. Maybe she'd be sympathetic enough to back away from this project. Damn. Why did he still have principles? "The tree beat you to it. Just a few scrapes. Sorry. This whole morning has been a bad dream. I took out some of my irritation on you."

"Some? Remind me to leave town when you're really in a bad mood."

"Yeah, well, I thought I could talk him out of this ridiculous project."

"Good job. Now you've made it impossible for him to drop it and roped me into the fray to boot."

"You forged into the fray under your own power, lady. What were you thinking when you told him this place had great possibilities?"

She raised her shoulders and cleared her throat. "It does. Look around. Doesn't it seem peaceful? Just the place for a retirement home."

"Homes! This is to be a development, not an institution."

She blinked, spilling more blueness his direction. "Okay! What's your problem, Scott? You obviously resent my presence on this project. What have I done to offend you?"

She'd picked up on his frustration? "I don't have anything against you personally. I'm not used to working with a partner."

She studied him. "Some revelation."

"No, really. I served as assistant on the first few projects I was assigned to years ago, but since then, I've soloed. You were right. I don't *play well with others*. Hasn't been a job requirement in years."

She continued to stare at him, as if looking through him. Made him want to pull at his collar like a witness under cross-examination.

"Nothing personal?"

As long as you don't set your sights on my job, lady. "Yeah, although I disagree about this place. It's shot through with problems, which I still intend to bring to Cam's attention. Once he's calmed down."

"Fair enough. What do you—" The honking of the car interrupted her question.

Scott looked over her shoulder toward the road. "Later. Right now, the driver's a man possessed."

LACEY KEPT her own counsel during the ride back to town, deciding it was the better part of discretion. She had a lot to think about. It had been quite a morning. She'd been assigned to the biggest project she'd ever encountered, she was now on a first name basis with her boss and she'd mixed it up with the firm's superstar and survived.

She'd also mixed it up with him in other ways, when they were trapped under the tree. Every so often, she'd remember how her body had detonated while pinned there so near him. Working with him was definitely going to be a challenge.

Cam apparently couldn't take the silence. "How 'bout some music?" He pushed a button. The song throbbed with a heady Latin beat. Cam leaned over to change it.

"Would you mind leaving it on, Mr ... Cam? That's a favorite of mine," Lacey said.

Cam shrugged. "You like Latin music? This is Salsa, isn't it?"

"One of the group's best."

"You into the stuff?"

"I've been known to frequent a few of the Salsa clubs around town."

"Well, well." He stole a quick glance at Scott, seated next to him. "If I recall correctly from our last Christmas party, Mr. Dalton here is also a Salsa aficionado."

"Really?" She tried to keep her surprise out of her voice. Though his dark hair and eyes qualified him for the Latin part, she wouldn't have pictured him as a fan of Marc Anthony.

"Um," he returned.

"Oh, c'mon, Scott. Answer the lady."

A deep sigh emanated from the seat in front of her. "Yes, I do a little Salsa," he said, grumbling.

Cam reached over and nudged Scott's forearm. "See, wasn't so difficult. I'm glad you've decided to make nice again. Besides the project, you and Lacey have this dance in common."

Scott stared at the car's ceiling. Then he turned to Cam. "If I promise to remain civil, will you hear me out about this project?"

"Scott, Scott, Scott. You disappoint me. I thought we agreed you'd drop your concerns?"

Scott spoke to her over his shoulder. "Concert's over. I need for Cam to hear this."

"Go ahead." Maybe Scott had seen something she hadn't, although she doubted it. He'd barely had a chance to look around before he'd dive-bombed the tree.

Scott swiveled in his seat so Lacey could hear him as well. "I can't do anything about the clients you do business with, Cam, nor who you assign to projects. But I'd be neglecting my professional responsibilities if I didn't advise you about the liabilities surrounding the site we just viewed."

This was a different Scott. This Scott sounded logical, knowledgeable and concerned. This one she should maybe listen to.

Cam didn't say anything at first. He continued driving, eyes plastered straight ahead. Finally, in a lower voice, he said, "Okay, I'll humor you. Clue me in."

Scott began by saying, "Bringing us out here for a private looksee the day after a major spring storm didn't help with first impressions."

"Touché. Tell me about your concerns."

"Here's my take on the place. It's beautiful, yes. The rolling hills may cause a few problems, but all in all, they'll add to the charm. The place is also tranquil, which I presume retirees are seeking."

Cam seized upon his words. "See! Just what I thought."

Scott held up a hand. "Hold on. There's more. Excuse the pun, considering our recent mishap, it's all downhill from here."

Cam scowled.

"The location isn't practical. The suppliers and subcontractors will charge a fortune for mileage alone."

"Manageable."

Scott's hand came up again. "Still not finished. There's a stream cutting through the place—it may threaten flooding of the low-lying areas unless we spend extra on hydraulic evaluation. I didn't like the percolation of the land in some places following last night's rain either."

Why hadn't she noticed those problems? She'd been the one studying the maps. All Scott had done was fall down the hill.

"Fixable?" Cam's tone had grown quiet.

Scott shrugged. "Almost anything can be fixed, if you throw enough money at it. Are our client's pockets deep enough?"

Cam fell silent. A mile of countryside flew by before he replied. "I don't think money's an issue with this client. I know he's good for it. But—"

"Yes?" Both Lacey and Scott chimed in at once.

"He's more concerned about time. At least this conceptual phase. As soon as we lock down a design concept, the master planners and engineers can do their thing with layout—plats, individual sites, infrastructure, that stuff. I'd like to see our firm take up master planning one of these days. This project might give us entrée into that world."

"You said he's concerned about time. What's his timeline?" a skeptical Scott asked.

"One month."

"What!" Scott nearly ripped off his seat belt. "We usually have at least double that time, and for big projects like this, maybe even six months. What's the rush?"

"The guy's got a bee in his bonnet," Cam said. "He's slated to be in town in about four weeks, so he said to have something ready to present to him by then. Besides, this is merely the design concept. We don't have to put specific plans together so much as suggest a thematic approach to the project and provide some sketches and diagrams to illustrate our motif."

"He doesn't have to be here to approve whatever we come up with," Lacey pointed out. "On several occasions I've used delivery companies to send plans to clients."

"True," Cam conceded. "But since he'll be in town, he wants an in-person meet."

"But a month," she said, trying not to come off too negative. "That hardly gives us any time to do preliminary research before we develop the concept."

"Research, Lacey?" Cam asked.

"Well, yes. I've never done a retirement complex before, let alone dealt with baby boomers. My search engines and I need some time together."

"Yeah, sure." Cam didn't sound particularly sincere. "Just make sure we're ready to go in a month." One month. What had she gotten herself into?

BACK IN HIS OFFICE, Scott wondered the same thing, but for different reasons. He now had a partner and a new project plus the added disadvantage of an unknown client. To top it off, they had the accelerated due date to finish their plans. Only one month. Insanity.

He could cope with just about anything for a month. Except working with Lacey Rogers. He hadn't been prepared for the effect she'd had on him. Professionally, she was going to drive him nuts with her obsession for data. She'd even scared the Bejesus out of Cam when she talked research, but the boss had played it cool and encouraged—encouraged—her to carry on.

But professionally he could put up with her. Of course, he'd have to stock up on headache tablets and check a few books out of the firm's library to make it appear he was doing his part. But the woman herself was going to kill him. Her mere presence while they were imprisoned under the tree trunk nearly did him in. His body had reacted as if it were one of Pavlov's dogs and she was a doggie treat.

Damn! Just thinking about her now made him go hard. How was he going to deal with being around her constantly for the next four weeks?

He didn't need this in his life. He might have a reputation as a ladies' man around the office, hell, he'd even stoked the fires to make it seem real, but the image was purely for show. To enhance his superstar persona. He'd learned a long time ago to steer away from office romances when a female colleague he'd been seeing "borrowed" some of his designs for one of her own projects. These days, he needed to keep everyone focused on what a great architect he was.

He was going to be named principal … soon. Had to be. Maybe then his parents would sit up and notice.

His phone rang. His mother. She called so rarely. How'd she know he'd been thinking of her and Dad? Could she now read minds along with all her other achievements? This day just kept getting better.

"Darling! I know you're going to be disappointed, but your dad and I won't be able to make it back for Cam's birthday party."

Birthday party? Oh, hell, he'd completely forgotten about the event later in the week. "Didn't know you were planning to be here."

"No? I thought I'd sent you word through Cam."

Cam. Their long-term friendship with his boss continued to trouble him. Though he worked like a dog to prove himself, his performance didn't matter, if his job depended more on the good will between his parents and his boss. "Uh, no. Cam didn't mention anything."

"Maybe I called and left you a message. When were we last in town?"

"A while back. You were going to come for the Halifax Plaza opening a few months ago, but—"

" … your father wound up in the senior amateur tennis finals at the resort we were visiting. Now I remember. What was going on?"

"Halifax Plaza. My last project. The biggest yet."

"Right. So sorry we had to miss it. But I'm sure there'll be many more in your career. Cam tells me you're quite a help to him."

"Yeah, in fact I just received a new assign—"

"Must fly, dear. Give Cam our regards. We plan to be back in town sometime in the next few weeks. See you then."

The click on the other end of the line wasn't just the end of their phone conversation. It was a reminder of his relationship with his parents—detached and conducted on the fly.

He blew out a long, audible sigh as he continued to stare at the phone. Just once, he'd like to see some interest on their part about his life, but he was damned if he would give them what they really wanted: a daughter-in-law, which was all they talked about during their infrequent visits. Forget it. He didn't have the time or mental energy to dwell on their parental inadequacies. He had a more pressing problem at the moment, surviving four weeks of Lacey Rogers.

Why was Cam so fired up to involve her in this project? Did the guy think he needed a partner? The competition thing was a ruse. Cam knew exactly what buttons to push with both his ego and Lacey's and had played quite a tune putting them together.

Scott leaned on his desk, head between his palms. What was he going to do?

One of his drawing pads lay in front of him. He flipped back the cover, picked up a pen, and started to sketch, a habit since his teen years. Whenever his parents' lack of attention got to him, or he'd pulled a low grade on a test, he'd found solace in his drawings.

Before he knew it, he'd drawn the hillside where he'd plunged to his humiliation. He held the picture away from him to get a better view. Not bad. Almost total recall.

Left to his own imagination, what kind of boomer retirement community would he conceive? He took a couple stabs at producing one. Not very exciting. Stale. Must be his present mood. He needed inspiration.

Inspiration, huh? Like finishing the design concept before the novice input her first page? She wouldn't be happy. Right! As testy as she'd been when he'd tried to pull her away from her precious site maps, she'd be furious if he had a full plan done before she was ready to start. What would she do if she got upset? Go to Cam for support? Doubtful. She was too busy proving she could best the Great Scott Dalton. Quit the project? A possibility. One worth pursuing.

A slim shred of hope kept him drawing for a couple more hours.

About seven, he rolled his shoulders to stretch, a sense of calm streaming through him. Oh, yeah. He'd struck gold. Maybe not with this design concept, but the idea he'd produced it independent of any input from her would send Lacey into a tailspin, possibly never to return to Earth again.

CHAPTER 3

After her encounter with the underside of a tree trunk, it would have been so comforting to spend the evening with a microwave dinner watching television from bed. But it was Wednesday. Wednesdays Lacey played cards with her brother, Brian, his girlfriend, Celia Fairchild, and Brian's next-door neighbor, Ken Harper. Wednesdays were sacred.

She was already five minutes behind schedule. Her punctual brother was sure to be agitated. But she'd had to stop at the supermarket close to her office for cherry cheesecake, her usual contribution to the festivities, and had found the bakery shelves empty. Go figure. She'd had to wait for them to find more naked cakes in the freezer and apply the cherry topping. "Sorry, I'm late," she called as she sailed into Brian's living room.

Brian emerged from the kitchen. "Not a problem tonight."

"Where's Celia and Ken?"

"They won't be joining us," Brian said, his voice barely audible.

Great, a reprieve. "Wish you'd called before I fought the crowd at Dill's to get this cheesecake."

"I told Ken not to come, but I wanted to tell you this in person. Celia and I are no longer seeing each other. She's been hinting she wants a permanent relationship. As much as I care for her, I'm not ready." Lacey's stomach lurched like she'd consumed some of the mud encasing her earlier in the day. She gaped at him, attempting to collect her thoughts. Celia Fairchild was not only Brian's girlfriend—ex-girl-friend now—she was also Lacey's best friend and the office manager at Mackenzie and Associates. Lacey assumed someday they'd be sisters-in-law. She'd fantasized about Brian and Celia's babies. She'd be Aunt Lacey, the closest she'd allow herself to a family of her own. Brian's news meant there would be no nieces and nephews in her future. Despite her concern for her brother and friend, she felt cheated.

"Well, say something."

She collapsed onto the sofa, at the last second remembering the cheesecake and placing it on the coffee table in front of her before it fell on Brian's pristine carpet. "What happened?"

Brian settled beside her, his face wrinkling like an overripe grape. He hunched forward, folded his hands together. "Celia isn't one for confrontation. But she's not above hinting. Or making assumptions about the two of us."

"That's what couples do."

He shot her a sardonic look. "Like buying a condo together?"

"Whoa! When?"

"A few weeks back. Came as a complete surprise to me when she informed me she'd made an appointment to see the place. I must not have appeared enthusiastic enough during the tour. Afterwards, she called me on it, so I let her have it. She went all weepy and started questioning how things stood between us."

Of course Celia was pushing for marriage. She and Brian had been dating for close to two years. "Don't you want to settle down?"

He pulled at his collar as if it were shutting off his air supply. "Maybe. Someday."

"Someday? You're almost thirty-two. How many oats do you have left to sow?"

He bristled. "At least I've been seeing someone. You flit from one relationship to another."

"Suits me just fine. Better than getting left at the altar again."

"Alex called it quits years ago. Time to get on with your life and start trusting men again."

It still alarmed and mortified her how, during her sophomore year of college, she'd so readily given her heart and body to the law school student who'd convinced her she was ready for marriage. Ever since their mother's death five years earlier, Brian had taken his role of surrogate parent very seriously. Though she'd needed the stability at the time, by the ripe old age of nineteen, she'd wanted her independence, whether she could handle it or not.

Then Alex announced his plans for her to quit school and work full time to support him during his last two years of law school. She'd been fool enough to think she could appease him by working part-time while still going to school. He'd supposedly gone along with her plan. Then a month from their wedding date, Alex broke off the engagement. Two months later, he was engaged to a senior, who apparently had no problem dropping out of school just months from her own graduation to support her new husband's schooling. They were married six months later and divorced two years following.

Though Alex's rejection hurt and humiliated Lacey, she blamed herself for making such a foolish choice. She suspected she carried the loser-in-love gene just like her unfortunate mother, whose spouse abandoned her. Unlike her mother, though, she'd been fortunate enough to discover her mistake before saying her vows. Couldn't subject herself to such heartache and disappointment again. Recovery had been too painful and too long coming. These days, she kept her social life light and uncomplicated. Her looks, not-so-bad body and reputation for no commitments kept the men flocking to her. Just the way she liked it—flings with no strings.

Darn! Brian had almost gotten her off track, making her remember Alex. "We're talking about your love life, not mine."

"There's no point beating this subject to death. Celia and I are through. I want her to move on. Find someone who'll give her the type of life she craves. A house and children."

"So now what?" Lacey tried not to think about her own regret. She'd been looking forward to having Celia in the family.

Shrugging, he patted her knee. "Guess your brother will have more time to spend with you. While Celia looks for the father of her children."

With no card game, it would have been such a relief to seek the comfort of her own apartment and pig out on her half of the cheesecake while she absorbed Brian's news. But Lacey chose instead to stop off at Celia's townhouse and hear her side of the story.

She knocked on Celia's door, not knowing what to expect. Anger? Tears? Accusations? She wasn't prepared for a sweaty, panting thirty-year-old woman garbed in a pink sweat suit. It shocked her to learn Celia even did perspire.

Towering over Lacey by several inches, Celia leaned against the doorjamb, wiping her neck with a delicate white towel embroidered with tiny pink flowers. "Lacey? No cards tonight? I thought Brian would have arranged for my replacement as swiftly as he disposed of me. I take it he shared his *news* with you?"

Lacey invited herself in and plopped on Celia's pale pink chintz-covered couch. Celia followed her into the room but avoided taking a seat.

"What's with the outfit?"

Her friend checked out her top and pants, then toweled away more perspiration on her forehead. "Working out. Just bought an exercise bike. Thought I'd get in shape before joining a club."

"A fitness club? You?" This was clearly not the Celia Lacey knew.

"Yes, me." A defensive air edged the response.

Realizing she'd inadvertently miffed her friend, Lacey attempted to undo her previous question. "Doesn't hurt to stay in condition. But I've never seen a spare inch of fat on you."

"Thanks. I've been fortunate with my weight, but lately I've been feeling a little worn down. Need to get back in shape."

"The *down* part. Brian's fault?"

"We had a very heated discussion the other night. A fight, actually. A rarity for us. Brian thought I'd taken too much for granted concerning how things were going between us and called things off."

"Just like that?"

"Just like that. I had no idea it was coming, although in retrospect, I think he may have been considering his decision for some time. Our misunderstanding about moving in together was all the excuse he needed."

So far, Celia's explanation more or less mirrored Brian's. Still, it didn't make sense.

"It's all so … unexpected. I thought things were going well between you two. So, give, girl. What's the story?"

Celia shrugged hopelessly. "I wish I knew. Obviously, he's not ready for a deeper commitment than steady dating. Living together, and—God forbid—marriage, aren't in his orbit yet. If ever."

"I didn't realize he was so commitment-shy," Celia said, straightening the cuff of her sweatshirt. "Maybe it's been there all along and I chose not to notice. We didn't socialize much with married couples. There always seemed to be a reason why he couldn't accompany me to friends' weddings. But I never put two and two together."

Come to think of it, Lacey had observed some of the same signs over the years. Their mother was an only child and their father's family lived on the East Coast, so there'd never been other relatives around. No family models to influence either one of them. Lacey had always envied the people with families, seeing them as living fuller, more fun-filled lives than her. But as much as she wanted a family of her own, her track record with the men in her life, the father who'd abandoned the family when she was six and Alex, the fiancé who jilted her, kept her from believing she'd ever find a man she could trust to stay in her life. Which was why she put so much stock in Brian and Celia giving her a family. Probably what had lured her to specialize in single-family dwellings.

"What am I going to do, Lacey?" Celia cried, the strain clearly coming through in her tone. "I love him so much. I could kick myself for pushing him too soon. I thought he needed me to make a statement about my feelings before he'd commit. That's why I dragged him out to see those new condominiums in West Des Moines."

"Brian loves you, Cee. I can't believe he would permanently walk away from someone he cares so much about. You've got to be patient and give him time to figure out you're what he needs."

Celia turned wide, panicked eyes on her. "I can't wait forever! Besides, Brian won't let this float. He's bound to take steps to separate us even further."

Lacey went over to the other woman. "I'll figure out something to get the two of you back together."

"You? This is my problem. And Brian's."

Even though Celia was a planner, she wasn't terribly assertive. Most likely, she wouldn't purposely take action or take action fast enough to get her man back.

"His decision affects me too. I've been counting on the two of you giving me nieces and nephews."

"When Brian sets his mind on something, I don't know what either one of us can do to change it."

Lacey took Celia's hand. "Don't give up. I need a little time to figure out how to handle this. I've been so distracted today, right now, it's not easy to focus."

"Distracted? You mean working with Scott Dalton on Project Arabella?"

Cam said the project was hush-hush. Best to play dumb. "Project Arabella?"

One corner of Celia's mouth went up. "I work directly for Cam. Remember?"

"Well, yes, but—"

"All the senior staff know you've been paired with Scott on this special project. Aren't you excited? You can finally show your stuff with something other than single family homes."

"I like doing those. Especially working with the families. But you're right, it's my chance to prove myself. I don't want to blow it."

"What's got you distracted? Scott Dalton? He is a bit to handle. A real maverick. The only reason he's been able to get away with such behavior has been his incredible ability to charm the clients and bring in the fees."

The mention of *charm* sent Lacey's mind off on a course she'd been fighting hard to avoid since morning. The man didn't have just charm. There was a magnetism about him, which made him mighty difficult to resist.

"Lacey? Did you hear me?"

"Never mind." Celia had enough on her plate.

But Celia persisted. "Never mind what? Is something going on between you and Scott? You've only worked together a day."

How to respond? It was so tempting to seek her best friend's counsel. But she couldn't. Shouldn't.

Celia raised an eyebrow. "Lacey? Obviously something is going on. Has he criticized your work? Knowing Scott's preference for autonomy, he's probably already tried to get you to quit."

"I can handle his criticism of my professional opinions. It's the other … stuff … that's got me, I don't know … confused."

"What *stuff*?"

"He … I … oh, God, Cee, I've got the hots for him. I don't want to. I've been fighting my libido all day, but I don't know how long before I do something stupid."

"Scott's a pretty spectacular-looking guy, but you've been around yourself. You've had more than your share of boyfriends, lovers. Why him? And why so fast?"

"Don't you think I've been asking myself the same questions? He's so full of himself. Thinks he can get by simply by turning on his killer smile and improvising as he goes. I doubt he's ever done a preliminary design study in all his years with the firm."

"He's the firm's superstar, hon, whatever his style. Maybe it's the 'opposites attract' thing." She stopped, bit a lip as if there was more she wanted to say. "Surely you haven't—?"

"Slept with him? Of course not. We just teamed up this morning. But the idea's already occurred to me."

"What if you do? There's no company rule against it."

Had she heard right? Celia was actually advocating going to bed with the man? "No! I need to maintain all my wits and creative energy to keep up with him. Sleeping with him might turn my brain to mush."

Celia leaned back in her seat, studied her. "I've never seen you like this. Are you sure this is just some physical thing?"

Lacey recounted the incident of the slippery hill and landing under the tree trunk on top of Scott. "My body goes crazy every time I'm near him." There, she'd finally said it out loud. That brought a certain relief. Then guilt. "I'm sorry, friend. Here you are in the dumps over Brian and all I can do is go on about Scott Dalton."

"Actually, you helped take my mind off your brother for a few minutes. I'm glad you told me. Even though it looks like we won't be family, I hope we'll still continue to confide in each other like sisters."

"I refuse to believe your split is permanent. Brian needs to realize what he's given up." She considered her words. "He told me he wanted you to find someone else to build a life with. I wonder what would happen if you actually followed through."

Well, duh! There it was, the way Celia could get Brian back. "We need to find you a new boyfriend, Cee. Someone so fantastic, Brian will forget about his commitment phobia and come running back to you."

"Good idea, but easier said than done. It's not like I keep a bullpen of potential suitors just waiting to take Brian's place. Most people, like me, think/thought Brian and I are/were headed to the altar."

"I don't mean a real boyfriend. Just someone who'd be willing to play the part long enough for Brian to wake up and take notice."

"Someone like … say, Scott Dalton?"

"Well, yes, but—"

"Lacey! Scott Dalton. If you were serious about wanting to stifle your libido while you're working with him, he would be perfect."

Lacey started to negate Celia's suggestion. It was such a bad idea, because, because why? She didn't want to give him up? She had to. "You wouldn't actually … "

"Sleep with him? To make it appear more real? Or to save you from yourself? No to both," she chuckled. "This would be clearly pretend and only at times when Brian would see us."

Celia wasn't at all Scott's type. Yet, if it helped her get Brian back, Scott Dalton was probably the one candidate they knew who wouldn't misunderstand his role and get his feelings hurt in the offing. "Would he do it?"

Celia rose and squared her shoulders. "We won't know until I ask."

"Keep my name out of this, okay?"

"Okay, but why? You're already partners on this big secret project."

"Because if he knows I'm in on this, we lose the buffer part. Yes, I'll know it's fake, and he'll know it's all made up, but if he thinks I don't know, he'll sell it better."

Celia's eyes narrowed, apparently processing Lacey's premise. "I feel like I'm Ethel Mertz and you're Lucy Ricardo, conning me to help you with your latest scheme."

"Okay, here's another reason. The guy's very competitive. I'm going to be fighting him at every turn to get him to take me seriously. If he agrees to be your new boyfriend, the less he knows I'm in on this plan, the more likely he'll be to listen to my ideas about the project."

"Now you're scaring me, because you actually made sense.

CHAPTER 4

Lacey barely had a chance to settle at her desk the next morning when she received a text summoning— not inviting —her to Scott's office. Already attempting to show her who was in charge? She grabbed her tablet and set off to meet with the great man.

His office, along with those of three other senior architects, was located down the hall from Cam's quarters. Unlike Lacey and several other junior architects who had to fend for themselves, Scott's group shared a secretary. Lacey tried to recall her name as she breezed past the woman. She couldn't, so a wave had to suffice.

She was about to knock on Scott's door when the woman showed up at her side, slightly breathless. "You can't go in there without an appointment."

"Watch me." She knocked and opened the door in one movement and swooped into the room. "Here I am, as ordered."

He looked up from something he was sketching, a comma of hair punctuating his forehead. "It's okay, Jean."

"I'm sorry, Mr. Dalton." The woman clasped her hand to her chest. "She charged right by me."

"This is Lacey Rogers. She works on the second floor."

"Oh?" The older woman actually sniffed. Turning to Lacey, she raised heavy, dark eyebrows and said, "I didn't realize."

Lacey started to say something conciliatory when she was cut off.

"Next time, please check in with me first." The secretary exited as quickly as she'd arrived.

Lacey could have sworn the woman clicked her heels before leaving.

"Do we need to discuss protocol?" Scott asked.

"What century is she from?" The firm operated on an open-door policy.

"Jean, Miss Sarducci, is a little more formal than we're used to, but she makes a mean cup of coffee."

"Oh, well, I didn't realize she making coffee was such a talent. A thousand pardons."

"What can I do for you?"

"What can you do?" She flounced into one of the leather chairs facing his desk.

"Have a seat." He extended a belated hand.

"I received a text to come here as soon as I arrived. To discuss Project Arabella, I assume."

"Pretty late arrival time for a newbie, Rogers. Especially with our priority project looming. I've been here for hours. In fact, I just finished some preliminary sketches."

Finished? "You've been working on it already?"

"Do I need to remind you this project is on the fast track?"

Lacey shot from her chair. She would have rushed around the desk to check what he'd been working on but caught herself at the last second. "We're supposed to team up on this assignment. That means work together. Like in, not by ourselves."

The man barely moved. He let her stand there tapping her foot for what seemed like an eon before he spoke. He even favored her with a condescending smile, a gash under his nose. "Lacey, Lacey. Calm down. It's not like I've finished the concept piece. I wanted to experiment with a couple ideas before showing you."

"Fine, but before we go any further, let's get this straight. I haven't signed on as your assistant or your intern. I do, however, realize I can learn from you, which is important to me. I want to be the next superstar."

"Duly noted."

She sensed the color inching up her neck. "What I meant was …"

"I know what you meant. Look, I'm all for ambition. Hell, I invented the notion around here. But I'm used to working at my own speed, using my own techniques. I'm not about to stop myself every time some brilliant idea strikes and wait for you to catch up."

"Then I expect the same understanding from you."

He blinked, like he wasn't accustomed to coworkers standing up to him. Good. She'd caught him off guard. Time to press harder. "As for your guard dog, I want free access to your office." Her own brilliant thought hit. Sure to make her point. "In fact, why don't I move in here for the duration of this project? Then, whenever *some brilliant idea* strikes, I'll be here to start the applause." She widened her eyes, conveying the epitome of cooperation.

"Share my office?"

She made a show of taking in her surroundings. "Sure. You've got an actual office. With a door. Triple the space of my little cubicle. Why, you even have a separate conference table over there in the corner just waiting for me."

He blinked twice before he scuttled over to the table, his arms splayed wide, like he was blocking her tackle. "I told you, I have my own work style, which doesn't include letting someone else into my space."

"'Fraid I'll discover you're a fraud who gets all his ideas from the internet?"

Triple blink this time. Had she gone too far? She was just trying to establish herself as strong enough to trade jabs with him. But having voiced the idea, she wasn't so crazy about it. Being in such constant close proximity to him the next several weeks would prove too tempting. She could only resist her attraction to the man so far. Why ask for trouble?

Her new partner didn't respond to her putdown. He appeared to be having difficulty breathing. Biting down anger. Had she struck a nerve?

"I'm definitely not a fraud. But, as you'll discover, I'm no computer geek. My ideas are organic." He touched the area around his heart. "They come from here. I listen to my clients. Get them talking about themselves. Then I translate those impressions to my plans."

Boy, he was even smoother than she thought. Hypnotic. Inspirational. She didn't need his smarter-than-thou attitude challenging her confidence every minute of every day of the next month.

"Hello, sunshine. Word has it you wanted to see me. Did I screw up my expense report again?" Scott draped himself in the doorway of Celia Fairchild's office. Though the office manager had a bit of a rep as a straight shooter, he liked her. She called things as she saw them and rarely let him snow her. Word had it she'd been going with some accountant for months, so Scott didn't worry about Celia being out to snare him. "Nothing so mundane. Have a seat."

He kept his smile intact, but a one-on-one with Celia, other than to hear how his latest attempt at creative expense reporting wasn't going to work, was rare. He settled his lanky form into the guest chair facing her desk. When she rose and closed the door, his foreboding meter kicked in.

"Don't look so panicked." She returned to her desk. "I have a proposition for you. You're the only person I know who can pull this off."

Interesting turn of phrase coming from her. "Pull what off?"

Celia fixed him with what appeared to be a sincere, self-assured smile. "I've been seeing Brian Rogers exclusively for almost two years. He's Lacey Rogers' brother?"

No kidding. Interesting connection. But then, until yesterday, he hadn't paid Lacey Rogers much attention period. "Yeah?" Blank face.

"He broke things off the other day. Didn't want to get too serious."

Nice going, guy. "Sorry."

"I want him back, but I need your help."

"Me? How?"

"I need a new man in my life to make Brian jealous. To make him realize what he's given up." Pause. "You fit the bill."

It took all of two seconds to react. He shot out of his chair, no longer in lounging mode. "Me? And you? No offense, Celia, but I thought you realized our little daily exchanges were pure banter. I never meant to lead you on."

She chuckled. "I know. But you're the best man I can think of to make Brian sweat."

He relaxed his shoulders and leaned against the chair he'd formerly occupied. Of course, he could make any man jealous, if he set his mind to it. But his mind was a fickle animal. Needed incentive. "You want me to act like I'm the new man in your life?"

"Exactly. Brian has to see us together a few times. I'll pay for whatever dinners, plays, etc. we take in. But you have to make it look real. Brian is slow to be convinced of anything."

Scott fingered a front button on his shirt and grimaced. "I'm no good at playacting."

"You deliver that charming playboy act every day, which makes you the perfect person to do this. It won't take Brian long to scout out my new man, and once he hears about your so-called reputation, I'm counting on his protective instincts to kick in."

"You really know how to stroke a guy's ego."

Her forehead crinkled. "Sorry. I was a little too candid."

"I appreciate how you don't mince words. But I'm not your guy." He headed for the door.

"What will it take, Scott?" she asked his retreating back. "Surely we can make a deal."

A deal? He knew her well enough to know she wasn't talking sexual favors. He stopped but continued to stare at the door for several beats. "What kind of deal?"

"I could put in a good word for you with the boss." Her faltering voice indicated she wasn't a particularly adept negotiator.

Did she know why he hadn't been named principal yet? He turned, faced her, one eyebrow raised. "You think I need it?

"No, of course, not. You're top of the heap around here."

Whew! In other words, though, an empty promise. "What else do you have to offer?"

"The graphic art for your next project? I'm the one who picks the vendor. I'll get you the best around."

Was she deliberately trying to talk him out of it? "I'm already getting the best."

She bit a lip, rose. "C'mon, Scott. Just for a few weeks."

He started to decline, but the time frame she proposed caught his attention. His parents were coming back to town soon. Their first question would be if he was seeing someone. A pretend girlfriend might be the answer. Besides, if his gut instincts about Lacey Rogers were on target, another love interest, even a fake one, might help keep his hormones in check. "A few weeks?"

"Six."

"Four."

"Okay, four."

They shook on it. "One more thing," he added. "This is just between the two of us. Everyone has to think this is the real thing." Especially their boss, who was sure to leak this to his parents once he heard Scott was seeing Celia. And Lacey. He wanted her to think his relationship with Celia was genuine, so she wouldn't encourage him otherwise.

Celia started to say something then merely smiled. "I won't tell another soul. We'll start at noon by lunching at Brian's favorite spot."

He opened the door and noted one of the other women in the business office coming toward Celia's office. Might as well get this show underway now. "It's a date, then. See you at noon."

Around one, Lacey's cell phone rang. With Scott out socializing, she was using her time to get ahead of him researching their project. With regret, she put her hamburger aside and answered the call.

"Who is Celia lunching with today?" Brian. A somewhat flustered Brian. Her plan seemed to be working.

"You must be talking about Scott Dalton, the company star. I heard through the grapevine they left together."

"A business lunch?" The curiosity coming through the wire was palpable.

She almost felt sorry for her brother. Almost. But he needed this wake-up call. "I'm pretty sure it wasn't a business lunch. My sources say he took hold of her hand as they left."

The other end of the line went silent.

"Brian? Are you still there?"

"Yeah," he returned begrudgingly.

Slang? From Brian? "Aren't you pleased to hear she's doing exactly what you told her to do? Getting out and enjoying herself."

"Not with a hotshot architect. Celia's talked about him before. Said he stopped by and chatted on occasion. Said his ego only slightly outdistanced his charisma with the ladies. I had no idea there was more to their acquaintance. Celia is a very trusting woman. He'd better not take advantage of her."

Brian's comment dispelled any doubts about his still loving Celia. "I'm sure she'd be pleased to know you still care about her, in a protective, brotherly way, of course. But she's also a grown woman, Brian. Nothing gets by her as office manager. She'll be on to Scott Dalton quite soon, if not already."

"Weeell …"

"How's this? I'll keep an eye on the two of them, at least around the office. If it looks like things are getting out of hand—" She paused for effect. "What do you want me to do then, Brian? Call you, so you can come charging in on your white horse? You gave up the role. Willingly."

"Just let me know. Okay?"

"Yes, brother dear. Anything else?"

"Keep me posted."

Lacey hung up, shaking her head at her brother's idiocy. Her idea had caught fire. She'd be maid of honor at Celia and Brian's wedding before the year was out.

CHAPTER 5

Lacey managed to walk into Scott's office unaccompanied the next morning. Jean was nowhere to be seen, although her desk lights were on. The watchdog must have made herself scarce at Lacey's appointed arrival time so she wouldn't have to acknowledge the fact Lacey could come and go as she pleased.

Engrossed studying a group of sketches fanned across his desk, Scott eventually glanced up to acknowledge her. "Got the concept nailed down." He shoved the top drawing toward her. "Shared communal areas for every four or five houses. Gardens, walkways, barbecue pits, anything for entertaining that's only used occasionally."

Lacey pretended to study the drawing, but she could barely concentrate. He'd done it again. So much for waiting to consult with her. She attempted to keep her voice level and noncommittal. "This is, uh, interesting. Where's the research?"

"Research?"

She offered a frosty smile, although it pained her to lift the corners of her mouth. Her fingertips prickled as she itched to reach across the desk and grab him by the neck. "No, I meant, what information have you gathered on the target population indicating this group of retirees wants shared communal space?" He tipped his head to the side, scrunched his eyebrows, like she'd spoken a foreign language. He pointed to his forehead, presumably where his brain, what there was of it, resided. "My research is all up here."

She tried not to snicker. "Thought as much."

"What do you mean?"

"You're a shoot-from-the-hip creative type whose hits outweigh your misses." She waited until the predictable self-serving smile claimed his scowl before proceeding. "But your success rate could increase considerably if you did your homework first."

The smile immediately disappeared. "I studied the project files. All the homework I needed."

She untied the folder she'd brought with her, having stayed up late surfing her computer to do her own research. "I found a few articles about baby boomers on the internet that provide a better clue about what they want in a retirement home."

Scott rolled his eyes.

"Born between 1946 and 1964, many have already retired. Like every generation before them, they don't want to age. Unlike their predecessors, however, technology and science are on their side, helping them maintain a youthful lifestyle."

Scott yawned.

"Which means, by calling it a retirement community, we may be limiting ourselves."

"What's your point? The name's up to Marketing, not the design team."

The man's attention span was smaller than a gnat's. He was already fidgeting. Time to wrap up. "Recent studies indicate only part of this age group plan to spend their retirement years in what's euphemistically referred to as an *active adult community*. If we concentrate our efforts solely on this demographic, we may find ourselves with an investment that's undersubscribed."

The economics got him. She could see it in his eyes. "Still not our problem. We're just to come up with the design concept."

"When the development goes bust, do you think we'll be exonerated when we claim we just developed the design concept? No, everyone involved will be tainted."

He slumped lower in his chair. "Even if I were to agree with you, how do you propose to convince Cam and his client there's a problem?"

"In Cam's case, I need more data. He's appears to be a bottom line man. If the numbers aren't there, he'll be convinced. The client is a different story. Without knowing who we're dealing with, it's impossible to know what's driving him."

Scott appeared to consider her arguments, then scratched his head again. "Cam's harder to call than you think."

"How?"

"Though he's motivated by the bottom line, his first task is to please the client."

"As he reminded us the other day, we're not his partners on the project," he said, hunching forward, palms on thighs. We're highly paid talent. We do what we're paid to do."

Burning pools of liquid mahogany bored into her. Despite the fact he was once again lecturing her, he was mesmerizing. Commanding.

She couldn't think of an immediate response. She could barely remember her own name.

His phone rang. He gave her one last penetrating look, as if to put a period on his statement. "Scott Dalton," he said into the phone. "Yes, Celia, I remember." He screwed up his face in a frown but then seemed to catch himself, molding his mouth into what appeared to be a fake smile. "Okay, pick you up at seven."

Right on time, Cee. Tonight was the fiftieth birthday party Marianne Mackenzie, Cam's wife, was throwing for their boss. Fortunately for their plan, Scott hadn't lined up his own date yet when Celia asked him to be her escort.

Since this call was for her benefit, Lacey played along. She raised a brow. "Celia Fairchild? You're taking her to Cam's party tonight?" She kept her tone ingenuous.

"Uh, yeah."

"Lunch yesterday, now Cam's party."

"You heard? The office grapevine is faster than Cam's new sports car."

Deflecting. Next, he changed the subject. "What happened to yesterday's *great possibilities?*"

"Haven't changed my mind about the property. But now we're talking concept. My research suggests we're limiting our options if we come right out and call it a retirement community or say it's aimed at boomers, even though that's what we'd actually be doing. I thought you were opposed to it too. You couldn't wait to tick off everything wrong with it as we drove back."

"I still don't like the whole idea of this project, but to borrow your expression, we're just the foot soldiers."

She played with her pen. Lacey wasn't naïve and she knew her place. But she felt a responsibility to the client's best interests, whoever the client was. "Foot soldiers protect the main flanks behind them. Sometimes protecting them means reporting the dangers that lay ahead before plowing into battle."

He could stay seated no longer. "Where are you getting these metaphors? Were you in ROTC?" He lifted a restraining hand to prevent her from answering. "You realize you could be ruining your career chances around here if you try to talk Cam out of this?"

"That realization hasn't escaped me. But I have to give the boss my best professional opinion." *Stupid, Lacey.* Talk about cutting her own throat. She steeled her resolve for his reaction.

But he surprised her. He shrugged and settled back in his chair. "When I consider my concerns about the property and yours about the concept, I have to agree with you. However, my career can probably recover from Cam's wrath, if he feels we've turned against him. Just want to make sure you know what could happen to you."

She released the breath she'd been holding. "You're not telling me to forget it?" Would she ever figure him out?

He sighed, as if she'd depleted his patience. "No. Just wanted to make sure you wore your Big Girl shoes today."

She sat back, relieved. "I'll draft a memo right—"

"Not so fast, newbie. We need solid, indisputable evidence to even have a chance of convincing Cam. I can't believe I'm going to ask this, but what else did your research uncover?"

She handed him the pages she printed off the night before. As he read over them, she cited the high points.

"Good start," he said when he finished.

"Good start? That's great stuff."

"You got names and dates, but we need the original source before moving ahead. Plus, the studies are over two years old. You need to find something newer or confirm what you've got still holds true."

"Okay."

"This stuff about home offices, computer labs, and lifelong learning will be great for add-ons."

"Terrific! Then we've got ourselves a profile to work from."

"Not exactly."

"What else do we need? I thought I had more than enough."

He gestured toward her stack of printouts. "For me to really get into design mode, I need to know my client. Since we don't currently have such information, and the only thing we know our client wants is a retirement community for baby boomers, words which you say we can't use. We have to focus on who baby boomers are, the whole ever-lovin' demographic."

Was he playing her? Outresearching her for sport? She had no choice but to play along. "How do you propose we obtain such info?"

"Probably'll take at least a week, maybe ten workdays, to do the plan itself, leaving us a week or two for research.

"Us? Research?"

His brow furrowed like he'd been insulted. "Yeah, field research. We need to get up close and personal. Follow the lives of real people, not just search the internet. My parents are in their fifties, but they're so unlike everyone else, I can't go by them. How about you? Do you know anyone in their fifties or early sixties?"

She shook her head. "Not really. My parents are no longer alive."

He seemed to sense her discomfort talking about her parents. "Oh. Sorry," he quickly added.

"I don't talk about them much. My brother Brian's my only family now."

"No uncles? Aunts? Friends of the family? Teachers?"

She did a brief mental run-through of all the people she knew, then shook her head. "How about here at work? Cam! He's turning fifty."

"Cam isn't your typical boomer. He's in a category by himself."

She chuckled. "We finally agree on something." Maybe he was actually serious about conducting research.

"But his birthday party tonight gives me an idea." He smiled. "Marianne, his wife, will probably include some of his cronies on the guest list. Why don't we study them? Might make the party a little less boring."

"Study them?"

"Talk to them. Find out their retirement plans."

"Great idea." Then she remembered he wouldn't be a free agent for such reconnaissance. "What about Celia?"

"What about Celia?" He seemed mystified by her question.

"Since she's your date, won't you have to tell her what we're up to?"

"Won't be a problem. She'll probably be helping Marianne run the show."

"Then it's settled." In her enthusiasm, she spilled her papers on the floor. Scott reached to retrieve them at the same time she did. Their hands barely touched, but it seemed as if she'd come in contact with a live wire as the shock of his touch coursed through her.

Scott jerked away and Lacey came to her feet. "I'll, uh, spend some time following up on those reports this, uh, afternoon." She breathed deeply and tried to make light of the situation to conceal how his mere touch affected her. "Tonight I become Lacey Rogers, Special Investigator."

"We'll compare notes first thing tomorrow."

"That's it? That's our work plan, we spend half our time stalking people over fifty and the other half writing up our findings and turning them into a design concept?"

"Works for me."

Of course it worked for him. These few action steps were probably more structure than he'd ever worked with. But the nebulous nature of his proposed approach made her knees buckle. Or was their accidental contact responsible for her lack of balance? "I need more detail."

"There, there, newbie. You sure you're up to this? Cam'll understand if you ask to be excused from the project. But do it soon, so I have enough time to do your work as well."

"Look, Scott, you may have more years' experience than me, but you don't know anything about timelines and action steps. Apparently you think you can just throw something together and the client will be forever grateful to have benefited from your creative genius."

He shoved back that intransigent lock of hair that had once again sought his forehead. "Hey, I've already agreed to do the research, but I'm not about to tie myself down with a to-do list. If you need that kind of crutch, be my guest. But do it on your own time."

"Fine."

"Fine. Now, go tell Lacey Rogers, Special Investigator she's needed. Her over-organized alter ego is giving me a headache."

ONCE LACEY LEFT for her own office, Scott summoned Jean. He could have sworn she saluted as she approached. Must've have been his imagination, or a thought planted the day before by Lacey.

"I need to do some computer research, Jean. I'm, uh, sorta hard-pressed for time with this new project and could really use the assist."

The woman studied him before replying. "Certainly, Mr. Dalton, although I assumed Ms. Rogers would handle those details."

"Uh, yes, she is. But just certain aspects. After I volunteered to split the work with her, I realized I'd overcommitted." He leaned closer. "Okay, I don't know the first thing about research. I'm great with Computer Aided Design, but search engines, not so much."

"You don't want Ms. Rogers to find out." It wasn't even a question. The woman knew him better than he knew himself sometimes. No need to concede the point, though.

"Find me everything you can about baby boomers, especially the oldest in the group, and what their plans are for retirement."

"No problem. I'll have something for you by the end of the day."

"Thanks." Didn't want Jean to think she was indispensable, although she was. Jean he could deal with. She just wanted to be acknowledged and appreciated. Flowers should do it.

His sentence as Celia's beau was only for four weeks. All he had to do was live through the next twenty-eight days when it came to dealing with her.

Lacey was the real problem. Keeping up with her was proving harder than he thought it would be. How much younger was she? Three-four years? Enough to label it a generation gap? Internet research. He'd been so quick to mock her, until she laid those numbers square in his face. Who could dispute the logic of her findings? But as with Jean, no way was he letting her know.

She presented another kind of problem as well. One he couldn't offset with his own—well, Jean's, research. The woman had his hormones raging. Though he'd only touched her hand for a matter of seconds when he helped her gather her papers, he'd come away with the distinct memory of skin as smooth as a rose petal. He'd had to drag himself back into his chair to keep from touching her again, prolonging the sensation.

The sooner he got rid of her, the better.

Then realization hit. Damn! He'd blown his own plan. Proceeding with the project without her input was supposed to get her so irritated and huffy she'd quit. But he'd become so engrossed in her research and not letting it make him look too uninformed and stupid, he'd forgotten to make the most of his sketches.

How was he supposed to deal with her now?

Lacey plopped the folder containing her research on her desk. So her proclivity for order and method gave Mr. Shoot-from-the-hip a headache? His noggin hadn't seen anything yet. Wait 'til she over-whelmed him with her project plan.

With no time to waste on dead end theories, they needed every tool available to stay on track. Her head swirled with information, unex-pected insights and questions. Questions about penetrating the Great Scott Dalton's armor and about her own physical response to the man.

Her fingers tapped a frenetic rhythm on her desk, her body a boiling caldron of energy. She'd been on the right track with her research on boomers. Even Scott had begrudgingly admitted as much. She could knock out a project plan and the additional research to answer Scott's questions in a few more hours.

What troubled her was the guy himself. He was an enigma. The day before, he was adamantly opposed to the project, and today, if he'd been working solo on this project, he would have settled for the drivel he tried to peddle. What had he been thinking, dashing off all those sketches? Did he really think she'd be impressed? Or the least bit ready to agree to his ideas so quickly?

"What are you up to, Scott Dalton?" she said to no one in particular. Though they'd worked together no more than a couple of days, she was pretty sure he didn't extend himself for nothing. There'd been a reason for those sketches. She just hadn't identified it yet. But she would. She had to be leery of the man. Ignore whatever physical reactions his touch or his look produced. Which reminded her—she picked up her cell phone and hit speed dial. "Got any plans for tonight, Brian?"

"No. Why?"

"I'd like you to be my date for an office shindig. Sorry for the late notice. I forgot about it until someone just reminded me." She told him about Cam's party, as she and Celia had discussed previously. "I have to warn you, though. Celia will be there. With Scott Dalton."

The other end of the line remained silent several moments. "She's seeing him again? So soon?" he said finally, in a lower, less enthusiastic voice.

"I heard him confirming the date with her not long ago. I could use your company, but not if you're going to fixate on Celia all evening."

He cleared his throat. "Fixate? Of course not! I'm happy she's found someone else so soon. I don't know this Dalton guy very well, but from what I do know of him, I find it difficult to see the two of them as compatible, is all."

Bluffing. She couldn't wait to tell Celia how well their plan was working. "Okay, it's a date. Pick me up at six thirty."

The call finished, she returned to her earlier speculations. If she'd read the signals correctly, Scott Dalton designed what he wanted and then sold his product to his clients with his more personal qualities. Until today, he hadn't put much stock in research. She could see it in his eyes the minute he realized she'd provided a missing element to their puzzle.

Whether he liked it or not, he needed her for this project. Lacey was no secondary player. The knowledge alone spurred her on through the afternoon, checking one resource after another.

When she finally thought to check the time, she realized she only had forty-five minutes to get ready for the night's big event.

CHAPTER 6

"You surprise me, Celia." Scott darted a glance at his date as they drove to the party. "All these years I've thought of you as a sensible, open, no-nonsense person. The what-you-see-is-what-you-get type. Who'd have thought you capable of a charade like this?"

"Until yesterday, I was the person you described. Look where it got me. Dropped like a hot dish after two years, when it started getting serious."

"Most men shy away from commitment. Look at me."

"Yes, look at you. How have you managed to elude marriage so long?"

He returned his eyes to traffic. "Me? I'm not the marrying type."

"What do you mean?"

He opened his mouth, then clamped it shut. What did it mean? He was never able to answer it for his parents, either. "Guess I'm comfortable with the way things are going in my life."

"Comfortable, huh? So you're happy? Content?"

"Of course I'm hap—never mind. Don't concern yourself with me. And don't play matchmaker. I'm fine. So drop it."

She seemed to study him a little too long before replying. "Just making conversation."

It was going to take all his energy tonight to play the dutiful escort. He wasn't up to defending his bachelorhood as well. It was tough enough dealing with his parents' questions on the same subject every time they were in town.

Fortunately, his car was nearing the country club, which ended the inquisition. Celia turned her attention to gathering her things and mercifully complied with his request to forget about his personal life.

"See, Lacey. We're not the first ones here," Brian reassured her as they strolled into the ballroom of the country club twenty minutes early.

"I still don't see why you were in such a hurry to get here." She reached behind her neck to assure herself the zipper on her black crepe cocktail dress was pulled up. "I had to dress so fast, it feels like something's missing or undone."

He turned her around to check her out, then stepped around her to study the front. "You look fine. There was no point wasting time at your apartment when we could be here selecting the best seats in the house."

"I don't want the best seats if they're anywhere in the vicinity of Cameron Mackenzie, or he'll be wanting a progress report on my new project, which I'm not ready to discuss." She spied a round table in the middle of the room, which appeared to be reserved for the birthday boy, so she made her way to a point several tables away. Once everyone else arrived, the location promised relative obscurity.

"New project?" Brian pulled out a chair for her.

"Can't talk about it. The boss is being very closemouthed about the client and has sworn us to secrecy on the few details we do know."

Brian took a seat beside her. "Sounds mysterious."

"Not the cloak and dagger kind. The secrecy thing is probably unnecessary, but since this is bigger than my previous assignments and potentially a huge career step, I'm not going to question it or do anything to jeopardize my part. "

"Congratulations. Guess I was so wrapped up telling you about Celia and me the other night, I didn't ask what you'd been up to. Sorry."

"There wouldn't have been anything to say. Uh, except one thing. Scott Dalton is my partner."

Brian swiveled in his seat to face her. "You and Scott Dalton? The same guy who took Celia to lunch?"

"Yes. He's considered the firm's golden boy, so working directly with him is a bit of a coup."

"Golden boy or not, you're pretty talented yourself. Don't let him take credit for your ideas."

"I'm touched. I didn't realize you paid much attention to my job."

"I've driven by every house you've ever designed." He rearranged his place setting. "Since discussing your new project is off limits, let's decide on the type of flowers to place on Mother's grave this year."

She'd forgotten about the approaching event. Every year since their mother's death, she and Brian placed fresh flowers on her gravesite on her birthday. "Does it really matter? Mom loved all flowers. She didn't have a favorite."

"We have to choose something meaningful. To honor her memory."

This really wasn't the place to examine Brian's inability to move on, but since the room was still relatively empty, she plunged ahead. "Do we really need to continue this practice? Mom's spirit is inside me. I don't need the flowers tradition anymore."

"How can you even suggest such a thing? We don't want to forget her."

In some ways, their mother's death had affected him more strongly than Lacey, because he'd had to become the surrogate parent at the same time he'd been the grieving child. Although it was long past time to get on with his life, in some ways he seemed to fight the idea.

Obviously making no headway, she acceded to his wishes, saving this conversation for another day. She suggested pink roses and he agreed, said he'd take care of it. He always took care of it. But at least, for now, he was pacified, willing to drop the subject. She was grateful to have it decided for another year.

They sat in silence a bit. "I could use a drink. Do you want something?" Brian asked.

She sent him for white wine while she debated if she'd forgotten to change shoes. Brian had been in a bigger rush to get going than usual. She leaned down to reassure herself the shoes were the right ones. While her head was below the tabletop, she thought she heard voices but couldn't make out what they were saying.

When she popped up, she discovered she was no longer alone. Celia and Scott stood on the other side. Scott was about to pull out Celia's chair. Neither appeared to notice her until Celia was seated.

Her friend winked. "Lacey. Fancy seeing you here."

"Small world," she replied. "But why aren't the two of you finding seats closer to the birthday boy?"

Scott gave her a knowing look. "We're keeping our distance tonight. Allowing the boss to be surrounded by friends and family rather than fawning employees."

Did he mean her? Or was she overly sensitive to anything Scott had to say?

Before she had a chance to think of a pithy retort, a wine glass appeared in front of her. "Here you go," Brian said. "The bar line's—" Then he noticed their dinner companions. His voice grew strained. "Celia. Dalton."

"Brian! What a surprise. I didn't expect to see you here tonight." Celia made a show of appearing embarrassed, her eyes growing wide with surprise, then shifting away to focus anywhere in the room except on her former beau.

"I forgot to get a date, so I asked Brian to accompany me," Lacey explained. She had no idea what Brian would have blurted out if left on his own to greet the two new arrivals. She wanted him to feel uncomfortable, but she didn't want him to make a scene.

She turned a bright smile his direction, placed her hand on his forearm. "Thanks for the wine." As unobtrusively as she could, she pressed down. "Have a seat and enjoy your drink."

Brian gulped his scotch, then spent the next few minutes clearing his throat, trying valiantly not to cough. Though he appeared to be focusing on the glass before him, he kept sneaking glances at the other couple. Each time, his expression more closely resembled a glare.

The four of them sat in uncomfortable silence. Finally, Scott remembered his manners and offered to get Celia a drink.

"Yes, thank you. I believe I will have something," Celia said. "How about a champagne cocktail?" As soon as Scott left, Brian went on the offensive. "You've started drinking?"

He leaned so far into the table he nearly spilled his drink. Lacey placed a restraining, sisterly hand on his leg.

"I've never been a teetotaler, Brian. I simply refrained from indulging these last few years for your sake, although I see you've hit the hard stuff tonight yourself."

"I never said—"

"Not in so many words. But you had a way of imposing your preferences nonverbally."

"I didn't mean—"

"Water under the bridge. This is the new, improved Celia Fairchild you're speaking to. She's trying different things these days, like champagne cocktails."

On cue, Scott arrived with the drink in question. "What have I missed?" He glanced from Celia to Brian to Lacey. "My, my. Should I retrieve your wrap, Cee? The temperature seems to have dropped several degrees since I left."

Celia patted his hands. "No need, Scott. We were just reminiscing."

"Uh-huh. How about we find a new topic, then, before I freeze?"

"Good idea," Lacey agreed. "Any suggestions?"

Scott looked at Celia, then back to Brian. "How about antiquing? Cee and I plan to spend Sunday checking out some shops in the area. I understand you're a bit of a collector yourself, Brian. Where would you suggest we go?"

Lacey held her breath. Brian was too much a gentleman to answer Scott's question the way he'd really like to. What would he do instead?

Brian shot a questioning look at Celia. "You hated going with me to see antiques. You said the moldy smell bothered you. Now you're interested?"

"Scott's been telling me about some of his recent finds, and the search sounded so intriguing, I asked to go along."

Scott's facial expression portrayed innocence. "Didn't realize it was a sensitive subject."

Brian folded his hands in his lap. "Many of the shops in the smaller towns won't be open Sunday. I'd suggest you stay close to the city. Valley Junction's always a great place to look." He sounded so stiff, would his face crack?

She searched her brain for something else they could discuss without friction. The party was barely fifteen minutes along. They still had a couple hours of small talk and social amenities to wade through, but no topic seemed to be safe. She turned to the tried-and-true. "Your dress is beautiful, Celia. It's new, isn't it?"

The recipient of the compliment sat a little straighter and offered a grateful smile. "Yes, it is. Everything I owned seemed so frumpy, so I went on a little shopping spree. I'm glad you like it."

"It's a little too—," Brian started to say. He stopped when three sets of eyes stared him down. "Red for your coloring," he finally said, "but you look very nice."

"Thank you," Celia replied.

Just as a waiter approached, Brian pushed away from the table. "I, uh, just remembered something I was supposed to do tonight." He turned to his sister. "Sorry, Lacey. You stay. I have to take off." He skittered away, not looking back.

Lacey mumbled a quick apology and ran after her brother, catching up with him near the front entrance. "Are you okay?" she asked, pulling him aside by the cloakroom. "You've grown pale, although there are red blotches on your neck."

Brian pawed the floor like a caged animal. "I underestimated my ability to deal with Celia in a social context. It's too soon. I want her to be happy, but I can't watch. Not yet."

"Do you regret cutting her loose?" She tried to keep her tone inquisitive, not hopeful.

"What's the deal with the new dress and drinking? Especially with Scott Dalton! When did they get so close?"

"You threw her a real curve, breaking up like you did. She's trying to bounce back by changing her image."

"There's nothing wrong with her old image." He shot a glance back at the table they'd just left.

"Although, I kind of like her dress."

"I'll tell her."

"But encourage her not to go overboard." He made no move to leave. "I never meant to hurt her," he finally added.

"I know. Deep down, Celia does too."

He massaged his temples. "It wasn't easy breaking up with her. I contemplated it for weeks, listed all the pros and cons. I figured she'd see other men, eventually, and someday, she'd find one to spend the rest of her life with. I just didn't think she'd rebound so soon. With a guy like Scott Dalton, no less."

"Even you would have to admit he's fairly good looking, and smart, and well, attentive to Celia."

"Watch out for her. She's obviously not thinking clearly these days."

Who's not thinking clearly, dear brother? "Are you sure you have to leave?"

He nodded vehemently. "Yes. Apologize for me. I can't watch her rebounding."

Even after her brother left for the parking lot, Lacey continued to stand there. Had they succeeded or failed miserably? They'd certainly gotten quite a reaction from Brian. But now, would he simply double up his efforts to separate himself from Celia?

At the table, she discovered Celia had fled to the women's lounge soon after Brian's departure. Lacey left Scott chatting with the newest arrivals and made her way to find her friend.

Celia blotted her lips with a tissue. When she saw Lacey, she quickly wadded it up and threw it away. "What did he say? Did we get the point across?"

Lacey studied her face in the mirror. It had grown pale with bright pink spots on her cheeks. "Brian's no good at spontaneity. He was totally flummoxed seeing you and Scott together. We all witnessed raw need. He seems to have no idea how to deal with it."

"Are you sure this is the way to change his mind?" Celia's voice carried its own rawness.

"No. I hated seeing him so miserable. But other than waiting to see if he ever comes to his senses, this was our best course of action." She didn't mention the other reason she'd pushed this idea on Celia, to help her cool her own jets around Scott.

Celia smoothed her skirt and made ready to leave. "I should get back out there. Even though the main event for us is over, there's always Cam's show."

"Brian asked me to apologize, so we're making progress. Of sorts. We're getting to him. He didn't trust his resolve." Okay, her comments were a bit of a stretch, but her friend needed a lifeline.

"What do we do next? Scott agreed to this farce for a limited time. As awkward as tonight was, we have to follow up with something else soon. Before Brian goes off the deep end or the strain forces Scott to beg off."

"Are you really going antiquing with Scott this Sunday?" Scott and antiques didn't mesh.

Celia released a drawn-out sigh. "He improvised, apparently wanting to give Brian something more to chew on. He had no idea Brian was actually into the stuff."

"Good, because Brian needs a few days to calm down before we confront him with you and Scott again." Plus, her new project needed her immediate attention. She couldn't afford the time and effort worrying about Brian would take out of her. "Tell you what. Let's forget about Brian for the rest of the evening. It's been a long, exhausting week. I could use some relaxation."

Celia slanted a smile her direction. "You actually think you can enjoy the rest of the evening?"

"At least it's a free meal."

CHAPTER 7

Once dinner had been cleared and dessert was underway, their host began to work the room.

"Uh-oh," Scott said under his breath, leaning in so only Lacey and Celia could hear him. "Birthday Boy Boss at two o'clock."

Lacey broke her concentration on her crème brûlée. Two o'clock? It was well past eight. By the time Scott's warning clicked, Cam was bearing down on their table.

Too late to make a hasty retreat.

"Good evening, folks," Cam said.

They greeted him and wished him well on his birthday.

He displayed a ludicrous grin. "My goal is to dance with every woman here tonight," he announced in a slightly tipsy voice. "Celia, you're next." He extended an arm to guide her to the dance floor.

Celia smiled on cue and followed him.

Lacey and Scott found themselves alone with each other, the other two couples at the table having sought out the dance floor as well. Scott sipped his drink, then exhaled at length. "Would you like another glass of wine? Your brother truly left you high and dry."

"No, thanks."

"You want to join the others?" He raised his eyebrows suggestively toward the dance floor.

"Thanks, but—"

"Your turn with Cam is next, unless you're already out there with me."

Three days ago, she'd been floating on air to have been included in the site inspection. Especially when the big boss told her to call him Cam. Now, she wanted to avoid him at all costs so she wouldn't have to discuss Project Arabella. She was pleased with the project plan she'd developed and the direction their research was taking but not prepared to explain it all on the dance floor. Though the admission pained her, Scott was a better spokesperson.

"Okay," she conceded, choosing what she hoped was the lesser of two evils. She rose and let him guide her out to the tiny slab of hardwood floor where numerous couples were jammed together swinging and swaying.

She almost jumped out of her dress when his hand touched her back. She reacted the same way back in his office earlier in the day. Why was this happening? She'd been in close contact with many a man over the years, but their touch had never affected her this way. What was there about Scott Dalton?

She allowed herself a quick peek to see if he'd felt it too. If possible, his eyes had darkened beyond their usual chocolate color. A glint she hadn't noticed before gleamed back at her.

The dance was a light-hearted love song. Even though he held her at arms' length, she continued to be very aware of him. His aftershave, something spicy, tantalized her nostrils. The rich fabric of his close-cut tux couldn't disguise taut shoulder muscles that rippled slightly each time he shifted his weight.

Stop it, Lacey! It's just a dance. She willed herself to think of something else besides this vibrant hunk of man, but her body wouldn't obey. Maybe it was simply the excitement of being out on a dance floor for the first time in months causing her breath to catch and her heart to bang against her chest.

"How's the detective work going?" he asked, his mouth so close to her ear, his breath tickled.

Detective work?

He nodded in the direction of the other dancers. "You know, interviewing the baby boomers at the party?"

"Oh, right." Brian's outburst had driven her assignment for the night to the back of her mind despite the opportunity it presented for their rushed project schedule. "How're you doing?"

"As dismally as you," he admitted. "I've been occupied entertaining Celia."

"So I've seen."

"And your excuse?"

"Sorry about my brother. He asked me to apologize to both you and Celia."

"What's with him? If I didn't know better, I'd think he was the wounded party. Not Celia."

"I wish I knew. But it appears his loss is your gain."

"You mean with Celia?" He started to say something but stopped, started again. "No offense, but regarding Celia, the guy's a fool."

She couldn't agree more, but thought it wise to end further discussion of Celia and Brian, or she might let slip she knew about his deal with her friend. "About my detective work? I was waiting to take my lead from you. But since you're here with Celia, looks like I'll have to strike out on my own. As soon as I find some boomers."

He pulled away slightly, crinkling his forehead. "What's the mystery? They're all over the place."

She was about to reply when the music ended and another tune started. Salsa.

Scott cocked his head. "Cam's doing?"

"The dance? Surely he's forgotten our conversation in the car the other day?"

"Don't underestimate the man, even when he's tipped a few too many champagne glasses. Shall we?"

Had it been any other dance, Lacey would have politely said no.

But she loved Salsa and, of late, she'd been short on dance partners. She agreed without hesitation.

The next few minutes were a blur of sound, blinking lights and weaving bodies. Scott guided her through the complicated footwork like a champion quarterback running a play. He brought her body up close so their moves matched each other perfectly. As they grew more comfortable with each other's styles, his hand stole slightly below her waist to guide her hips.

The movement had her gasping for air, but she attributed it to the thrill of the dance.

Scott took them through routines she had never encountered despite numerous visits to Salsa clubs. But she met him step for step, exhilarated by the challenge. Scott's eyes burned. Her skin glistened from the exertion and the heat of the moment.

They floated and swirled, awash in the music, but her eyes couldn't leave Scott's. If possible, the glint from earlier had sharpened into the undeniable look of desire every woman instinctively recognized. In response, strange sensations pulsed through her body— sensations which blended physical arousal with emotional need while her heart pounded in rhythm to the Latin beat.

She noted vaguely how the crowd parted to make room for them. When the dance ended, the two of them stood there, chests heaving, suspended in a moment only they shared.

A wave of applause broke the spell, as other couples came up to congratulate them.

"You were fantastic!" a fiftyish-looking woman cried.

The man with her chimed in. "The couple on our CD does similar steps, but I've never seen them done in person. You guys are great."

"How long have you been dancing together?" another woman asked. "You were so well synchronized."

Fanning her face, Lacey didn't know what to say. "Uh, well, uh, no. It was spontaneous."

Apparently Scott's lungs had survived better than hers as he was able to address the crowd. "My partner's still a little winded, folks. We're giving a class, if you're interested. Monday night at seven.

Mackenzie and Associates." Announcement delivered, Scott grasped her hand and led her back to their table.

"A class?" she gasped between breaths. "Are you crazy?"

"I enjoyed dancing with you, too." He pulled out her chair for her. When she was seated and he was in his own chair, he leaned across the table conspiratorially. "Did you happen to notice anything our group of admirers had in common?"

She chugged down her entire glass of water before replying. "They were able to breathe normally?"

"Try again. Never mind, catch your breath. I'll tell you. They were all boomers!"

His statement left her cold, struggling to put two and two together.

"Don't you get it?" he asked, losing patience. "We won't have to go chasing after them. Now they'll come to us and fall all over themselves supplying details about their lifestyles."

It clicked. "What a fabulous idea." She didn't even cringe at the thought of congratulating him.

"It's about time you caught on."

Another thought tugged at her. "You had us grabbing the spotlight out there for this very result." He'd sucked her in as well as the boomers. She'd actually enjoyed dancing with him. All part of his grand scheme. How deflating.

He studied her a moment as if deciding what to say. Then a self-satisfied smirk stole across his face. He pulled at his lapel. "I'm good, huh? It came to me during the first dance. I've heard boomers have this thing about being on the cutting edge, including the latest dance craze. When the Salsa piece came on, it was as if it was meant to be."

She forced herself to smile. "You're good all right. I'll bet you've already figured out how to get Cam's blessing to use the office."

The light went out of his face temporarily. Brightening, he shrugged. "No problem. Didn't you notice his wife, Marianne, in our crowd of admirers?"

"Okay. Which leaves only one stone unturned."

"Yes?"

"Neither of us has the slightest experience teaching Salsa."

He was still giving her a blank look when Celia returned to the table. "Some show out there, you two."

"Did you hear his announcement? We're going to teach a Salsa class."

Celia's gaze went from her to Scott. "Really? Why? Don't you have your hands full working on Cam's special project?"

"This is research for the project," Lacey reassured her.

Celia's eyes narrowed, as if attempting to catch up as well as figure out why Lacey had agreed to spend more time with Scott. "For the project?"

"Sorry," Scott said. "Can't say more. You know how hush-hush this project is. The idea for this class just came up. Apparently we gained some fans out there on the dance floor. They want to learn to do what we did."

Celia turned to Scott. "I thought we had plans for next week."

"This will just take one night. It's important, Celia."

Celia glanced back at Lacey, who was still absorbing this new development herself.

A dance class for boomers was an absolutely brilliant stroke of luck, but it meant spending more time wrapped in Scott's arms and telling her body it didn't mean anything. The Salsa wasn't exactly a minuet. "Why don't you take over for me, Celia?" she suggested.

"Me?"

"Celia?" Scott replied in a surprised tone.

"You know how to Salsa, too, Cee. Then I wouldn't be cutting into your time with your, uh, with Scott."

"No offense, Celia, but Lacey needs to be there with me. We only agreed to teach this class because we're studying these folks for our project."

Chalk off one ploy. Time for another. "You're welcome to attend, though," Lacey added. "Right, Scott?"

Dark brown murderous eyes bored through her. But before Scott could say anything, Celia added, "Never mind. I get it. As long as it's just Monday night?"

"Okay, then," Scott put in before either woman said anything further.

Damn! She needed Celia there to run interference for her. Now she'd have to figure out some other way to avoid too much contact with Scott.

CHAPTER 8

Monday morning found Scott staring at the Newton's Cradle on his desk. The tiny steel balls swung back and forth in their relentless quest for order. They didn't have to think, didn't have to do anything other than hang there suspended, waiting to be hit by their neighbor and follow the orbit designated by physics. The Yin and Yang of their life was so less complicated, so less critical than his life at the moment.

Teaching a dance class for boomers had been genius, if he did say so himself. Teaching a dance class was also the stupidest thing he'd done in a long time.

Intent on checking out his desk toy, he didn't focus immediately on the figure in front of him. Jean. "This is what I've managed to gather thus far about baby boomers." She handed him a three-ring binder.

He'd been so focused on the dancing class as a research tactic, he'd forgotten about the assignment he'd given her. "Thanks, Jean. This looks great." He flipped through her work product.

Her lips formed a shape vaguely resembling a smile. "If there's anything else you need?"

"As a matter of fact, there is."

"More on baby boomers?"

"Not exactly, but related." How much to tell her? "I got roped into giving Salsa dance lessons here tonight to some friends of Cameron Mackenzie. The instruction part I can handle, but I'm at a loss how to set it up. Got any ideas?"

"I witnessed you and Miss Rogers at Mr. Mackenzie's birthday party. It's a Latin American dance, isn't it?"

"Yeah, it's become quite popular in this country in recent years. Some places even have Salsa clubs."

Not a muscle on her face moved, yet her eyes seemed to widen slightly and take on the glow of the explorer summoned on yet another safari. "You'll need refreshments. Hot, spicy things to go with the dance theme but plenty of bottled water and veggies for when their stomachs rebel." She couldn't resist the challenge.

Refreshments. Of course! You could get away with almost anything if you served food. "Terrific! You take care of the food. I'll provide the music."

But Jean wasn't finished. Her head remained cocked, like she was still running through her own to-do list. "What about decorations?"

"Not necessary. These are only dance *lessons*, not a dance."

"Read my report. Baby boomers are into ambience. The affluent ones spare no expense to obtain all the accouterments of their latest obsessions."

Now he had both Lacey and Jean quoting their research efforts to him. He'd created a monster with this previously accommodating woman. "Spend the rest of the day putting together whatever you need. If the other architects complain, send them to me. Or, better yet, invite them to the class." She eyed him.

"Something else?"

"Do you have room in the class ..." She hesitated.

"Yes?"

"For me?"

No-nonsense Jean Sarducci wanted to take Salsa lessons? The idea amused him. Lacey would be delighted. Well, no. Lacey didn't want Jean anywhere near her. But the idea of Jean taking dance lessons was sure to tickle her. "Uh, okay. I had no idea you'd be interested, but feel free to join us. The more the merrier."

Jean taking dancing lessons? Couldn't get his mind around the idea.

He arrived at the Mackenzie and Associates conference room that evening thirty minutes early to set up. The minute he turned on the lights, he realized this would be no ordinary dance class. Jean had struck already, and as usual, the overachiever had executed her assigned task superbly.

Life-sized palm trees surrounded the perimeter of the room. Colored lights and paper lanterns stretched from one tree to the next. A couple of fancy birdcages occupied the corners. One contained what appeared to be a multi-colored parrot and the other a macaw. Tucked away in another corner was an actual fountain with flowing water.

You've only got yourself to blame. You're the one who asked for her help.

While he was setting up his sound system, Jean arrived with the refreshments. At least, it appeared to be Jean, although this woman wasn't wearing Jean's hallmark dark suit and white blouse. She was decked out in a bright yellow dress, with ruffles around the bottom, no less. And orange shoes.

"Oh, Mr. Dalton. I hoped I'd beat you here and get these goodies out before you arrived."

"No problem. Besides, it looks like you've already spent considerable time getting the room ready. It looks great."

Her face assumed a needy expression. "You really think so?"

"Definitely. It looks like a slice of the Caribbean."

She scanned the room, admiring her work. "I'm glad you like it. I had fun and I kept expenses to a minimum. A friend at a local department store cleared out her tropical storeroom for me.

"And the birds? You know someone at a pet store too?"

He'd been teasing, but she took him seriously. "No, they're mine."

"Oh … my … God!" Lacey stood inside the door, surveying the room as if she'd just landed on the moon.

Scott moved toward Lacey, signaling with his eyes not to spoil

Jean's handiwork. "I asked Jean to help provide a little atmosphere. She did a great job, don't you think?"

Lacey glanced at Scott and then to the ever-efficient Jean, who was peering around his shoulder. "You could say that again." She nodded in disbelief.

"You don't think it's too much?" Jean's voice had lost its usual supercilious quality.

To Lacey's credit, she allowed the look of incredulity she'd entered the room with to mellow into a softer smile. "No, of course not, Jean. You've provided quite an atmosphere."

Jean slipped in front of Scott and stood straighter. "Thank you, Miss Rogers. When one of you creative types gives a compliment, it means a lot. Now, if you'll excuse me, I have jerk chicken to warm."

As the woman scuttled off to tackle her next task, a bemused smile played across Lacey's face. "What potion did you use on her?" she asked once Jean was out of hearing.

Scott scratched his head. "Damned if I know. I didn't want to plan the chips and dip part, so I asked her, and voilà." He gave his assistant one last indulgent glance, then returned his attention to his dance partner.

"Talk about getting into this." He'd been so busy making sure Lacey didn't hurt Jean's feelings, he hadn't noticed his partner's contribution, her, until now. The straight black dress from the other night had been replaced with a bright fuchsia number. It was shorter and more flowing, and, whoa! From their experience under the fallen tree, he already knew the woman was well endowed in the chest category, but this was the first time she'd actually revealed her ample wares. The piquancy of the goodies Jean brought faded next to this spicy dish.

What had he been about to say? Didn't matter. His mouth had gone dry.

"Scott?" Lacey tilted her head, reminiscent of the wildly plumaged birds gracing the corners of the room.

"Huh? Oh. You look great, Lacey. You women have really gotten into the spirit." He took in his black shirt and slacks. At least his pants hugged his butt like a glove. He could show off too.

"Thanks. Since I have no idea how to teach others to dance the Salsa, the least I can do is dress the part."

Scott continued to admire how, when she turned slightly, the skirt flounced across her legs, rippling like the rolling rush of a wave upon the shore. What had she said? Something about no idea how to teach others. "You'll, uh, do fine. Just follow my lead."

"Fol ...?" A gleam of understanding came into her eyes. "Now I get it."

"Get what?" Her brain could skip around more quickly than a propellant pinball.

"You've found the perfect way to keep me in check. You lead, I follow. I take the fancy steps and look good to the crowd, but you control the moves."

How had complimenting her deteriorated so fast? God, she was suspicious of his motives. He stepped toward her, but she backed up. "I wish I could take credit for the deviousness you're crediting me with. But so clever I'm not. The other night I saw an opportunity to gain some information without appearing to be amateur detectives and I took it."

She continued to glare at him.

Had her nostrils actually flared? "Look, you don't have to do this. I can manage the class on my own."

Her eyes flickered. Good. His suggestion hit its mark. "I-I—" She stopped and scrutinized him as if trying to read his thoughts. "Good one, Dalton. If you can't dominate the act, eliminate the other person."

He opened his mouth in protest, but what was he going to say? Whatever he told her, she'd find a way to read the worst into it.

Before he had a chance to find out what she'd do next, they were joined by Marianne Mackenzie, Cam's wife. "Hi, you two. Hope you don't mind if I invited myself to this shindig."

"Of course not, Marianne," Scott said, assuming his most ingratiating air. Taking the back of her arm, he led her into the room. "How's the place look? Remind you of the Caribbean?"

"I had no idea it was going to be so festive," she gushed. "My new dance dress should fit right in." She pirouetted for him. "What do you think? Does this say Salsa?"

She seemed to need his good opinion. As Cam's second wife and several years the guy's junior, the tall brunette was always trying to validate her worth. Probably why she'd gone overboard with Cam's birthday party and why now it was so important to be a part of this gathering. He kicked himself mentally for not inviting her personally.

"It says more than Salsa. It screams Latin Lady. You'll be a natural."

She seemed to visibly relax as she touched his arm. "Thank you, Scott. Cam looked at it and laughed."

Years of practice as Debonair Dalton kept the chuckle begging release from his throat in check. Hopefully, she'd interpret the twinkle he knew must be in his eyes as admiration. But Cam did have a point, even though he'd been rude enough to let his wife know. The woman had selected a tight-fitting green satin dress trimmed in black lace. Somewhere along the line, she'd confused Salsa for Flamenco. No way, though, would he be the one to set her straight.

"How about some hors d'oeuvres before we get started? My secretary outdid herself."

Lacey watched Scott escort Cam's wife across the room and put her in Jean's charge. The guy had a way of making women feel special. He'd taken in Mrs. Mackenzie's emerald green get-up and never missed a beat welcoming her to the class. She herself had stood there stupefied.

Or was she still reacting to his reaction to her own get-up? When he'd spotted her in this hot pink number, he couldn't stop salivating. Those brown eyes seemed to penetrate the fabric, as if he could see her naked underneath, which left her gasping for air. She'd panicked at his libidinous scrutiny and done the only thing she could think of, started an argument. Dumb.

"Excuse me, are you here for the Salsa lessons too?"

Lacey turned to find a middle-aged woman not three feet from her. Tall, she wore her salt and pepper hair back in a long braid down her back. Unlike the other early arrivals, she was dressed in a baggy, white gauze blouse and black slacks set off by an oversized necklace of red, black and gray stones. She must have come in during the exchange with Scott. "Actually, I'm one of the instructors," Lacey replied.

"Then you're just the person I need to see." She offered Lacey a hand ringed in three clunky bracelets. "I'm Janice Collier. A friend of mine saw you dance last week. She intended to be here tonight but last-minute houseguests changed her plans. She suggested I take her place. Do you mind?" She offered an anxious but pleasant smile.

"Sure, Janice. No problem. But you understand this is probably for one night only? The other instructor and I don't have any experience at this. The people who saw us dance last week coaxed us to show them a few steps."

The woman continued to hold her hand, but her expression mellowed. "Don't worry. I'm not really here to learn the Salsa, although it sounds like fun. Apparently my friend thinks I've been spending too much time rejuvenating my business and I need to get out more."

"Oh?" Now they'd become someone's excuse to get away from home?

Janice Collier blinked, as if she read Lacey's thoughts. "I'm a widow. Two years now. I think I'm doing fine adjusting to being on my own, but my friend believes otherwise." She smiled shyly.

The woman's revelation of such personal information surprised Lacey. "I'm sorry. I didn't mean to make you uncomfortable."

"You didn't. I don't usually mention being a widow. It felt right to tell you. By way of explanation."

"You don't need to explain anything. We'll do whatever we can to make it fun for you. As you can see, they've gone to a lot of work to get us all into the spirit."

Janice Collier took in the room's decorations. "Wow! I had no idea this was going to be another party."

"None of us did, until Scott asked his secretary for help with refreshments. She tends to get a little carried away at times."

"I say let her do her thing more often," Janice replied. "I'll check out her efforts before everyone else arrives."

Others were now streaming into the conference room, oohing and ahhing as they took in the atmosphere. Almost all of them were dressed as if they were attending a fiesta. Even the men. This was getting exciting.

"Lacey? You ready to get started?" Scott pulled away from his entourage of gushing females long enough to check on her.

"No time like the present." Her stomach wasn't exactly unsettled, but until this shindig got underway, she had no idea what to expect. Maybe Jean would stand in for her?

"Okay, folks. Gather round." Scott signaled for everyone to join him near the dance floor. "Pull up a chair for now, if you will. Lacey and I want to get to know you first."

Introductions filled the next fifteen minutes. Scott told them a little about himself, then turned the spotlight over to Lacey, who, though not prepared to say much, surprised herself with her little speech. Then everyone else got into the act.

One by one, the rest of the group spoke up.

"I'm a gastroenterologist at a local clinic. I'm pretty good doing the jive and the swing, but Latin dances have always intimidated me."

"My wife and I became empty-nesters this year. With so much more time on our hands than we're used to, we're trying our hands, and tonight, feet, at several new outlets."

"I write a blog on wine tasting, although my day job is teaching American History at Roosevelt High School."

And so it went. Their comments didn't shed any light on their retirement aspirations, but it was clear they were all individuals with unique interests. They certainly didn't fit the *over-the-hill* stereotype society liked to pin on those over fifty. Strangely enough, those who indicated they were retired from active careers appeared to have even more interesting lives than those still working. They described encore career jobs like lobbying for better child care facilities, teaching fly casting, selling sex toys for bachelorette parties and serving as marshals at a local golf course.

Some had grown children; some were even enjoying the wonders of grandparenting. Others had started families later in life and now spent the better part of their time at their children's soccer games, dance recitals and martial arts classes. One thing for sure— they didn't consider themselves old. Mature maybe. But they were still hard at living and enjoying their lives.

"Great getting to know you all," Scott announced, when the last person concluded. "But now, I know your feet are itching to get dancing." He gave them a smile only he could deliver. It was more than warm. It was the patented Scott Dalton look which said, *trust us, you're amongst friends. This is going to be fun.*

Heaven help her when he turned it her direction. Thank God she'd taken steps to avoid the Scott Dalton charm machine by setting him up as Celia's fake boyfriend. After the project ended? Maybe, since neither of them seemed interested in long-term hookups, but probably not, since she didn't want to get involved with someone within the firm.

Scott held out his hand in invitation to Lacey, focusing his same *trust me* smile directly on her. She couldn't swallow. Her heart seemed to have broken loose from its moorings and lodged in her throat, where it continued to beat erratically. *Move it, kid.* The curtain had risen on their one and only performance.

He placed his hand over hers and drew her to him, smiling down at her like the dentist saying *this shouldn't hurt … much.* Then a strange thing happened. The moment they came in contact with each other, she relaxed. Not in the go-limp sort of way, but like the practiced musician forgetting stage fright to launch into the familiar and practiced concerto.

They started with the fundamentals. Box steps. A dip. After a bit, a twirl. When the song transitioned into a faster tempo, Scott increased the difficulty of the steps. For not having practiced, they were in perfect synch with each other.

It was as if Scott sensed her best moves and concentrated on those, although a few times he took her through new combinations, challenging her to keep up. The sense of exhilaration coursing through her body was almost as great as completing a design to the delight of her clients.

Her heart raced, which only added to the thrill. As her comfort level increased, she dared a peek at Scott. Was he enjoying this as much as she was?

He noticed her checking him out and returned her gaze with a deep, penetrating look of his own. His eyes had grown cloudy and dark.

When she thought her senses could be aroused no further, the song ended with a dramatic climax. With a flourish, Scott swung her into a one-handed death grip. She hung on for dear life, determined not to spoil the effect with an amateurish release.

Then it was over. Scott pulled her to him, gave her a collegial hug and whispered in her ear. "You did great."

She struggled to catch her breath. Though winded from the dance, she was more discombobulated from the thrill of contact.

The class members jumped to their feet in applause and admiration, crowding around them to shake hands and pat them on their backs.

"Even better than last Friday," one of the more familiar-looking men told them. "But I don't think I'm up to the fancy stuff you did."

"Oh, but I want to try!" the woman with him cried. "It looked like such fun."

"Good attitude," Scott said. "I hope the rest of you feel the same way. We'll start slow. What you just saw was," sheepish grin, "Lacey and I showing off."

Lacey and I showing off. Right, Scott, I couldn't wait to break my neck on that last move. At least she hadn't fouled up and embarrassed herself. Yet.

"Let's get to it, everyone." Scott moved farther out on the dance floor. "Line up in rows of four so you can all view our feet. Jean, how 'bout turning up the lights so we can see better?"

Jean did as asked and then raced back to find a place in the first row.

For the next fifteen minutes, Scott led them through a few basic steps, adding music after a bit. Then partners.

At first, this part was awkward, except for one couple who'd obviously been dancing the Salsa for some time. When Scott noticed them, he conned the guy into dancing with the extra woman. Though the guy's partner didn't look too pleased, Lacey moved over to her to go through some more advanced steps.

When they took a ten-minute break, people clustered around the room in small groups, chatting and drinking. Scott motioned for Lacey to start mingling.

No rest for the wicked. But then, this class was about information-gathering. Scott approached the Salsa-trained couple and congratulated them, so she moved off in the other direction, passing Janice Collier, who seemed quite engaged talking to Jean, and sought out Marianne Mackenzie. "Mind if I join you? My feet could use a rest."

The woman rewarded her with a broad, welcoming smile. "By all means, Lacey. This is a hoot, although I'm having to concentrate more than I thought I would."

"I had the same problem at first, too," Lacey said. "But it got easier. Just a matter of relaxing and letting the music guide you."

"If you say so."

A few minutes later, Scott called them back together and he and Lacey walked the group through a new routine, one where they turned and Lacey was twirled away from Scott. The difficulty level was considerably ratcheted up from the first routine, but the group seemed up to it, even the infamous Death Grip.

Jean wound up with the guy who knew as much as Scott about the dance. Lacey couldn't believe her eyes when Jean flung herself back with a dramatic flounce of her arm and closed eyes. Not bad, if she held on. Which she did. Where was the real Jean tonight? Never mind. Lacey liked this one better.

Although most of the students appeared beat and a bit out of steam when the lesson ended, they enthusiastically praised their two teachers and thanked them for the class.

"When's our next session?" Marianne asked.

"Next?" Scott's voice rose in surprise. "This was just a one-time deal." He looked helplessly at Lacey, his eyebrows lifting, as if to say, "Get me out of this!" Though her body still buzzed from prolonged contact with Scott, a niggling whisper of disappointment wormed its way into her brain. She'd expected to gain more information from the evening than she'd accomplished.

"Would you consider at least one more time?" one of the women asked. "I learned a lot tonight, but I need more practice."

"Me, too," another woman added.

"I'm sure Cam wouldn't mind our using this room again," his wife reassured them.

"I think I can get these decorations one more time," the ever-helpful Jean said.

"I'll bring the food next time," Janice Collier offered.

"Uh, well, I don't think Lacey and I have any more to add to your repertoire, folks." Scott was actually stammering. "What you saw tonight was as good as we get."

"Then just repeat this stuff," suggested one of the men. The one who'd looked so put-out to be there at first.

"Next Monday night?" Scott asked. How would he ever get Celia to agree to another night off from their so-called courtship?

He never should've agreed to the arrangement at a time when he needed every waking hour for this Arabella thing. But since he hadn't been very successful gleaning information from the group tonight, maybe a second run at it would help. Their time for drafting the design concept was fast disappearing. Even his breakdancing approach to work might not be enough to salvage this project if their boomer research didn't net a viable concept soon.

Lacey stood across the room from him sending him a bewildered and scathing scowl. He was getting pretty good at sizing up the degree of her displeasure, and this decision was right up there with his being born.

He'd set her straight later. For now, this was too good an opportunity to pass up.

The group agreed to meet the following Monday, then partook in Jean's heartier refreshments. They seemed to enjoy the social time and were slow to break up and leave. Several stayed to help Jean take down the decorations and load them in her car.

Scott was tired. No, exhausted. Not even thirty and he was ready to crash. Exuding charm and being on all evening he could handle. It had been taxing to invent the lesson as he went, but all his efforts seemed to go well. He was used to thinking on his feet.

But being in constant physical contact with Lacey? Grueling. He'd never had such a responsive dance partner. But those evocative blue eyes and bouncy blonde hair, not to mention her luscious, tiny body, had his own body on alert all evening. Executing all those moves while attempting to avoid an imminent hard on had not been fun. *Stupid idea to wear such tight slacks.* No fun at all. The breaks he'd called had been just as much for his sake, to cool down, as they were for the sake of the class. Now, he was ready to drop.

They still needed to compare notes about the evening, what she'd learned about boomers. He hoped it was more than he'd been able to unearth. These were interesting people, but other than the idea of adding a Salsa club on the property, they'd contributed very little to his ideas for the retirement community.

But his discussion with Lacey would have to wait until the clear light of morning, when she'd hopefully return to the confines of a business suit and after he'd submitted his body to at least two cold showers.

CHAPTER 9

Although he arrived home by ten, Scott didn't sleep well, still pumped from the success of the class. The lesson part had gone much better than he'd allowed himself to hope, even though they still knew very little about boomers. But they now had a second chance to tap this gold mine next week. Tomorrow he'd worry about what they were going to teach, once he got some sleep.

But every time he closed his eyes, he saw Lacey. Remembered how those cornflower blues had turned to molten sapphires as their dance imitated the heated rise of passion. Nor could he forget how well she molded herself to his body as they performed those tricky steps. The faint whiff of lilacs. *Cool it, Dalton. The lady is off limits.* But his mind and body weren't listening. How could a guy sleep when his body was ready for other things? The greenish light on his alarm clock mocked him the rest of the night.

Now, in the bright light of morning, too bright, he lounged at his desk, chin supported in his palms, trying in vain to keep his mind on Project Arabella. God, his body hurt! He sipped the lifesaving coffee Jean set before him five minutes earlier. Unlike him, his lieutenant hadn't shown any signs of wear from last night. She'd even been humming!

"I have just one word for you this morning, Dalton. Why?" Lacey stood in the doorway, her expression pinched, last night's gravity-defying dress now replaced with a pair of olive green slacks, a light blue blouse and tan blazer. Very businesslike, very no-nonsense, very "no, I'm not going to do another Salsa class." Still, she was a vision, even to his fuzzy eyes.

Had to do something to relax those wrinkles lining her forehead, though. Fortunately, he was prepared. "Here, have a seat, enjoy one or two of these doughnuts and finish the question." He flung open the lid of the pink carton and shoved it toward her. He'd driven out of his way and suffered the early morning drive-through traffic to procure it. How could she appear so alert and put-together while his own body had already checked out for the day?

"Let me spell it out for you. Why did you agree to another class? Granted, we may have gleaned a few clues to understanding boomers, but I'm out of Salsa moves to demonstrate. My body is on strike today. I'm in flat soles and slacks because I can barely stand. Your body, too, if not your brain, seems to have realized it was a wash."

As if sensing his need for reinforcements, Jean appeared out of nowhere with a mug of something which she offered Lacey. "Coffee. One sugar, right?" God, the woman was good. He hadn't even clued her in to Lacey's resistance and yet Jean seemed to sense it on her own.

"Uh, yes. Thanks." Lacey narrowed her eyes. "I know what you and your cohort are up to," her expression said as she accepted the mug and approached his desk.

"You're most welcome, Lacey. I really enjoyed our class last night."

Lacey's frown melted into a tolerant smile. "Due in large part to the mood you set."

Whoa. The ladies were actually chummy this morning. At least the class had accomplished something, gotten these two talking.

"What's with her?" Lacey asked once Jean left. "Why so chipper? She danced as much as we did last night."

He did a shoulder roll. Shrugging would expend too much energy. "Beats me. She really seemed to find her groove. Who'da thought?"

"Maybe she should teach the class, then, because I don't want to."

She headed back to the door, coffee mug in hand, doughnuts untouched.

"Hey, wait! I didn't realize you were so against repeating our efforts." *Liar.* "Come back and let's talk."

She halted, cocked her head, as if weighing his sincerity. In the end, she did return and take a seat. But she didn't look at him. Instead, she sipped the heart rate-restoring liquid and rooted around in the pink box for just the right goodie. "Why subject our worn-out bodies to additional punishment when every minute counts on this project?"

He offered the easy reply first, while his brain attempted to manufacture a plausible reason even he would buy. "Marianne Mackenzie wants it. Her friends want it. We don't want her to lose face with them by chickening out."

She took another bite of her doughnut, swallowed. Her expression suggested a mother refusing to believe her son's explanation of the newest dent in the family car. "That's bull, Scott, and you know it. If Marianne Mackenzie really wanted to impress her friends, she'd hire professional instructors."

Saw right through his gambit. She was right. It was a bunch of bull. Since he hadn't come up with a better rationale yet, time to employ one of his time-tested client techniques. Admit defeat. Turn the tables. Smile ingenuously. "You got me. But, look, *tempus fugit.* It's all we have at the moment, unless you've got a better plan?" He offered his patented ingenuous smile and cast a surreptitious glance at Jean's binder of boomer info resting on his conference table. Damn. Should've taken the time to study it yesterday, then he could be more directive in this discussion today.

She fell back into her chair. "Finally, some candor. I suppose we could start with the few tidbits I picked up last night. Haven't had a chance to write them down yet. Too tired when I got home."

At least she had something to document. He'd been so busy praising Jean, charming Marianne Mackenzie, and trying to avoid any missteps in his dance routine, there'd been no time or energy to absorb boomerspeak. "Me, either. Why don't we go over your findings?"

She ticked them off on her fingers. "They adore their grandchildren, follow them anywhere: soccer games, school plays, band concerts, and when Mom and Dad aren't able, babysit, pick them up from school and take them to doctor appointments."

He entered "grandkids" into his tablet. "Check."

"They're really into finances," she continued. "Savings, bonds, stocks, tax write-offs and part-time jobs. And traveling, whether it be weekend trips to see their kids in St. Paul or ten-day Mediterranean cruises."

"Whew! Breathe. Give me a chance to get all this down. Thought you said you came away with only a few ideas?"

"Just those three, although they do seem to be promising clues."

Promising clues. Great opportunities. Was she putting him on? Time to find out. "Clues to what?"

She squinted. Like she couldn't believe he had the audacity to ask. Then her expression morphed into one of authority, eyes clear and wide, chin up. "Guest rooms are no longer *de rigueur* in single family homes. The 'extra' bedroom is there, but since visiting relatives and overnight guests are no longer as frequent as they used to be, because a lot of travelers prefer staying in motels now, the extra bedroom now is more a hobby room convertible to an extra bedroom should guests arrive."

No kidding? "I may not have done many single family residences of late, but I do keep up with the trends. What's your point?"

"These days, Grandma and Grandpa are more likely to go visit the grandkids on their home territory, since kids' lives are so overscheduled. Should the grandkids come for a visit, sure there ought to be adequate sleeping facilities for them, but those are more likely to be in finished basements which feature state-of-the-art flat screens equipped with internet hook-up for gaming, movies and cable networks." She folded her hands and sat back, as if to say, "Were you able to keep up?"

He really had to take a closer look at Jean's binder. "You got all that from 'grandkids'?"

"Want more? Consider the travel part. Almost everyone I talked to or eavesdropped on had either just returned from somewhere out of town or was planning a trip in the near future. While they're away, three things concern them: home security, home maintenance and care for their pets. Our plan needs to include top-notch security systems, a range of concierge options to keep the grass cut, snow plowed, plants watered, and low-cost, highly sensitive animal care."

Now she was just showing off. His job. "Sounds like you heard a lot more than you thought you did. You just made my case for doing another class next week."

She blinked. "Excuse me?"

"You did good work. Just think how much more we can pick up doing the class one more time."

She slumped in her chair. "Well, I got my answer to why. I don't like it, but in your own convoluted way, your reasoning makes sense."

One point for him. Time to quit while he was ahead. "You should probably round up all those thoughts and get them into the computer before you lose them." *Hint, hint. Go, so I can do a crash course on Jean's findings and develop my own list.*

But Lacey made no move to leave. "What? You weren't done?"

"Are you trying to get rid of me?"

I hate bright women. "No. Like I said, I don't want you to lose your train of thought."

WHAT WAS GOING on with Scott? She could take a hint, especially one offered twice. Why was he trying to get rid of her? Their meeting had barely lasted a half hour. He'd listened to her thoughts, grilled her, actually, and then almost threw her out of his office before sharing any of his own findings. And of course they hadn't even discussed the project plan she'd thrown together the day before.

She was so intent on figuring out her partner's motives, she walked right into another woman. Janice? The woman who'd attended last night's class under protest? "Mrs. Collier? What are you doing here?"

"Hello, Lacey. Call me Janice. I'm here to meet with the woman who helped arrange last night's lesson. Jean. Jean Sarducci. She invited me to tour the building, thinking some of the artwork at my gallery would fit in well here."

"You own a gallery? I didn't realize—"

"That I was in charge of a functioning business and not cloistered at home, afraid of my shadow?"

"Uh, well …"

"I came across somewhat wimpy last night, probably because I felt pressured to attend. But I'm really doing quite well and I'm glad I came to your class. I enjoyed myself immensely, and it was a welcome break from gallery work."

And I made a new friend. Funny how life had a way of surprising one with unexpected gifts when least expected. "I'm glad. I had no idea what we were getting ourselves into, but I had fun also."

The other woman brushed off her sleeves.

"I hope I didn't hurt you," Lacey said. "I wasn't paying attention. Too busy trying to decipher the meeting I just had with my partner."

"You wouldn't be talking about Scott Dalton, would you?"

"You're quick."

"The fireworks between the two of you were hard to miss last night. They probably contributed to your great dance style."

"Actually, we're not a couple. He's seeing my best friend. Scott and I are just partners on a design project right now, and we seem to have totally different approaches."

Janice studied her. "Oh. I see." She didn't sound convinced. Then she appeared to remember her business inside the building. "I need to get going, but I plan to be there again next Monday."

"I'll see you, then. Jean's office is a little farther down the corridor."

They said their good-byes, then went their different directions.

Rather than return to her office and computer, Lacey headed off to the fitness center down the street where the firm maintained a membership for all its employees. Cameron Mackenzie believed inspiration occurred in many ways. He encouraged his architects to grasp hold of their ideas whenever and wherever they occurred. A little exercise might revive her aching bod and at the same time help her put her finger on what just happened in Scott's office.

Ten minutes later, she was on the indoor track, striding vigorously and seeking creative genius. She let her mind go blank—it was almost there anyhow—and sprinted around the track. She focused on breathing, swinging her arms and increasing the pace.

After two laps, her brain was ready to engage, just not on design ideas. Instead, her mind took her back to a day when she was six, sitting on the front porch swing while she played with the dress-up doll her daddy brought her the week before, waiting for him to come home from work. He'd be there any time now. She loved this part of the day, when Daddy arrived to scoop her up in his arms and make a big show of asking her about her day.

Only today, Daddy was late. Her mother had come out twice to tell her dinner was on the table. Lacey had stubbornly refused to eat before Daddy got home. What would he think if his little girl wasn't there to greet him?

But Daddy didn't come home that night. Nor the next night or the night after. He didn't come home again. Life had never been the same. Her mother told her Daddy had an illness and had gone away to get better. He still loved them all very much, but he couldn't be with them anymore.

Night after night, Lacey cried herself to sleep, hugging her dolly to her chest and wondering if somehow she'd been the one who made her daddy sick so he had to leave.

One night, she heard her mother crying. She left her doll on the bed and went off to comfort her mother. Pausing near the top of the stairs, she heard her mother, between sobs, tell her big brother Daddy wasn't coming back ever again. Family life had become too much for him, so he'd left them.

Brian was now the man of the family, her mother said. The three-some began a new life. Lacey abandoned her doll to the bottom of her toy chest and never asked for another doll again.

She pulled up, leaned a palm against the cool poured concrete wall of the gym to catch her breath and snap her head back to the present. Why had she been thinking about her father's desertion? Memories of those sad times, especially the doll, rarely occurred anymore.

The doll! The doll was the connection. Her father had given it to her knowing it would be the last thing he gave her. A bribe.

Scott tried to bribe her this morning. Nowhere near as profound as a father about to abandon his child, but the same self-serving premeditation was there. He knew before she arrived she didn't want to teach another class. She'd made no secret of her reaction the night before, but until now, she hadn't realized he'd caught her scowl. For some reason, he was willing to put up with the backache and foot strain another class would inevitably bring. Willing enough he'd stopped off for doughnuts on his way to work to coax her to say yes.

Why couldn't he have just asked her outright? Better yet, why didn't he check with her last night before caving to the group's demands? Because, even with her only feet away, he momentarily forgot they were partners. He took charge yet again. But unlike their first meetings, he didn't appear to have done it to anger her enough to quit the project. Oh, yes, she'd picked up on that ploy after a few days. Last night, he'd just forgotten himself. Until he saw her scowl. The doughnuts weren't a bribe. They were an apology minus the "I'm sorry" part.

So why the bum's rush? Embarrassment? No, Scott didn't get embarrassed. She played back the last few minutes of their meeting. She'd been reporting the few clues she'd picked up during the class and hypothesizing how those elements could be used in their design concept. Though she'd gotten a little carried away, she surprised herself with how much she'd gleaned. He'd actually listened, agreed with her, though his eyes kept wandering to something across the room. Then he'd shooed her away. Afraid to acknowledge her success? No, he'd used her findings against her to justify doing another session.

She couldn't figure him out. But for now, it was enough she knew he hadn't been entirely forthcoming. Though she was getting used to his ways and even sort of liked him, she'd have to be on her guard even more than she'd ever imagined necessary when this project began.

Returning to her office, she raced through her documentation so she could get back to Scott's office as soon as possible. He'd wanted her out of there. Time to find out why.

JEAN DESERVED A RAISE. No, a promotion. Hell, if she had any design talent, she could do his job. Her boomer research was a treasure trove. Like Lacey, she not only listed various characteristics, demographics and so-called wants and needs of boomers, she also went on to list her conclusions about how such data could and should be used in a design concept, even though he'd never actually told her the nature of the project.

Women. They couldn't leave well enough alone. They had to show you they knew everything better than you.

Good thing. He doubted he would've come up with half the suggestions she made.

He returned to the first half of the report, a scrapbook of sorts, clippings from the AARP magazine, a global study on boomers, the Wall Street Journal, Scientific American, all more or less expected. But he also came across a hodgepodge of other items: restaurant listings and menus, college course descriptions, flyers for manicures and pedicures, auto ads, theatrical film box office numbers. She did this in three days?

"Ahem." He'd been so absorbed in the binder, he hadn't heard Jean enter. "I trust I completed my assignment to your satisfaction?"

"Good job, Jean." Telling her it was brilliant would only raise unnecessary expectations.

She lingered, waiting. For what, he had no idea, unless he hadn't laid on enough praise. "Yes?"

"I wanted to tell you how much I enjoyed this task. So much, I may have gone overboard. Overkill?" she added when he didn't reply.

Overkill? How about totally over the top? It would take weeks to absorb all this, and he only had days. "It is thorough, but I appreciate having so much to choose from."

"I thought this might help." She handed him a one-page document containing a list of five items: health concerns, higher education, volunteer work, small business ownership and spiritual needs.

Bless her needy, bragging little heart. Even his tiny male brain could understand her one-page summary. It didn't escape him she'd withheld this part until she was sure he'd at least opened her magnum opus before she handed over the bottom line. His job wasn't good enough for her—she should be CEO. "Why yes, I think this list will help me formulate my plans. Thanks."

When he didn't add anything further, she backed out of the room. Maybe he should be thankful Lacey and Jean still considered themselves on different teams. If those two ever got together and compared notes, he'd be out of a job.

He was still contemplating how to incorporate Jean's list into a design concept when there was a light tapping at his door and Jean reentered. Hah, this time she knocked. "I'm going to be leaving shortly for an early lunch." She placed a cardboard mailer on his desk. "This came for you a little while ago." Curious, Scott ripped it open after she'd left.

Son:

Dad and I have met the most marvelous couple from Kuala Lumpur. They were here on holiday and will soon be returning home. They invited us to join them. Imagine! We've never seen that part of the world. We're really looking forward to it. It means, though, we won't be back for another month. By now, you should be quite familiar with the routine of checking out the old homestead to assure all is well, so this shouldn't be any great task for you. Take care.

See you soon. Mom.

Scott stared at the letter a moment longer, then ripped it up and threw both it and the mailing folder in his wastebasket. He wondered if he'd ever receive a registered letter or phone call from his parents inviting him to join them. Better yet, telling him how much they missed him.

CHAPTER 10

"Okay, Dalton, time to come clean." Lacey froze in her tracks, her eyes riveted on Scott and Cam standing in the middle of Scott's office, hands joined.

Cam turned to Scott, raising his eyes in response to Lacey's statement. Then he seemed to realize what she was staring at and quickly released his grip.

Did the woman have radar? Even though he'd shooed her away just an hour ago, he was glad she'd returned. "Come in, Lacey. Close the door."

She switched her attention to Cam. "Hi, Cam. I didn't know you were in here. Sorry to interrupt. Scott's been doing some research I wanted to hear about."

Thank God. She'd read the situation correctly and adlibbed a different reason for her visit. And once he got rid of Cam, he was about to snow her with his newfound boomer insights. Okay, Jean's insights.

Cam gave her a knowing smile. "Our boy's doing research these days? Sounds like you've made quite an impression on him."

I'll say.

"Oh. Right."

"Since you're here, why not give us a hand? To replace the one I just removed from Cam's." Scott put as much distance between himself and his recent student as he could in the confined quarters of his office.

She lifted an eyebrow. "What were you doing? It looked like a two-person version of Follow the Leader."

"Good description," Scott said. "I think you've identified our problem. Cam's agreed to join our dance class so we'll have more men. I was catching him up on the routine we taught the class last night."

Her frown relaxed. "Welcome to the club, Cam." She beamed. "So, you need a partner?"

"One of the feminine variety," Scott added. "You walked in on two men trying to lead. You're just what we needed."

"Back to that following thing again? Thanks," but she was smiling as she said it. "Since for the moment I'm the best game in town, looks like I'm it." She approached Cam and reached for his hand, placing her left hand on his shoulder. Lifting her chin, she flashed her baby blues his direction. "Ready?"

"Uh, okay. I guess," responded a surprised Cam.

"You'll be a natural," she said, her smile broad and reassuring.

They spent the next fifteen minutes going through the drill, Scott talking them through the steps first, and Lacey talking them through as they went. Even though Cam tripped up every so often, including stepping on Lacey's instep twice, she retained a fixed smile. "You're doing fine," she responded each time. "The main thing is to keep the time and remember the steps." Just that morning she'd been comparing notes with Scott about whose feet hurt more.

"I don't know, Lacey," Cam complained. "I'm messing up more than I'm getting it."

She patted his shoulder where her left hand lodged. "You're doing better than you think. It takes a while to catch on to this beat."

"What do you think, Scott? Have I got it down well enough to survive?" Cam called.

"Huh, oh, right." He'd been admiring Lacey's swishing derriere. Even with a jacket covering her slacks, the swaying motion of her hips hypnotized him. He coughed, attempting to get his breathing back to normal.

"I think you've got it," Scott said in the style of Professor Henry Higgins to Eliza Doolittle, bringing the session to an abrupt end when Cam's hand strayed an inch or so beneath her waist.

"You think?" Cam couldn't contain his relief. But his eyes glowed excitedly.

"Definitely," Lacey added. "Keep practicing and you'll do fine next week."

Standing behind Cam, Scott closed his eyes and said a silent prayer Lacey hadn't promised Cam the moon while mouthing his thanks to his dancing partner. In fact, she'd done a credible job of coaxing and convincing Cam he was ready to join the rest of the class despite his obvious lack of rhythm. She seemed to have picked up on his own glib turn of phrase.

"I'm outta here, then. Thanks, guys," Cam beamed, his hand already on the doorknob. "By the way, let's keep this our little secret, okay? Especially from my wife."

"No problem," they promised.

"Oh, and about Project Arabella?" Cam delayed. "The client ... did I mention he's originally from this area? Which is why he wants to build here. Another factotum for your research folder. He's moved the due date for your design concept up a week." He was out of there before either reacted, as if a magician's wand had zapped him from the room.

"Did I hear what I think I heard?" an incredulous Lacey asked Scott. "The deadline's been moved up?"

"So it would seem."

He kept his expression impassive as he doodled on a notepad. The news had knocked the floor out from under him, but he didn't want to alarm her. He'd worry enough for both of them.

She fell into the chair next to his desk and rubbed her temples. "I feel a headache coming on. Nausea, too."

Scott settled behind his desk. "Must be catching. My stomach's doing somersaults."

"Do you believe our boss? He let us give him a short course on Salsa, then he dropped this little bomb." She leaned back and cradled her head against the back of the chair. "This day just keeps getting better."

"What are we going to do about it?"

Lacey twiddled her fingers on the armrest then switched to her hair instead, twisting one strand back and forth over and over. "Dance lessons aren't enough," she replied finally. "They're a great idea, but we have six days 'til the next class, and we just lost seven days of our planning time. We've got to go into warp speed studying boomers. Got any ideas?"

He could share Jean's ideas with her, but something told him they weren't enough, just a bunch of unrelated thoughts. They needed some way to unify them into a concept.

"I really thought I had something when I input my notes from last night," she said. "It was good stuff, but once I finished and read back what I'd written, I realized I had filled in some of the detail we need, but it wasn't the foundation. You know what I mean?"

"You put your finger on it the day we received this assignment when you asked Cam about theme." Who would've thought back then he'd be admitting as much to her now?

"You're right!" she said. In her exuberance, she touched his arm. Bolts of sensation shot up his arm. He glanced up, saw the same recognition of feeling in her eyes as must have been in his. She removed her hand as fast as she'd placed it. "Theme to me means something broader than blueprints and layouts. It's the essence of this collection of buildings we'll be planning, what ties them together. It's eluding us right now, but we'll know it when we see it."

"Nothing we haven't heard in countless college lectures and professional seminars, but for once it makes sense in the context of this project. You done good, kid." He reached out to pat her arm, remembered the surprise of their last contact and withdrew his hand.

"Thanks, but now we're back to Square One. Where can we observe boomers?" she asked.

"What do people over fifty-five do? Where do they go?"

"Let's not waste time," she said. "What's happening today? Right now, at two o'clock in the afternoon. Restaurants?"

He wrinkled his nose. "Not this time of day. From what I hear, seniors eat around five."

"A grocery store?"

"A thought, but we want to be able to observe as well as overhear them. People are too scattered in a grocery store."

Her fingers went to her hair again, twisted a strand. Just for a moment, he pictured his own fingers in those spun-silk tresses. What he wouldn't give to switch places with her hand right now.

"Too bad there isn't an AARP meeting in session," he said. "At least we'd know our target group would be there. Why not one of those super discount stores? Now there's an idea."

"Same problem as a grocery store," she reminded him. "But what about a collection of stores?"

"Huh?"

"The mall."

"You want to go shopping?"

She returned a broad smile. "Now you're talking. To think, it was your idea." She rose and made for the door. "Meet you in ten at the front door. You drive."

"Hey, wait. I was kidding."

Though she was already out the door, she stuck her head back in. "I wasn't."

THE MALL on the southwest side of the metro was the area's most recent sprawling retail complex. They parked near the movie theatre on one end.

"Confess, we're here because you need to pick up a blouse or pair of shoes," Scott speculated as they made their way to the nearest entrance.

"Would it be so horrible if I did?" He wasn't correct, but wouldn't it be fun to drag him into one of the ladies' underwear stores on the pretext of buying a new bra? Never mind. Knowing Scott's reputation with the ladies, he was probably already more than familiar with those places. "My blood sugar's low. I feel like an ice cream cone." She made a sharp turn to the left and headed toward a place that specialized in the delicacy.

Scott joined her, treating her to a single dip of chocolate chip mint while he ordered rocky road. Cones in hand, they seated themselves in the black wrought iron tables flanking the main eating area in the food court and spent the next few minutes licking their treats before they dripped down their hands. "We could've gone to several restaurants, if ice cream was what you were after," Scott said at length.

"Shh. I'm trying to hear what the couple over there is arguing about."

"What couple?" he whispered.

"Behind me, on the left. They look to be about sixty."

His brow furrowed. "How do you know?"

"His hair's totally white, hers is died dark brown, but short, so she doesn't have to mess with it much. Now, shush, I can't hear."

"What did the doctor say, Marty?"

"Same old, same old. Stop eating, drinking, smoking. In other words, might as well pick out my coffin now, because life ain't gonna be worth livin' once I stop."

"You're exaggerating. Stop smoking, yes. Drinking was probably more like cut back. And eating was eat better. Don't you want to live longer?"

"Told ya, not if I have to give up all my pleasures."

"I thought I was your pleasure."

"Sure ya are, when it fits your schedule. Before Colbert, not during the weather, and only if I shower first."

"Not so difficult."

"Stop eavesdropping," Scott chided, sotto voce.

"They're getting into really personal stuff."

"It's the personal stuff we're here to investigate."

"You're getting something from their conversation?"

"Well, they still have sex."

He raised an eyebrow. "Didn't know you were into kinky stuff."

"Sex after sixty is not kinky. At least, it doesn't have to be. It's just reassuring to discover they still indulge."

He stared at her with an expression she hadn't seen from him before. Disbelief. But in a flash, his eyes softened. "I forgot. You don't know many seniors."

"What about you?"

"You mean my parents? Let's not go there. The thought of those two doing it," he shivered, and not from the ice cream he was consuming, "almost makes me want to consider celibacy." He gave her a lascivious grin. "But not quite. Actually, given their globetrotting lifestyle, it wouldn't surprise me a bit to learn how much they're into it."

His admission halted further discussion. They turned their attention to finishing their cones.

Why had she even mentioned the subject? She felt a bit like the kid who, when threatened with getting her mouth washed out with soap for repeating swear words, couldn't wait to go off on her own and swear up a storm. Only in her case, the subject was sex. The ice cream hadn't frozen her brain, it softened it. She wanted Scott Dalton, but better sense told her to pass on this particular treat. At least until the project was over.

So instead, what was she doing? Indulging her sweet tooth and talking about the very thing she'd sworn off.

This line of thought needed to stop. Now. *Finish up the cone, Lacey, and get out of here.*

Scott did nothing to help get her mind off the forbidden fruit as he relished his cone, taking long, leisurely licks. She had to swallow, twice, each time he retracted his tongue, coated with melted chocolate cream.

When he glanced up, he seemed to note her interest in his ice cream consumption, and a smoky haze curtained his eyes. Was he reading her thoughts? A part of her wished he could.

Before she realized what was happening, he reached across the small table to touch her lips. His fingertips caressed the side of her mouth for less than a second, but her sensory bank recorded the touch forever.

"You've got a few pieces of chocolate there. Unless you're saving them for a snack later?" His eyes sparkled with humor and glowed with heat at the same time.

"Uh. No. Didn't realize. Thanks." Could she sound any more awkward?

He withdrew his hand. "Let's check out some other parts of the mall."

She swallowed the last bite of cone, swiped a napkin across her mouth, just in case he missed a stray particle and rose along with him. "Where to next?"

They strolled down the corridor connecting the food court/theatre area to the main leg of the mall, no particular destination in mind.

Scott gestured toward an open bench down on the main level. "We could park ourselves in the central court and people watch."

"Or we could pick a direction and see what there is to see. There are some children's stores off to the right on the lower level. The grandparent thing, remember? Maybe we'll find our prey there."

They passed several high-end clothing stores. "Not there. Those are the territory of teens with money and young professionals. How about the sporting goods store? My research said boomers were really into recreational sports. Fishing, golf, tennis, you know?" he suggested.

On their way to the sporting goods store, they passed the children's play center. The indoor forest-themed playground featured a myriad of "climb on" toys. A small army of preschool age and younger children swarmed over each plaything, guarded by numerous moms, dad, aunts, uncles, older siblings, nannies … and grandparents. Aha! She'd proved her theory.

Without realizing she was going to do so, Lacey stopped, mesmerized by the scene before her. One little girl in particular caught her attention. She must have been around three, because her mobility was good, but her words still sounded somewhat infantile. She was dressed in a one-piece pink and white striped knit playsuit. Shoes off, all the kids had to shed their shoes on the sidelines to protect the toys, her tiny feet were tucked into pink and white polka dot ankle socks.

"Lacey? See someone you know?" Scott asked, having retraced his steps to where she stood.

"Huh? Uh, no. Just watching."

"Those kids? What's so intriguing about a bunch of little rug rats?"

She knew this playground was here. She gravitated toward it every time she came to the mall. How could she explain this was as close as she'd allow herself to get to what she couldn't, wouldn't, allow herself to have? "Rug rats? Term of endearment or a dig?"

"Came to mind first. Why?"

"No reason." She resumed her trek to the sports-nuts mecca, nodding for him to follow.

"Something you want to talk about?" he asked as he joined her, apparently not ready to drop the subject.

She shouldn't have paused at the play area. Didn't want to get into this can of worms. "No. Children fascinate me. I played with other kids when I was younger, but since I've become an adult, I'm not around them very much. I thought my brother and Celia would get married someday and give me nieces and nephews, but as you know, not going to happen now."

He halted, gripped her arm. "You're not blaming me, I hope. For breaking them up?"

Uh-oh. She'd wandered into a minefield with this subject. Since she was supposed to believe his pretend relationship with Celia was real, it wasn't prudent to mention anything about what might have been between Celia and Brian. "No, of course not. My brother made a poor decision when he broke things off with her. I'm glad she has you to help her, uh, regain her self-confidence."

Fortunately, he let it go as they entered the massive sporting goods store and made their way up the center aisle, seeking inspiration. Near the golf department they slowed, where two older men, probably in their late fifties, were trying out various clubs.

"What do you think?" the first guy asked the second. "Can I justify this new nine iron when I've already got three?"

"After that bungled chip shot I saw yesterday, I'd say buy this one and five more," his friend replied.

"Yeah, but if I come home with this, Sandy will have a fit."

"Don't tell her. You pay the bills, right?"

"I write the checks, sure. But we both are bringing in the bacon, and her pension is bigger than mine."

"O-kay. In that case, put it back. I'll work with you on your chip shot, and you can use the one you already have."

Lacey and Scott sped past the two golfers, waiting until they'd rounded a floor-to-ceiling display to burst out laughing. "Too good," Scott got out while still bent over.

"Do men really buy one club after another, even though they already possess the same club?" she asked.

"How many pairs of shoes are in your closet?"

"Nowhere near the same thing."

"How many pairs of black shoes?"

"Do you really want to know or are you just attempting to make a point?"

He gave her question some thought before replying. "I'm curious. I really want to know."

"Five."

"Five?" His voice rose.

"All for different needs: a pair of sandals for summer, a pair of flats for slacks, a pair of three-inch heels and a pair of four and a half-inch heels for dressy, and a pair of black patent strappies for really dressy."

"Ah, well, who could dispute such a list? Makes perfect sense."

"How many pairs of black shoes do you own?" she asked in rebuttal.

"Me? I don't know. Never counted, but I need every last one of them for meetings with clients."

"How many?"

"Six."

"Aha! Good lesson for me. Always follow up whenever you're trying to best me."

He opened his mouth and shut it again, apparently bereft of a pithy retort. Eventually, his tone changed from kidding to one of more personal interest. "Speaking of follow-ups, you didn't answer my question back there about kids. You never mentioned someday having your own kids, just nieces and nephews."

"You're getting pretty personal now. What if I told you I was unable to have children? Wouldn't you feel bad to have pursued the subject?"

He waited a couple beats. "Can you?" he asked in a softer tone.

How had they gotten this far off the topic of boomers? She didn't want to answer his question, but if she didn't, he wouldn't let it drop. "I'm physically able. I just decided children, my own children, aren't in my future. Even though some women are content to be single mothers, I'm not, not after watching my own mother struggle to keep our family together after my dad left."

"You don't have to be a single mother, you know."

"Marriage isn't for me. I've seen and experienced too much heartbreak." There. He'd pushed, so she'd pushed back. "Are we finished here? I've seen more than enough for one day."

CHAPTER 11

"**Y**our turn to come up with something, Scott." Lacey massaged her temples as the two of them went over their notes from the previous day's shopping mall excursion.

"We did pretty well yesterday. We added 'continued interest in sex,' 'hiding unnecessary purchases from spouses,' and 'insatiable devotion to sports' to our list. A few more outings and we should be ready."

"We don't have time for many more outings, Scott. By now, we should've had a concept well in mind so we could spend the rest of our time drafting the plan. All we have so far are footnotes. We still need an overriding theme."

She was right, but he hated hearing their predicament pronounced out loud. "Too much to do, too little time."

"At least I feel more human today. I can actually walk without grimacing. Do you want to return to the mall? Try another area?"

God, no. He was so not into shopping. Time to bring up Jean's findings. "My research pinpointed five areas of interest to boomers in their retirement." He repeated the list to her. "We saw evidence of the recreational part yesterday. We could maybe visit the volunteer bureau or someone at Drake University who deals with Lifelong Learning. Or one of the hospitals?"

Jean entered the room with two mugs and a carafe. "I thought you could both use more caffeine. I'm trying to cut back myself, but sometimes you need a pick-me-up to revive the gray cells."

"Thanks, Jean." Lacey reached for her mug.

Although Scott thanked her, too, Jean didn't leave. "I take it your expedition yesterday wasn't a huge success?"

"Are you psychic, too?" Scott asked.

"No. But part of my job is to observe the body language of those with whom I work. I'd say you with your head on the desk and Lacey sprawled in her chair signal all is not well. Yet."

Lacey raised her mug in salute. "Nice optimistic touch, Jean. *Yet.*"

The secretary stood there, hands clasped in front of her. "I'm not supposed to know much about your project, but as your secretary, it's impossible for me not to be aware of some things. Like, baby boomers. Your project has something to do with them."

"Good observation," he replied, knowing full well how much she knew. "In spite of its supposed hush-hush nature, you might as well hear the rest. We're to come up with a design concept for a boomer retirement community. If this were my project alone, based on my gut instinct, I'd whip up several possible approaches I think the client would like. But Lacey is heavy into researching the subject population. Since neither of us has much personal experience to go on, we've been making ourselves crazy trying to study boomers and figure out what makes them tick."

Jean was savvy enough to act like this was the first she heard all this for Lacey's benefit. She took her time, appearing to think through Scott's *revelation*. Then she brightened. "From what I know about boomers, the problem is, they're not exactly into the idea of retirement. At least not the same way their parents viewed retirement. *Retire* means something else in their vocabulary."

He found himself shaking his head at her, marveling at her insight and wondering why they hadn't talked to her, really talked, and listened, sooner. "Where did you learn this?"

"Without realizing it, I probably walked away from your dance class with the results you've been seeking. I hit it off with one of the other women who was there. We had lunch together yesterday." She turned to Lacey. "You met her, Lacey. Janice Collier?"

"Oh, right. Nice woman."

Jean continued, "Janice is in her late fifties. She's been a widow the last two, but prior to then, she was happily married to the same man. They had one child, a son. He's some kind of musician and travels a lot, so she's pretty much on her own, and she seems to be thriving."

"She told me she runs her own art gallery," Lacey added.

"Right. In fact, she was here yesterday at my invitation, surveying the building to determine if she might have some items to bring to Mr. Mackenzie's attention."

It was so unusual for Jean to insert herself in his meetings, Scott let her go on for a bit about her new friend, although he failed to see where she was heading. "Uh, that's all very good, Jean, but—"

"Why am I rattling on like this?" she finished for him. "You said you wanted to study baby boomers. Maybe you should consider doing so on a case-by-case basis. In other words, why not interview Janice and see what she can tell you? Seems much more civil than stalking them in malls."

Scott broke away from his desk and grabbed Jean by her arms. "Jean, Jean. Why didn't we just hire you as our consultant?"

"You're not upset?"

"Good grief, no! Do you think we could meet this woman? Talk to her ourselves?"

"Well, yes. I'm sure she'd be delighted to help. You'll remember her when you see her. She looked a bit like a refugee from the seventies. Should I make an appointment for her to come in and talk with you?"

He was all set to say yes, when he noticed Lacey watching him as if just waiting for him to take charge again. If he'd learned anything about the woman, she hated to be one-upped, especially by him. "I remember the baggy outfit, however I didn't get much chance to talk to her. But you did, Lacey. Why don't you handle this?"

"Me?" Lacey replied, a note of surprise in her voice. "What's wrong with this picture, Scott? Why don't you want to deal with her?"

"You begging off? Fine, Jean, set up an appointment for me with her later today, if she's available. We need to do this fast."

"Never mind, Jean. I'll be happy to talk to her," Lacey said, her distrust of his motives apparently giving way to her ambition.

"I'll call her right away," Jean said.

Once Jean departed to carry out her mission, he leaned back in his chair, hands behind his neck. "Well? I'm waiting."

"For what?" Lacey asked. "For me to *thank* you for *letting* me talk to Janice Collier? Don't hold your breath."

"Give me a break here, Lacey. I'm trying to play by your rules and share the lead with you for once. What I meant was, I was waiting for you to admit Jean does more than make great coffee."

She bit a lip. "Oh. Well, I'll give you this much: she did come up with a new angle, although technically, Janice is a result of the dance class."

"Which was my idea."

"Give your ego a rest, Scott."

As it turned out, the Collier woman loved the idea of helping them with their project and made room on her schedule later in the afternoon to talk to Lacey. While his partner was off, Scott remained behind sketching. Didn't produce much, other than several views of Lacey's behind. He spent great effort getting that cute little butt to look just right, firm, round, daring a guy to get his hands on it. Damn! He couldn't even draw a house right now, his mind was so caught up imagining what it would be like to … *Don't go there, Dalton.* Frustrated with his lack of progress, he gave in to a more cerebral pursuit, sailing paper airplanes across the room, his rejects.

His hand reached for his cell, but he restrained himself from hitting Lacey's number despite his desire to hear about the interview. *Be patient. Show her you can be a good partner.* But, damn! This wasn't easy.

He should've followed through himself on Jean's suggestion. He could've charmed a lot more from the Collier woman than Lacey. And a lot faster.

~

"I HAD no idea I'd see you again so soon, but I'm glad you're here," Janice Collier told Lacey at the door of her gallery. "I was surprised when Jean Sarducci called to arrange this meeting."

"Thank you for seeing me on such short notice."

"C'mon in."

Lacey followed her through a large main room, noting a few smaller rooms off to both sides. In the back, they found Janice's office. A massive desk, piled with folders, brochures and artsy odds and ends, was surrounded by boxes, cartons, papers, packing material, etc. In one corner, a rocking chair occupied the space in front of the room's only window.

Janice settled behind her desk, indicating a side chair for Lacey. "Jean said you want to talk about my life as a baby boomer. I rarely think of myself as one, but what do you want to know?"

About fifteen minutes in, it became apparent to Lacey this method wouldn't net the information they needed. Still, she continued with her list of questions. She liked Janice. The older woman wasn't exactly self-deprecating, but neither did she demonstrate an ego.

"Would you like to see the gallery before you're on your way?" Janice asked when they finished.

How could she turn down such an invitation, even though she should get back to the office and see what few points she could salvage from this interview? "I'd love to."

Janice steered her into what appeared to be the main room. "I like to think of my gallery as an eclectic boutique since I show a little bit of everything."

"I'm impressed. I've driven by but never stopped. Didn't realize what wonderful treasures this place holds. You should be very proud of what you've accomplished."

Her new friend leaned against a doorframe and smiled shyly. "Thanks. I am. The last two years have been difficult, taking over my husband's end of the business. I was familiar with the inventory data but not the artwork itself. Now that I have a better feel for our offerings, I've been considering some changes to give it a facelift, like painting the walls and replacing the old carpeting with hardwood floors. Dan, my late husband, was more the traditionalist, but these days the walls seem to be closing in on me. When I'm done, I want the place to feel like a walk in the clouds."

"I like that. Very ethereal. True serenity."

Janice blinked. "I like your word for it. If you don't mind, I think I'll rename the gallery to Serenity once these changes are made."

"I'd be honored. Glad to help. Be sure to let me know when you hold the grand reopening."

Lacey drifted off by herself, taking in all the visual wonders the place offered. Would Scott have taken the time to humor the woman? Scott. Why couldn't she go a full hour without thinking about her new partner? And what was he up to, *suggesting* she handle this interview on her own? Why couldn't he act like a partner all the time, as had been the case with their trip to the mall yesterday, instead of subjecting her to these moments of doubt, like this interview and driving her out of his office the day before?

Get your mind back in the moment, Lacey. She came upon a framed photograph of a man near the back wall. "Is this your husband?" she asked.

Janice rejoined her. "Yes. That's Dan about five years before he died. We met in a college art history class and were inseparable from then on."

"It must have been difficult going on without him."

Janice took a long breath before replying. "At first, I didn't see how it would ever be possible. But with the help of friends and my family, I gradually made it through the abyss of grief I felt."

She touched the picture. "I don't need this picture to remember him. Dan's spirit permeates this place. This is more for the benefit of our long-time customers who still remember him as the inspiration for this gallery. In those days, I stayed out of the limelight doing the accounting and inventory. Dan was the real salesman."

Janice's reflection on her late husband reminded Lacey of her reaction to her own mother's death. Brian kept several pictures of their mother in his apartment and insisted Lacey do the same. Over the years, they'd more or less melded into the background so much, she hardly noticed them anymore. "How about your son? What does he think of the changes you want to make?"

Janice turned her direction, a melancholy expression tinging her features. "Haven't really discussed my plans with him. He didn't share his father's and my interest in art."

"Are there pictures here of him, too?"

Janice shook her head sadly. "I keep those at home.

He's pretty private. Doesn't like me showing him off."

"Does he get back home much?"

Janice looked away. "Not much. He travels a lot. He calls every few days, though not as much as he did right after his father's death. He still worries about me being on my own. Wants me to come live with him. Same city, at least."

"Why haven't you taken him up on his offer?"

Janice didn't answer at once. "This is home for me. We worked so hard to make this place a going concern at a time when people weren't spending their money on art. I couldn't give it up. At least not yet. I sense there's another chapter ahead for me. Whatever it may be."

Janice's statement impressed her. The older woman seemed so at peace with herself, even though she was still grappling with the grief of her husband's passing and not sure what the future held. She wasn't ready to give up, retire and take it easy.

Whoa, back up. Though their interview had gone nowhere, unwittingly, Janice had just handed her a key to the boomer puzzle—the organic piece Lacey had been seeking.

Lacey nearly stumbled she was so excited. She grabbed Janice and hugged her. "You are a genius."

Janice gazed back at her, perplexed and a little surprised by the gesture. "Really? What did I say?"

"You said you weren't through yet. Reminded me of the optimism underlying everything I've learned about baby boomers."

"My generation also grew up with bomb shelters and protested the Vietnam war."

"That's the point. You haven't given up. You're still planning ahead." Flinging her purse strap over her shoulder, she ran out of the gallery, anxious to share her discovery with Scott. "Thanks for every-thing today," she called. "You're a life saver."

Scott's tenth paper airplane sailed across the room and dropped to Earth just in front of the door. He'd switched to a "safer" way to kill time than drawing Lacey's ass and torn up and disposed of all vestiges of his fantasies. A split second later that same door burst open and Lacey exploded through. "I just had the most terrific chat with Janice Collier."

"The hippie?"

She bent to retrieve the fallen paper aircraft and return it to his desk. "She's not a hippie. She dresses for comfort more than the rest of us. I got an earful of what it's like to be on the cutting edge of the boomer generation."

He jumped out of his chair. "Spill. What'd you find out?"

She was so hyped. She couldn't stop smiling. God, she had a nice smile.

He moved closer.

She grasped his hands and her force field grabbed a chokehold on his senses. "I think we've got it this time, Scott."

He gazed into her eyes. Those baby blues just begged him to … to … God, she looked adorable, so animated. Her hands felt so good in his own. Like she actually trusted him. No, something more. Like she was pulling him into her sphere, inviting him to get lost in her vortex of energy.

It would be so easy to simply follow through. He certainly wanted to.

But just as he reached the brink, better sense yanked him back to earth. He dropped his arms to his sides.

As he did, the look in her eyes changed. What had been enticement changed to determination. She reached up, grabbed his face and pulled his lips into hers.

The pleasure crew manning his hormones woke up and went to

work. Heat fanned through him, taking a short cut from his head to his groin. The team running his breathing apparatus went on strike.

"Oh!" She gulped released her hold before he could respond. "I'm so sorry. I got carried away with my excitement." She backed away 'til she was almost at the door.

Scott struggled to reply. Had she really just kissed him? "Uh, no problem. But signal a guy next time before you come flying at him."

She returned a horrified expression, as if he'd struck her rather than been the recipient of her lips on his. "No next time. We're partners. Work partners. Can't mix … you know." She reached behind her back for the doorknob. "Brief you later," she called as she sped off. "Need to write up my notes."

After Lacey's strange, abrupt departure, Scott stared at the door, replaying the last few minutes in his head. Though he'd controlled his urge to take her in his arms, she'd followed through for him, tugging him into her pulsating energy field. He'd allowed himself to be swallowed up in it. Who wouldn't? She'd been like a magnet, overcoming any resistance his gentlemanly hesitation could muster.

He touched his lips. They still tingled and tasted of sweet berries.

She'd kissed him with the same ferocity with which she attacked her research. Just as fast, she was apologizing and looking embarrassed and running off so she didn't have to deal with the aftermath of her actions.

From the taste of her, he knew she hadn't been drinking, which left only one explanation. The idea made him scratch his head and grin from side to side. She was attracted to him. Oh yeah, the Old Boy still had it. She could deny it and run away from it all she wanted. He was on to her.

What was he going to do about it?

CHAPTER 12

"We have to stop meeting like this," Lacey told her locker at the fitness center. For the second time in as many days, she was headed back to the walking track. This time to burn off the self-loathing eating away at her after forgetting the resolution to keep her distance from Scott Dalton. Okay, so it was just one kiss. Spontaneous. Celebratory. Harmless. No, not harmless. It was insane to let slip even the slightest hint she was interested in him.

Now she had her work cut out for her to convince him the kiss meant nothing. Because it didn't, did it? No, of course not. "You enjoyed yourself, didn't you?" the little devil sitting on her shoulder goaded. "You want to kiss him again. And again. You want him to kiss you, too. If it leads to something more, all the better."

"Be still," she told the little nemesis. "Giving in to what you suggest would be highly unprofessional. I can't risk my career over a disobedient libido." Oh, but what a ride it would be. One kiss and her heart, no, her whole body, had gone into overdrive.

Although she really needed to get back to her computer and record her thoughts following her meeting with Janice, she needed to get her head and body under control first, because this wasn't the last she'd see Scott today. She nearly fell over her feet when she remembered it was Wednesday, cards night. She had arranged for Celia and Scott to make a "guest appearance" at Brian's apartment. Damn! She needed more time to get past the kissing incident. Not gonna happen, so she'd better power up and keep walking.

After twenty minutes of firm strides, she finally felt ready to return to the office. Just so Scott stayed out of her way.

She hid out the rest of the afternoon and finished her task, leaving herself all of a half hour to pick up dessert for the evening's activity and arrive at Brian's apartment promptly at six thirty.

Unfortunately, she hadn't planned on the crush of customers in the express lane of the supermarket. She picked up the naked cheesecake she'd ordered from the bakery, this week deciding to purchase a package of crushed pecans and a can of cherry pie filling to finish it off herself.

In front of her, a younger woman in denim cutoffs, T-shirt and flip-flops struggled to pull out coupons and a credit card with one hand while preventing the toddler she gripped by the other from feeding a cookie to an infant seated in the grocery cart.

The little drama held up the rest of the line. This delay would make her late once again. Good. Maybe she should skip the evening's *festivities* altogether, knowing what was coming. Why had she allowed Celia to talk her into this?

"Jimmy has his own treat, honey. He doesn't need your cookie," the young mother told her older child.

"But he already ate his treat, Mommy. And he's still hungry."

"You're a very thoughtful big sister, Lindy, but we don't want Jimmy to get a tummy ache from overeating, do we?"

The little girl slumped her shoulders, bowed her head, but went along with her mother.

Okay."

The exchange intrigued Lacey. How in the world was the woman, who couldn't be more than twenty, maintaining her sanity? Scenes like this probably repeated themselves throughout the day as new ideas for *helping* Mommy care for her baby brother occurred to the little girl. What Lacey wouldn't give to be the mother. But not at the sacrifice of her independence to some guy who probably had no idea how hard it was to raise two small children. Some guy who'd get her pregnant and disappear, leaving her to raise the kids on her own.

Stop yearning for something you're not allowing yourself to have. What was this new fascination with young children, anyhow? Of course, with nieces and nephews no longer in the picture, she was probably fantasizing, filling in the void. Bad habit.

Fortunately, the woman's sale finally concluded, and she and her children headed off for the parking lot.

"I hope Ken is bringing something scrumptious to augment your measly offering of sherbet," Lacey said for effect when she arrived at Brian's apartment ten minutes later, although she already knew the answer. "Where is he anyway? And who's he bringing to replace Celia?"

"Ken's not coming. Something came up at the last minute. But don't worry, he found alternates."

"Did he say who?" she asked with uneasiness she didn't need to feign.

Brian shrugged. "I should have pushed him for names, but I was so anxious to play, since we didn't play last week, I let it slide."

"So some stranger, some potential rapist or arsonist, could be sitting down to a friendly game of cards with us this evening?"

Brian rolled his eyes with brotherly tolerance. "Calm down, Lace. It's just for tonight. Ken's still working on a permanent replacement for Celia. Probably'll find one long before I do," he mumbled.

"What?"

"Nothing."

Before she could pursue what she suspected was an unstated cry for help, the doorbell rang.

Brian rose and gave her a hopeful smile. "Let's see how well Ken did."

Yet another time, she asked herself why she'd allowed Celia to talk her into this. They'd decided to stop throwing Scott in Brian's face for a few days, then it had occurred to Celia what a shame it would be to waste cards night. In Celia's defense, she didn't know about Lacey's impetuous kiss, and Lacey had no intention of bringing her up to speed. This evening promised to be some kind of interesting with three of the four participants ill-at-ease with each other.

A churning tornado of trepidation swirled inside her as she followed Brian to the door. Should've begged off tonight. Caught malaria or something equally as radical. She really didn't want to spend her evening with Scott, pretending the kiss never happened. It was just asking for trouble by seeing him again so soon.

The door opened, revealing Celia and Scott, one with a nervous, tentative smile on her face and the other's eyes nearly closed, obviously there under duress.

"Surprise!" Celia swept into the room, her unwilling partner following behind.

Brian remained wide-eyed by the door, as if solidified in a gelatin mold.

"Celia. I didn't know you were coming," Lacey said, taking over hosting duties from her tongue-tied brother.

"When I ran into Ken at the dry cleaner's the other day, he asked if I wouldn't stay on for at least one more session. Apparently he hasn't yet found a replacement for me and some teachers' meeting had come up unexpectedly for him. I relented and brought Scott so we'd have a foursome."

Though returning to her former boyfriend's apartment may have been somewhat daunting, Celia didn't appear to be the least bit embarrassed.

If she can do this, so can I.

Celia breezed off to the kitchen, carrying a large paper sack. Scott hovered just inside the door, studying the floor while he balanced a couple of containers of food.

"Bring those out here, will you, Scott?" Celia called from the kitchen.

Scott dutifully complied, still not looking at either Lacey or Brian.

Lacey stole a glance at her brother. Lips pursed, hands clenched together, he didn't appear to be taking this turn of events particularly well.

"Did you know they were coming?" he whispered.

She pretended not to hear.

"What do we do?" He appeared as if he might escape through the front door any minute.

She moved closer. "Play it through, I guess. What else can we do, other than throw them out?"

His eyes brightened at the thought, but she quickly squelched the suggestion with a decisive shake of her head.

Celia popped back through the kitchen door. "I brought lettuce wraps filled with cold vegetables and portabella mushrooms for you, Brian. For the rest of us, cold cuts and corn soufflé. We're late because we waited for the soufflé to finish baking."

Brian continued to stand there motionless. Lacey took her cue from the scent of warm butter and corn permeating the air. "I love corn soufflé. Do you need help, Cee?"

Celia shook her head. "No, I know where everything goes." She breezed past her statement with no discernible reaction. "Ready to eat?"

"Great idea. I'm famished," Lacey replied. "We're eating in the dining room," she told Scott.

His eyes finally lighted on her. Though he must have known she'd be there, he blinked in a sort of doubletake. Was he surprised she dared show her face after their earlier encounter? He even smiled. Not one of his client charmers and not a leering one. A genuine, gratified-someone-was-making-an-effort-to-be-pleasant type of smile.

Brian remained on the sidelines while the other three prepared the table. They ate dinner in silence, much like they had the previous week at Cam's birthday party. Lacey tried without success to think of a suitable topic of conversation. At one point, the quiet was so palpable, she thought she heard the cuckoo clock in Brian's bedroom ticking.

Finally, when she could bear it no longer, she jumped up and started clearing away what was left of the meal. Celia joined her, stuffing trash in the wastebasket. Brian went off to find the cards. Scott remained seated, drinking his beer.

Once Brian returned with the cards, he pointed to the seat opposite him. "You sit there, Lacey. You'll be my partner tonight."

"Whose turn is it to decide on the game for the evening?" Celia asked.

"Mine," Brian announced with a little too much vigor. "I choose Euchre."

"Not that again," Lacey protested. "None of us really enjoys it, Brian."

He returned a self-congratulatory smile her direction.

"I thought we were playing poker," Scott said.

"No, I said *cards*," Celia replied.

"I just assumed … well, that's the only card game I know."

"You'll pick up on Euchre fast," Brian returned, obviously over-stating his glee to be in the driver's seat.

"We should go, Celia. I won't be much help as your partner," Scott said.

Celia grabbed his hand. "Please stay. Brian's right about it not taking long to learn the game."

Scott seemed to remember his role as Celia's attentive beau. "Okay," he said in a begrudging tone. "I'll give it shot."

The first few games went fast. It was obvious Scott had no idea what he was doing, and though Celia put up a valiant defense, they were no match for Brian and Lacey, who ruthlessly staked out their plays with no consideration for the newcomer.

"Too bad. You came close," Brian said when Scott missed completing a play Celia had worked so diligently to set up.

"Huh? Oh, right. This goes so fast, my head's spinning."

Though Scott's understanding of the game improved considerably during the next few rounds, Brian and Lacey continued to win except for one fluke. At one point, Scott flopped his chin in his hand, shaking his head. "How much longer does this insanity go on?"

Brian checked his watch. "Another hour or so. Unless you're ready to concede?"

Lacey winced inwardly. Brian was laying it on a bit thick. But then, he was jealous, the result they were shooting for. However, she considered throwing a couple games to reduce the growing tension. "How about a dessert break? I've been salivating all evening in anticipation of the cheesecake."

Scott perked up. "You like cheesecake, too?"

"One of my downfalls. I bring it whenever it's my turn to provide dessert, to Brian and Celia's dismay."

When she returned with two plates of cheesecake, she discovered that Celia had excused herself to use the facilities and Brian was off checking his phone for messages. That left her alone with Scott. Okay. She could do this. Just focus on topics other than the kiss. Topics like cards night. Right. It'd been fun to watch Scott scramble to learn the game, but he'd taken enough punishment. Time to come to his rescue.

She carried her cherry-laden plate of cheesecake over to the table to sit across from him. "What do you think of the game so far?"

He stared back at her, as if to say, "I can't believe you'd ask."

"You don't want to know."

She took the bait. "Try me."

Sighing like a man under duress, he set down his plate and fork and gave her his full attention. "The game's okay, I guess. But Celia and your brother can barely tolerate each other. Each seems to be taking great pleasure in besting the other. I can think of a lot better ways to spend my evening."

"Sorry we interfered with your evening with Celia," she said, since she wasn't supposed to know he was only pretending to date Celia.

"Huh? Oh, right. No need to apologize. This was all Celia's idea."

He seemed ill-at-ease, so she glanced away, took a bite of cheesecake.

"There was no need for you to apologize earlier, either."

Their eyes met. Had his grown dusky or was it just the darkening sky outside? Did she see an unspoken message in his expression? Or was she kidding herself? "I, uh—" She glanced away, not wanting her eyes to betray her true feelings. "I know you're with Celia. I'd never, uh, betray her."

"There was a moment ... I almost forgot," he said.

"I didn't notice." *Liar.* Of course, she noticed, and when he hadn't followed through, she'd taken matters into her own hands.

"Something came over me. Just for an instant. Call it battle fatigue or whatever. I was so anxious to hear if you'd been successful, I couldn't get much work done all afternoon. So when you announced you had the key to the puzzle, guess I let myself get carried away. For a moment."

"So, we're okay?" she asked.

"More than." He extended a hand. When she took it, the same unaccountable bolt of electricity zapped up her arm as had attacked her with every contact she'd had with the man thus far.

"Just so you know, the same thing's been happening to me. The shock waves. We must be polar opposites, or whatever they're called. I never did well in Physics class," he said.

"We should, uh, get back to the game, that is, if Celia and my brother ever appear again." She needed to have a little talk with Celia about how to treat her boyfriend, real or not. The goal tonight had been to raise Brian's level of jealousy. Instead, all they'd done was raise his gaming ego.

"This card game is getting old fast. Do you think I can get Celia out of here in the next hour?"

"She isn't one to back down easily. You guys have to win a few rounds first."

Scott leaned in conspiratorially, his breath tickling her ears. "Thank you for stating the obvious."

Even given the understanding they'd just reached, Lacey fought to keep her mind on the situation at hand and not let other parts of her body take over. Just a whiff of Scott's aftershave was attacking her gray matter.

Ten minutes later, stuffed with cheesecake, the four resumed play. The carbs in the dessert must have recharged his brain, because before long, Scott won a game.

Celia arched a brow in surprise and surveyed the board. "Scott! You did it!"

"Yeah, yeah, yeah," Brian said. "But it's only your first this round.

Keep playing."

Lacey mouthed *bravo* to a grateful and excited Scott, who seemed to be in a mild state of shock at finally having done something right. He nodded, then turned his attention back to his cards.

Scott and Celia won the next two rounds. Celia became even more animated, tsk-tsking when they blocked several of Lacey and Brian's attempts.

"It appears the tables have turned," Celia announced.

"Pure dumb luck," Brian retorted, emphasizing the word *dumb*.

Scott threw down his cards and half rose from his seat. His eyes flashed with unleashed anger ready to explode. "Look, buddy, I've been more than patient with your attitude. But we don't need to sit here and be insulted."

Brian picked up his own cards and started arranging them.

"I think Scott deserves an apology, Brian," Celia said.

"Ah, it's not worth it, Cee," Scott told her, his voice more even. "I'm done for tonight." He rose and gave Celia an expectant look.

She set down her hand and also rose. "Until tonight, I've never known you to be ungracious, Brian." She grabbed her purse and accompanied Scott to the door.

The door didn't actually slam shut, but the sound of it closing echoed through a room grown quite still. Lacey continued to stare at the door, not believing the outburst she'd just witnessed.

The cheesecake and cherries warred inside her stomach, though her conscience suggested the pain was more from the aftermath of messing with others' lives. If she hadn't given Scott the pep talk, perhaps he wouldn't have caught on to the game so quickly and helped Celia win. If they'd continued to lose, Scott and Celia would have left frustrated but not angry. Celia wouldn't have poked Brian, and Brian wouldn't have … Oh, phooey! They were all to blame.

She rubbed her temples. She needed to clean up and get home to bed. She'd told Celia it was too soon to flaunt Scott at Brian. Just like the week before, they succeeded in getting Brian's attention but in all the wrong ways.

As much as she wanted to throttle her brother, she realized he was a man backed into a corner in his own home, which still didn't excuse his behavior.

"Damn! Why can't it just be over? Why does she keep coming back into my life?" His voice snapped with torment.

Lacey wanted to say, "Because she still loves you, you dimwit!" But instead, she kept her anger in check. "Maybe because she really hasn't left."

SCOTT WAITED until he and Celia were inside his car to detonate. "Consider this charade over!"

"You can't back out now, Scott. You still have two weeks to go." She smoothed her slacks and attempted to settle into her seat. "I'm sorry Brian was so brusque, but his attitude means our plan is working. I think we made progress."

"Progress?" Scott nearly shrieked, his hand arrested over the ignition. "By what stretch of the imagination would you call tonight's fiasco *progress*?"

Celia sat up straighter. "Brian hardly spoke to me or looked my direction all evening, which translates to I still matter to him."

"Never speaking to you again would testify to his undying love?"

"Don't be trite. Once you and I started winning, Brian was beside himself with jealousy."

"Do you need an eye exam? What you saw was a guy who can't take the heat of competition."

Celia fluffed her hair. "Right. Competition from you for me."

"Ugh!" He threw his hands up in the air, sighed and started the car. The sooner he brought this evening to a close, the better.

They drove several blocks before he was able to frame the words he wanted to say. "The way you're rubbing Brian's nose in our supposed relationship, hinting, no, downright boasting that you're much better off with me than you ever were with him, is the wrong approach."

Celia turned her head to the window, purportedly watching the lights of the city go by. But she seemed to be listening.

"I said yes to this plan because I liked you and wanted to help." *And I needed something to take my mind off Lacey, which is working so well.* God, he'd nearly kissed the woman earlier in the day. Who knew if it would have stopped there? He'd almost admitted as much to her tonight when she apologized for initiating the lip lock. "Our dating seems to be making the guy more resolute than ever in his decision to break things off."

There. He'd said his piece. It didn't make the gnawing sensation in his gut go away, but his breathing relaxed.

Celia took several deep gulps before the sniffles began.

He pulled up at her apartment complex and waited for her to make a move. She continued to sit there, dabbing at her eyes with a tissue she'd retrieved from her purse.

"I'll walk you to the door."

Slowly, she turned to face him. From the shard of light streaking through the car windows from the streetlight, he could see her eyes were still misty. She blew her nose and rolled her shoulders. "Could we talk first?" Her tone was meek.

"Depends. Are you ready to call our so-called relationship quits?"

"I'm ready to discuss a different strategy."

He collapsed his shoulders, released a few choice oaths under his breath. "Celia! Have you not heard any of what I've been saying?"

"Yes, Scott. You're right. Tonight wasn't the best tactic. Being back in his apartment reminded me of what I no longer had. I didn't behave so well myself."

"What are you going to do about it?"

She shrugged. "I don't know. What an admission. Celia the Planner, out of ideas."

"Good! First smart thing you've said in some time."

She put aside the tissue. "What should I do?"

"I know what you shouldn't do. You've been charging through this get-Brian-jealous plan like a herd of elephants going through a turnstile. The heavy-handedness has only served to rile him, not make him jealous."

She sighed. "Not very smart, huh?"

He nodded. "Since this routine of hunting him down in his haunts and flaunting our relationship at every opportunity isn't working, maybe you should go the opposite direction."

"Like in *hide out* from him?"

"More or less. You've been in his face at every turn. You haven't given him an opportunity to miss you."

"You're right," she said to herself, as if she'd forgotten he was there. "He has to miss me. Realize what he's given up."

Scott watched, fascinated, as she processed this new line of thinking, fearing he'd just let a pyromaniac into a dynamite shed.

She gathered her purse and opened the car door. "Thanks, Scott. For talking me down, and for the idea. See you tomorrow." And she was off, reanimated.

"But what about ending our deal?" Scott asked the air.

CHAPTER 13

"We need to talk."

Lacey emerged from perusing her Collier notes to find Scott leaning against the door to her office. Talk some more about the kiss? She thought her apology the night before had sufficed. Apparently not.

"I want to hear about your meeting with that hippie woman."

Oh. Her interview of Janice. Much better. "I emailed my notes to you last night."

"Right. Along with a rough outline for our design concept." He held out a blue folder. Jean's efficiency had struck again.

"I know, I know. I did this independently without consulting or informing you." He raised both eyebrows.

"Go ahead, say it," she replied. "If the reverse had been the case, I would have been raving mad at you by now. But I got going and couldn't stop. I'm starting to understand why you did those sketches. You seem to process your thoughts through pictures."

"Guess so. Interesting observation." He flopped into her one and only visitor chair, flipped through the plan, probably for effect. "Not bad. Takes us in a different direction, but I like it."

"Really? Thanks."

"Would've said so last night, but my, uh, mind was elsewhere. Sorry I left in such a huff, but your brother is a real …"

"Poor host at times," she said, avoiding the use of a more derogative term.

He crossed one knee over the other. "Have to say, the Collier woman threw you some real tidbits. For instance, boomers don't want to retire. Could've fooled me."

"They still want to retire, just not in the classical sense like their parents did. Boomers see retirement as a higher level of existence, a time to reinvent themselves from the type of work they did in the past. They want to live meaningful lives, not just sit around and idle their days away until they die as a reward for surviving thirty-some years of work."

"Heck, might as well plant them in the wilderness and let them dig their way out, if they want meaning in their lives." He laughed at his joke. When he noted she didn't join him, he caught himself up short. "Sorry. I wasn't belittling your ideas. You've spun a great theory."

"How do we translate this theory to a design concept?"

He shrugged. "Put something down on paper, I guess," he replied.

"Like what?" The idea had been so clear in her mind five minutes ago. Then he'd walked in and her vision blurred. Using Celia as her shield against Scott's appeal wasn't working. Why did he have to track her down in her tiny office? He was sitting less than two feet away. Too close for comfort. Her beating heart was on overload, which was nothing compared to the tightening of the muscles in her lower parts. "Other than a monastery, what would a place where people sought meaning for their lives look like?"

"Got a notepad?"

She tossed him one along with a pencil and hoped this would keep him busy while she got her shameless body under control.

He played around with several sketches before dropping the pad back on her desk, stood and shook out his shoulders. "This office is too confining. How do you ever produce anything?"

"I haven't known anything better, until I started working with you and learned how the top echelon lives."

He ambled over to her window and stared out aimlessly. "Some view they gave you. Bet you get a lot of kick-ass ideas from gazing out at the parking lot."

She chuckled. "Which is why my desk is over here."

He stalked back to his chair and collapsed into it, crossing his arms and sucking in his lips. After a bit, he thunked his forehead. "You know what I saw while I was over there admiring that asphalt ocean?"

She waited for the brainstorm she sensed was on its way.

"It's a beautiful day." He sat back smugly and eyed her as if expecting her to sing praises of his great revelation. When she didn't, he went on. "Let's go enjoy it. How about a ride in the country?"

In the country? "To the Project Arabella property? Didn't we suffer enough out there last week?"

"I need to see it again, get the lay of the land, crank up my creative juices. Want to go along? We can run out there for a couple hours. Grab some fast food. Picnic on the grass. It should be dry today," he said, looking down at his shoes, then grinning again.

The idea was staggering. She could barely breathe. Could she trust herself to be alone with him out in the middle of nowhere? "Okay, sounds like a great idea, but we've got to use our time wisely."

"What could be more inspiring than plopping ourselves down in the midst of the property?"

AN HOUR LATER, reclined on a blanket snatched from the trunk of his car, Scott sucked up rays from a friendly sun. Filled with fried chicken and potato salad, he was a contented man. So they were still struggling to develop the project concept, and he didn't know why he hadn't been named the firm's principal yet, and he'd committed the next few weeks to someone who'd turned into a wild woman in her quest to regain her boyfriend, right now, life was good. He plucked a sheath of a weed of some kind and crushed it between his fingers.

Across the blanket, Lacey occupied herself packing up food containers and stuffing them into an oversized garbage bag. She looked as yummy as any candy store concoction in the pink knit top she wore. And they hadn't had dessert yet.

He focused on the creamy shoulder escaping the neckline. So innocent, and yet so inviting. His imagination ran rampant imagining the safari his lips would take, starting there and meandering upward along her regal neck. Just the thought of attacking the earlobe buried underneath those flaxen curls made his blood run faster.

Great. He'd transformed from lunch companion to turned-on male.

"Scott?" Lacey's gaze was watchful. "Is the sun getting to you? You seemed miles away." She stared at him, her head tilted slightly, the sun's rays streaming through her hair like golden splinters, her face flushed. From the exertion of cleaning up? Or did she sense his crotch waking up?

For one moment, he considered letting her know. Hell, out here in this grassy meadow, far enough from the road where no one could see them, who knew where it could lead?

"Ready?"

Was he ever! Then, like the day before, his better judgment reappeared. They were here on a mission. A work-related mission. Lacey believed he was seeing Celia, her best friend. Technically, he'd ended his agreement with Celia last night, although he wasn't sure Celia had heard him. Lacey was certainly unaware of the change. So, no messing around.

He took several deep breaths to alleviate his physical dilemma. When those efforts didn't help, he subtly rolled away from the blanket and stood, pulling it up with him, presumably to fold the thing. For the next five minutes. "We'll get started as soon as I take this stuff to the car."

Task completed, he gave himself a mental buck-up lecture. He studied the landscape and tried to envision what he'd put there. Designing buildings was his second favorite thing. Today, Number Two would have to suffice.

Lacey was staring vacantly toward the horizon when he rejoined her. "What's up? Inspiration calling?"

She grimaced. "I was trying to empty my brain and simply let the spirit sweep over me. But so far, no go. How do you do it?"

A putdown? Nah, she was serious. "Same way you were attempting, more or less. I find a place to stand and take in the canvas before me. Focus on the totality of the scene, then let the landmarks populate it, one by one. The landmarks are the key."

She brought a hand up to frame her eyes and scope out the view before her. "The rise over there? When we were here before, I noticed a stand of oak trees surrounding it. Think we could incorporate them into our plans?"

"We can do whatever we like, if it makes sense. Want to check it out?"

Despite the steep incline, they headed off to inspect the hillock.

He hadn't paid those trees much attention when they were here before. Too busy extricating himself from under that other tree trunk. But Lacey spotted them. Good eye.

Anxious to see what was on the other side, he kept his impatience in check and walked alongside her companionably.

Once, when he glanced over at her, he caught her gazing up at him. She returned a broad smile, like there was nothing else she'd rather be doing. "This is fun, Scott. For a few hours I've been able to relax and my stomach has stopped churning at the threat of our deadline. I'm glad you thought of coming here."

A bubble of satisfaction bloomed inside his chest. He tried not to appear too pleased. "You've been having stomach problems too? Thought I was the only one feasting on antacid tablets."

When they arrived at the foot of the hill, he took her hand and helped her pick her way up. The side of the hill was covered with wildflowers. As Lacey and Scott passed through them, their movement set off a shower of fragrances. If he'd been a kid, he would have been tempted to stop midway up and roll down the scent-filled blanket.

Lacey slowed her pace as they neared the top.

"Tired? We're almost there."

"No. Just enjoying the trek. And the view."

Until then, he'd forged straight ahead, but her comment made him check for himself. She was right. Up higher, the property took on a whole new perspective. Much more rolling than it appeared at their picnic site, which could present a few more architectural challenges than a flatter landscape but would also add to the ambience. Home-buyers loved those things.

They reached the summit a few minutes later, both slightly breath-less but also invigorated by the trip.

Scott scanned the periphery. "I should've brought my camera. There's more here than I thought. Sketches won't do it justice."

The slope was less steep on the other side, the descent more grad-ual. A couple small plateaus dotted with trees cut into the side about a fourth of the way and halfway up.

"Maybe Cam and our client are really on to something with this place. Even though it's so far from town."

"I suppose we could follow through on Cam's suggestion to build a mini-town out here?" Scott could hardly believe his words, but the place was starting to get to him.

"I hope we can keep the creek down there. It lends a certain charm to the property."

"Sure, if the experts say it's safe."

"I wonder if there are other water sources on the property. Did you check the aquifer reports?"

He started to answer, but before she could hear him, she took off, scanning the ground for something. She toed a couple logs. He hoped they weren't home to any field creatures. She bent and picked up what appeared be a slender, forked stick. Fortunately, no wildlife struck back at her.

She set off down the slope, extending the switch in front of her at arms' length. She'd go a few feet one direction, then turn and head off perpendicularly, only to repeat the pattern a few feet later. When she'd gone about a hundred feet, she stopped abruptly, the stick pointing down.

Was she doing what he thought she was? He'd heard of witching water but never witnessed the process. He caught up with her. "Are you—"

"Do you see any other branches around here, about this size? But not forked."

He wondered if the country air had messed with her sanity. "You already have a stick."

"This locates a vein. I need a straight switch to determine its depth."

He couldn't get over what he was witnessing. The Internet Princess had reverted to a practice going way back in time. Shaking his head in amazement, he bounded off, searched in concentric circles, but came up short.

"Sorry." Scott returned empty-handed. "Nothing. How long have you been witching for water?"

She beamed a hundred-watt smile. "Picked it up from my grandpa when I was a kid. It's supposed to be handed down through generations. My mom couldn't get the hang of it, so my grandpa took me out with him when he'd witch for neighbors. I was a natural. He died before I could get the hang of it from him, so I taught myself."

Her resourcefulness continued to surprise him.

She moved farther away, heading downhill. "Got a notepad? I need you to jot down roughly where I'm getting these readings."

Though she'd put him in the position of playing recorder, he didn't mind. He was fascinated. He retrieved a pad and pencil from a pocket. "Okay. Shoot."

She looked up and seemed to freeze in her tracks. "S-S-Scott!" Her voice came in a hoarse whisper. "Don't move!"

"Huh? Can't hear you." What was up? Had she stumbled across one of those ground creatures after all?

"Lose the notepad and start backing up the hill as nonchalantly and quickly as you can."

"But—"

"Do as I say, okay? We're not alone. Hurry!"

"What do you mean not a—" Over his shoulder, he saw what she meant. A scruffy-looking bull stood no more than thirty feet away, pawing the ground. The animal didn't look the least bit happy to have company.

Scott tried to swallow and nearly choked, his heart hammered so furiously. Where had the beast come from? He must have been hidden behind the trees on the other side of the hill.

"Don't look directly at him!" Lacey commanded in a lowered tone. "Go!"

Warned not to, he resisted a powerful urge to stare down the animal. But he couldn't get his feet to budge, no matter how much he willed them to. "I-I-I can't move," he hissed. How much longer before the bull decided to rush? Couldn't be long. "Get out of here, Lacey. I'll distract him for you."

"I won't leave you!"

"Do it!"

"But—"

"Now!"

She backed up the hill a few steps at a time. He waited until she reached the crest and disappeared down the way they'd come. Then he began his own retreat. Bulls weren't typically part of the knowledge base of townies like him. Did you stare down the beast or pretend it didn't exist?

The debate came to an abrupt halt when the bull snorted, stopped his pawing and raised his enormous head. When he saw Scott, he snorted again.

Scott continued backpedaling up the grassy slope, keeping the bull in sight without looking him directly in the eye. As Scott arrived at the top of the hill, he chanced a glimpse of the other side to check Lacey's position. She'd reached the bottom and was making her way to the fence.

Time to make his escape. Could he outrun a bull? No time like the present to find out. Adrenaline he didn't know he possessed shot through him, propelling him down the slope. He sprinted like he was back on the high school track team, stumbling a few times but staying erect. He didn't dare look back until he'd almost caught up with Lacey.

His flight wasn't in vain. The bull was cutting the distance between them with each leap.

"Go faster, Lacey," he shouted. With the bull in pursuit, whispering was superfluous.

She jerked her head around. In doing so, she missed her footing and tripped. She went flying, landing face down, arms akimbo.

No time to spare. He caught up with her, swooped down, picked her up and flung her over his shoulder like a rag doll. Increasing his pace, he made the distance to the fence in four strides. He hoisted her over and out of danger. She landed with a thud, wrenching his heart.

"Are … you … okay?" he asked in broken breaths once he'd scaled the fence too. "I had to get you out of there fast. Keeping your bones intact was secondary."

"I-I think so."

His heart beat so frantically, it sounded like giant tympani in his ears. "Thank God!" Messing with the bull would have been bad enough for him, but he dared not think what the animal would have done to her.

Scott went down on his knees to help her sit up, his face inches from hers. The scent of lilacs hit him again. Mesmerizing. Without thinking, he wrapped his arms around her and tucked her into his embrace, squeezing her tight. Though she said she was okay, he rubbed her back nonetheless, as one would soothe a hurt child. But Lacey was no child. She was a grown woman with curves and heavenly scents and a fast-beating heart, which he felt pumping through his shirt.

He wanted to hold on longer. Despite how they got to this point, having her in his arms felt so good, so right, he didn't want to let go. Finally, past the appropriate amount of time to provide comfort, he released her.

She returned a quizzical expression, as if trying to read his mood. The azure depths of her eyes drew him in, and something inside him clicked. The attraction he'd been denying and restraining for days took over. Frenetic need claimed her lips that trembled slightly then parted a bit. Their tongues met. Tentatively, testing at first. Within seconds, they locked in their own mad Salsa.

He slid his hand up her back and felt her curl into him, setting off a spasm of shockwaves in his bloodstream. Her arms went around his neck, pulling him closer. She wanted this too.

In the background, their bovine friend snorted and whined. Even he sensed the world rocking on its axis.

Scott didn't care at this point. He wanted her now, bull or no bull safely behind the fence. To hell with his resolution to avoid office relationships. He'd deal with the consequences later.

He took his lips from hers long enough to lay her gently in the grass and hover above her. In her eyes he saw expectation, invitation and desire but no hesitation. Taking the cue, he kissed her again and moved his hand inside her knit top. Her skin felt soft as satin but also very warm. Heated.

He reached behind for the clasp on her brassiere, deftly opening it with one hand. Her moan made him grow bolder. He traced the bottom of the garment with his finger and brought his hand around to seek a breast. Her flesh molded itself to his grasp, so smooth, so firm yet pliable. "You feel so good." God, could he sound any more like a teenager feeling up his first girl. But those were the only thoughts in his head, other than wanting more of her.

She jerked beneath him, her eyes refocused into a look of alarm. "What about Celia?"

"Over, as of last night." At least, in his mind it was.

Her expression softened, then grew hazy as she relaxed. "Oh."

No need to tell her it wasn't because of her. Though, maybe it was.

"Then continue," she urged, arching her back beneath him, the pressure of her hips against his pelvis urgent, demanding.

He teetered on the edge of the abyss. One more move and he'd be free-falling, saying good-bye to reality and letting himself go with the moment and the pleasure. The bull was getting a show he hadn't anticipated. Vaguely, Scott thought about the nearby road and the view passersby might be seeing but dismissed his concern. He and Lacey were in a ravine behind a row of bushes. Secluded.

Lacey drew a hand down the side of his cheek. As if every nerve ending in his body wasn't already on heightened awareness, the receptors beneath her caress exploded. "Aren't you going to finish what you started?" she asked, her voice raspy.

"You're okay with doing this? Out here?"

"No. Yes. I can't think clearly," she replied.

"Me, either. Haven't stopped thinking about you, this, since we were here before. If Cam hadn't shown up when he did … But he's not here now to stop us. Nothing but our own better judgment to prevent this from happening," he said. "I'm tired of fighting my *better judgment*."

"Me, too. I want to, have to, see this through."

"No matter where it goes?" he asked.

"Shut up and kiss me," she said.

He readily complied. This kiss lasted longer than the first, as if their lips spoke a secret language to each other, sharing their sensations, their needs, their reactions. He couldn't get enough of her mouth, though his hand remained on her breast, his thumb making lazy circles around the aroused nubbin.

Lacey kissed back with great enthusiasm, like she'd been waiting for this for a long time.

Scott remaining on top of her, they rolled back and forth in the grass, each attempting to get more of the other. He glided his hand down from her waist to locate the zipper on her pants. As he started to pull down the tab, a far off ringing caught his attention. His cell phone. Should have left it in the car.

"Don't answer."

He didn't want to, but they were on company time. The last thing he needed was for someone back at the office, unable to reach him, to speculate, correctly, what he and Lacey were doing.

"Yeah?" he answered, his tone challenging.

"Mr. Dalton? It's Jean. I know you're in the middle of a site visit, but something's going on here I thought you should know about."

Now what? The client had decided to drop by today? "What's up, Jean?" he asked, attempting to breathe normally.

"Your parents are here."

His breath caught. What were they doing in town? They were

supposed to have extended their trip another month to visit friends in Kuala Lumpur. "In the office?"

There was a hesitation on the other end of the line. "You sound winded."

"I just ran down a large hill. Tell them I'm out for the rest of the afternoon doing field research."

"I already did, Mr. Dalton."

"And?

"They seem anxious to see you and they think you'd want to see them right away. So, I, uh, told them to wait in your office."

"Ah, Jean!"

"I'm sorry, Mr. Dalton." She sounded near tears. "I really tried to find an alternative solution, but they—"

"I understand. My parents can be quite persuasive. I'll be back in half an hour."

No, no, no, no! Why couldn't they stay out of his professional life like they did his personal life? But he knew the answer all too well. They'd made his professional life possible and wanted to check on their investment.

"Scott? Is there an emergency?" Lacey was redoing her bra and zipping up her slacks, apparently more aware than his body their romp in the grass was over.

He stuck the phone back in his pants pocket and offered an apologetic smile. "My parents have returned to town and are waiting for me at the office."

She looked confused. "Couldn't your bulldog put them off?"

"My parents, the jetsetters, think the world revolves around their timetable." She crinkled her brow.

"They're old friends of Cam. My career is their own little project, so apparently they popped in for a progress report."

"I see," she said, not sounding convinced. "We should go back." She attempted to stand and just as quickly dropped down again. "Oh." Her cry held pain.

"What's the matter?"

"It's my, my ankle. I must have twisted it when I landed." Face contorted, she rubbed the injured extremity.

"Let me see." He drew her foot into his hands, turning it just enough to get a good look. It definitely was swollen and turning purple. Damn his horny self! If he hadn't gotten them off on another tact, she would have noticed it sooner and maybe been able to do something more for it.

"It's pretty puffy. Don't put any weight on it. I'll carry you to the car."

By the time they reached the vehicle, any thoughts of the hot scene minutes before vanished. Before he could even deal with his parents, he needed to get medical attention for Lacey.

As he roared away toward town, he kicked himself mentally for failing to protect her from the bull, then giving in to his lust while she lay there hurt. "I'm taking you to the emergency room. Who's your doctor? We'll call from the car." He glanced her direction to reassure himself she hadn't fainted.

"Your parents are waiting. I'll be okay. Just get me back to the office."

"No way. You can't walk."

"Then drop me off at the hospital. They can take it from there."

Why did she have to be so cussedly independent? Did she blame him for her ankle? "I don't do drive-by emergency calls. This little junket was my idea. I'm not letting you out of my sight until we get your ankle checked."

She was about to protest when his cell phone trilled again. They exchanged looks, but in the end, he gave in and answered it. "Yes?"

"I'm sorry, Mr. Dalton. I tried to keep them occupied in your office, but your mother—"

"What's she doing?"

"She followed me back to my desk. Their surprise appearance left me so flummoxed, I left your calendar up on my computer screen and she started going through it before I realized what she was doing."

"She went through my schedule? I hope you closed the program on her right away. There's private information in there."

"I know, I know. I took care of it. I had no idea how inquisitive she is."

"Snoopy is more like it." He ended the call and mumbled a few choice oaths. Jean had no idea how his parents could take over. His general had met her Waterloo.

"It doesn't sound like you can afford the time to take me to the hospital, Scott. I'll call Brian." Lacey had her cell phone out before he could object.

When she couldn't reach her brother, she called Celia but got her office voicemail. "I know, I'll call Janice Collier." In the end, it was Janice who met them in the company parking lot.

Scott carried her to Janice's car. "Thanks for doing this," he told the older woman. "I've got a situation back at the office I've got to handle, or we would've gone straight to the hospital."

"Not to worry. I'll take it from here." Janice sent a shy smile Lacey's way.

He leaned in to Lacey. "Back there?"

"Just one of those moments."

"You're not angry?"

"I was as much into what we did as you."

"We need to talk. I'll get back to you as soon as I've dealt with my parents." God, he hoped she realized how much he regretted not going with her.

"Later," she said, lip trembling.

Seconds later, he found himself standing on the curb watching them take off in Janice's small car. He despised himself for being so weak. He should have put his parents on hold and taken her himself.

This was the last time Marcia and Gordon Dalton walked all over him. No sir, from now on, despite what standing up to him might do to his father's health, he would not let them take over his life.

CHAPTER 14

Scott trudged into the building to face the music. He discovered his parents in his office, huddled over his desk, their backs to him. He did a quick mental inventory of what he'd left out, but he couldn't remember anything of note.

He didn't cotton to anyone going through his papers, especially his parents. A sharp new wave of anger shot through him, joining his annoyance at having to cut short his time with Lacey, especially since she needed him right now at the emergency room.

He gulped a few calming breaths to get his temper under control. Yes sir, he'd set them straight. Tomorrow. But first he'd find out what the hell they were doing here. "Look who's back from their trip a month early."

In unison, his parents turned toward him, showing no signs of embarrassment. "Scott! Finally. We've been so anxious to see you," his mother said.

"Mom." He stepped forward to place a perfunctory kiss on her cheek. Still wearing the overpowering musky fragrance he found so noxious. Looked good, though. Even at fifty-nine, her eyes were still bright and clear, and her skin as dewy as a flower petal.

As he shook hands with his father, he took in the other man's appearance. Slimmer than a few months ago, although he seemed fit enough. Maybe a few more gray hairs feathering his temples but just as much hair as before.

"Scott, boy." His father kept holding Scott's hands. "Where have you been? Your secretary was very tight-lipped as to your whereabouts."

"She's paid to keep my doings private, including my calendar." He gave his mother a pointed look. "I was scouting a site."

His mother rolled her shoulders nonchalantly. He marveled at how well toned her arms still were in her sleeveless beige blouse.

"Not to worry. Cam kept us entertained."

"Cam? You've seen him?" A tiny alarm sounded inside his head.

"Caught up with each other's news," his father said.

His mother picked a stray piece of grass from his collar. "Cam tells us there's a new woman in your life," she said.

Cam told them about Lacey? God, the minute they saw her, they'd be on his case to do something about keeping her in his life. *Not happening, folks.* Sure, he'd just given in to his impulses out in the country. Those were pure libido. Hadn't been so charged up about a woman in a long time. But one didn't introduce his sex partners to their parents. Wait. Cam had no idea what was happening between him and Lacey. The boss had seen him with Celia. "Not exactly. We've only been out a few times."

"Cam seems delighted," his mother continued. "Bosses aren't always so open-minded. In our day, your father and I certainly foiled the fraternization attempts of our staff. Office romances can be so risky."

"You won't have to worry about this one."

"We're not," his father said. "She seems very nice."

"You've met her?" His voice cracked. Boy, they worked fast.

His parents exchanged looks, as if debating his sanity.

His mother tilted her head. "Cam had to leave for another appointment. You weren't here. So we took advantage of the opportunity to meet her."

They were mighty proud of themselves, like a pair of bantam roosters. Like he and Celia were the couple of the year and they'd made it happen.

"You've done well, son," his father added. "Celia seems quite agreeable. So well-organized. In no time at all, she had her plans for tonight rearranged and a reservation made for the four of us at seven."

"What? You. She. No!" He needed to get back to Lacey and find out how bad she was hurt.

His mother offered him one of her patented tolerant looks. "She's very efficient, dear."

She, Celia, not Lacey. "Not what I meant."

They both blinked, then waited for him to continue.

"I, uh, I should've been the one to make the reservations," he stammered, improving. "Not her." Lacey was getting x-rayed and checked out at the hospital while he was here discussing dinner plans with his parents. Unreal. Insane.

Once his parents finally departed to spread their cheer elsewhere, he tried calling her but got a busy signal. Hospital zone. Probably had to turn off her phone while there. He'd check back later.

The rest of the afternoon and early evening went by in a blur. What had his parents been up to in his office while they waited for him? What had they talked to Cam about? These questions nagged at him, eating away at any reflections about the property he might have brought back with him.

Just before he left the office, he tried calling Lacey again.

"Hello?" said a somewhat familiar voice but not Lacey.

"This is Scott Dalton. How's Lacey doing?"

"Oh, hello, Scott. Janice Collier. I brought Lacey back to her apartment about an hour ago. They gave her something for the pain, so she's sleeping now. She didn't break anything, but she has a nasty sprain that's going to keep her off her feet a bit."

Scott released a sigh of relief. At least nothing was broken, even though it sounded like she'd done considerable damage to her ankle. Damn! He'd never injured a woman, especially during sex. He hated seeing this happen to Lacey. "Thanks for taking her to the emergency room."

"No problem. Reminded me of my son's teenage years. He was always spraining this or hurting that. I hope you were able to resolve your situation back at the office."

About all he'd accomplished with his *situation* was to eject his parents from his office. He was still on the hook for dinner tonight. "Let's say I dealt with it temporarily, but it still requires my attention tonight. Please tell Lacey I called and I'll get back to her as soon as I can." He hung up and raced to shower and change in the next ten minutes.

"Thanks for going along with this dinner," he told Celia later, as he drove to the restaurant. "Especially when I was ready to quit our agreement last night." Despite his misgivings about the reason for his parents' visit, the look in their eyes when they told him they'd met his new lady friend had been too intoxicating. Their interest in his love life disturbed him, but their seeming approval felt great. He wanted to bask in the sunshine of their notice for a little while before setting them straight. Besides, he hadn't really lied about squiring Celia around recently. That much about their fake relationship was true.

"Actually, your parents didn't give me much chance to say no, let alone explain our situation, but I don't mind. You've been such a good sport to help me with Brian."

"They're a pair of human bulldozers. Don't let them plow you under."

"They seemed so pleased you were seeing someone, I hate to lead them on like this."

He pulled into a parking lot and located an empty spot. "Serves them right for preventing us from clarifying why we're together. But I agree, we need to let them know we're not serious about each other."

"Just so we don't let on about our arrangement," she said.

Despite their intrusiveness, he didn't want to lie to his parents, although that was pretty much what they were doing with everyone else. "Uh, sure."

His parents were waiting for them at Moliere's, a French contemporary bistro in Windsor Heights. His mother, her hair dark as ebony, was chic as usual in a gold linen suit. His dad, looking more debonair than ever, complemented his wife in a dark blue blazer, perfect on this late April night. Once the amenities had been seen to and their dinner ordered, they moved right into their agenda.

"How long have the two of you been an item?" his mother asked.

Scott gripped the edge of the table, reminding himself to keep his cool. "We aren't what you'd call an *item*, Mom. That's a term used by your generation. Celia recently broke up with her boyfriend, so she asked me to escort her to Cam's birthday party. We've only been out a few times."

"Ah, but according to Cam, you haven't tried to hide your association." His mother rested her gaze on Celia, apparently hoping to pry more information from her.

"Well, yes, that's true," Scott admitted. "But—"

"Sounds like you're an item to me," his father said.

Scott looked to Celia. Time for her to conclude this interrogation.

As she folded her hands, Celia leaned into the table. "I hope my agreeing to join you tonight didn't give you the wrong idea about Scott and me. He's been helping me pick up the pieces after my last relationship ended abruptly."

"Oh." His mother exchanged glances with his father. "Well, you certainly seem to be getting along well."

Gordon Dalton touched Celia's hand briefly. "We're happy you were able to join us tonight."

What was this? Nicey-nice all around. Another shoe was out there somewhere, about to drop. But at least he hadn't led them to believe he and Celia were serious.

As they were finishing dessert, his father set down his coffee cup and cleared his throat. "Did Cam mention our luncheon discussion?"

And there it was, the sound of footwear hitting the floor. Scott felt his dinner clump together in his stomach. "No. I didn't see Cam this afternoon."

"I'm sure he won't mind if we give you the news instead of him." His mother's eyes glowed with anticipation.

Scott wondered if his own eyes might not be glowing. With fever.

"Cam is elevating you to a new position," his father announced.

Scott sat up suddenly, his heart rate escalating. Celia's eyes widened. "Principal?" Scott said. Finally.

"Better." His father pulled at the hem of his blazer in apparent preparation for his big news. "You're going to be Cam's new marketing director." He sat back, issued a smug smile and eyed Scott, as if expecting a big hug. Except his parents weren't the hugging types.

"Marketing director? What the hell is a marketing director?" Scott's exclamation caused patrons at neighboring tables to glance their way.

"Lower your voice, darling. I'm sure our little announcement has you excited, but we don't want to make a scene." His mother chided.

"Okay, fine," Scott said in a less vociferous tone. "What exactly did you discuss with Cam?"

His parents gazed at each other, as if deciding how much he understood of their adult world. "I'm sure the projects you've been working on have been fine, son. You've cut your teeth on them, made a name for yourself, earned your co-workers' respect. But it's time to move up the corporate ladder. Especially since you may soon be settling down." He looked directly at Celia.

Celia studied her vegetables. Scott massaged his temples. The room seemed to be spinning around him. Or had the entire world gone into a tailspin? This was more than inquiring about his work. Once again, they were interfering in his career. Did they have no faith in his own abilities?

He wanted to scream and upend the table. Throw a child's tantrum like he never had when he was a kid. Why couldn't they simply appreciate him for who he was?

"Well, Scott? Isn't this great news?" his mother wanted to know.

He wanted to groan.

"Scott's overwhelmed by your announcement," Celia said for him, valiantly attempting to cover for his reaction.

"Ah," his mother replied, somewhat mollified.

Celia did what she did best, handled the situation. "While Scott digests this turn of events, why don't we celebrate with some bubbly? My treat." She didn't wait for their consent. For the next several minutes, she oversaw the ordering and toasting, making sure Scott kept his cool.

Having dropped their bomb, his parents departed shortly after taking a few courtesy sips of the champagne, claiming jet lag.

Scott hunched in his chair, hands clasped, twiddling his thumbs. "Thanks for rescuing me."

"The least I could do. Was tonight typical behavior for them?"

"Tried to warn you. Sometimes they do it long distance over the phone."

"Families can sometimes be a pain, but my parents would never insert themselves in my work life."

"Would you mind if we cut the evening short?" he asked. "This business about becoming Cam's new marketing director has me reeling."

"Of course not. You should check in with Cam as soon as possible."

"My plan exactly." Why would his boss agree to such a ridiculous idea? Scott had been dealing with his parents' off-and-on-again attention span since he was a kid. But Cam's part in this had him worried. He thought he knew his boss and had the man's support. What hold did his parents have over the guy?

LACEY AWOKE around eight thirty that evening, groggy from her lengthy, drug-induced nap.

"How are you feeling?" Janice asked from a chair in the corner. "You were out for some time."

"Like my brain has been stuffed with cotton. Those pain killers were potent." She swung her feet over the side of the bed, but as soon as the affected ankle touched the floor, her whole foot throbbed with pain. "Ouch! It still hurts, Janice." Could she sound more pathetic?

Like a little child rather than a grown woman who should be able to suck it in.

"It's not going to subside immediately, even with all those meds the hospital gave you. I hate to sound harsh, dear, but you'll have to deal with this for at least the next few days."

Gritting her teeth, Lacey pulled her feet back under the covers. "I thought the meds would block the pain."

"At least they helped you get some rest, so your body could start to heal. Are you hungry? You shouldn't take any more pills on an empty stomach."

Lacey really wasn't hungry but agreed to try something. She could only consume a few bites of the sandwich Janice fixed, but she was able to get down half a glass of water.

"Scott Dalton called while you were sleeping," Janice told her after removing the tray of food from Lacey's lap.

Lacey smiled to herself. True to his word, he did check on her. "Oh? What did he say?"

Janice filled her in on Scott's call, ending with his promise to check back on her later.

"Did he say when?" Maybe he'd come to see her yet tonight.

Janice shook her head. "Sorry. Perhaps I should've pressed him for a time."

Just in case he might still stop by that evening, although it was now after nine, she convinced Janice she was fine and could manage on her own. After Janice left, Lacey remained in bed, the pain of her sprained ankle fighting the memory of her romp in the field with Scott. She'd known their pent-up emotions were heading for an explosion, but she hadn't been prepared for the impact, interrupted though it was, let alone the aftermath.

Where was her head? She still couldn't believe they'd almost gotten naked right there near the roadside.

She knew the answer. She'd wanted Scott to take her right there, right then. Blame it on the bull. Their adrenaline levels had been sky-high as they'd barely outrun the aggressive animal. No wonder they'd collapsed in a heap in the grass. Of course, the bull hadn't forced them to remove each other's clothing and maul each other. No, their after-noon frolic in the field was all their own idea.

How the pain from her injured ankle had not permeated her passion eluded comprehension. Yet she'd been totally unaware of the sprain until she'd tried to stand. Scott Dalton was getting to her, as much as she hated to admit it. Not good. Couldn't afford to let herself get too involved. Yet the thought of his making love to her made her tighten her knees, bad ankle and all.

Who was she? Lacey Rogers, the woman who could have any man she wanted? The rising architect who'd learned she could hold her own with the firm's star player? Or a woman so wanton she'd almost given herself out in the open on the edge of a farm field? "What's with you, Lacey Rogers?"

Just weeks ago, she could have readily answered her own question. She wasn't so sure now. Scott Dalton was more than she'd bargained for. It went without saying he was the most gorgeous, charming man she'd ever known. His mere touch had her heart pumping at warp speed. The challenge of keeping up with him professionally gave her a buzz like none she'd ever experienced.

But there was something more about Scott. Whatever it was had been working its way under her skin the last several days. He possessed a certain decency, a humanity. Here, finally, was a man she might be able to trust. One who wouldn't take advantage of her and then run off.

Would he call or come by? If she allowed herself to fall asleep again, she might miss him. She had to know if he was still panting from the aftermath of their picnic. Around one in the morning, she finally decided he wouldn't be contacting her that night and gave in to sleep.

Though their deadline weighed heavily on her conscience, she stayed home from work the next morning, sending Scott a message saying he'd have to muddle through without her. That should generate a call. Though every step was slow and painful, she managed to drag herself from bed and throw on clothes. She could lounge on the couch and ponder their project just as well there as at the office. After all,

Janice's contribution had helped them turn a corner. The concept wasn't quite there, it still needed something she hadn't been able to define, but they were getting close, which was good, because the deadline was fast approaching.

Promptly at eight, her phone rang. Scott, at last! She grabbed for the cell, anxious to hear about his visit with his parents. But it wasn't him. It was Janice, offering to come over again. Lacey refrained from telling her friend how much pain she was still in. She wanted to savor yesterday's memories and ponder last night's dilemmas by herself, even though she'd have to struggle to get around. "You hardly know me, yet you came to my rescue when my brother and friends weren't available. I don't expect you to drop everything at your gallery and come over here now."

"I'm not leaving you alone today," Janice said, and within an hour, she was there making breakfast.

"You really didn't have to do this," Lacey said, wolfing down a homemade muffin, "but since you wouldn't take no for an answer, I'll have another of these."

"Good! Your appetite's returning. You had me worried last night when you could barely hold your sandwich let alone eat it."

She'd been preoccupied, wondering when Scott would check in. But she wasn't ready to share what was really troubling her, so she supplied another reason. "Hospitals."

Janice cocked an eyebrow. "Bad memories?"

"From when my mom was dying of cancer. I was old enough to visit her room but too young to deal with it."

"I experienced a similar feeling after my husband's death. Although Dan had been failing for months, he had a heart attack when he was out jogging and passed away two hours later in the emergency room. I couldn't go anywhere near the place for some time, even when close friends were hospitalized."

"I totally forgot about your situation when I asked you to take me to the hospital yesterday."

Janice placed a hand over Lacey's. "I wouldn't expect you to. I told you about my feelings just now because I wanted you to know it's possible to get beyond them."

Lacey studied the muffin she'd been about to bite into and sighed. "Next week would have been my mom's fifty-fifth birthday. My brother and I observe it every year by placing flowers on her grave."

Janice studied her. "Nice tradition."

"I suppose. But I don't feel it's necessary anymore."

Janice remained silent.

Unbidden tears welled up in Lacey's eyes. With Janice, she didn't feel the need to hold back. She wiped away the moisture with an index finger. "Am I so terrible? Brian won't hear of it."

"When you lose someone who's been close to you, one of the greatest comforts you have is sharing your grief with others. Trouble is, people don't always deal with grief the same way."

"That's it exactly! Brian thinks I'm forgetting our mom. No longer honoring her memory."

Janice got up and poured herself a glass of water. "My son and I are going through something similar," she said when she returned to the table. "I threw myself into keeping our business afloat, attempting to get through my grief by working round the clock. My son worries about losing me as well as his father. Since he lives so far away and is always traveling, I think he obsesses about my wellbeing."

"Sounds a bit tedious."

Janice considered the question. "I guess I worry about him, too."

"Losing him?"

"No. I don't think he's fully processed his father's death. Given in to the grief." Her eyes blinked with her own tears. "I worry about what will happen when he does."

"I went for years without fully accepting my mother's death. It finally caught up with me in college."

"What happened?"

"A broken romance. Though it wasn't as traumatic as losing my mom, being dumped by my fiancé brought back all those feelings of hurt and anguish. First I partied and let my grades slip. Then I dropped out of school for a year, ran off to France and lived with other students I met in the clubs. Slept all day, caroused all night."

"What turned you around?"

"One day, the shouting in the room across the hall sent me outside to escape. It was early spring, misty and cool. I wandered the streets of the Rive Gauche for hours. When I finally settled on a park bench, I was numb with cold. When I took note of my surroundings, I discovered I was sitting near the Cathedral of Notre Dame. This was before the fire. My eyes focused on the powerful lines of the grand old lady of the City—the parapets, spires, flying buttresses. Sketching them calmed me. I used an old letter from Brian I found in my purse for paper."

She hadn't even shared this story with Scott. "After I finished, I felt more at peace with myself than I had in months. Enough to finally read the letter. He said he'd given me my space long enough. It was time to come home and work through my grief."

She faced Janice, tears now flowing freely. "It all came together for me. Accepting my mother's death, deciding to go home and discovering how much architecture appealed to me. The irony of my brother's words, which snapped me out of my funk, hasn't escaped my current concern about him."

"Making your way through sorrow can be a circuitous journey."

"It's a strange emotion, isn't it?" Despite the tears, it had been comforting to share her story with someone who understood. "I think meeting you at the Salsa class was meant to be. You not only saved our skins with the project concept, but you've helped me see my family situation with new eyes. It's like"—she stopped for a moment, almost too shy to put her thought into words—"like having a mother to talk to."

Janice's eyes welled up more. "Thank you, dear. I appreciate the sentiment." She waited a beat. "Speaking of our class, how are things going with your dance partner?"

Back to Scott again. She'd managed not to think of him for at least two minutes. "It's getting complicated and a bit risqué. Might be more information than you want to hear."

"Try me."

Did she really want to tell a near stranger, growing friendship notwithstanding, what almost happened the day before? Too late. The subject was on the table. Not easy to back out now. "Things sort of exploded between Scott and me yesterday, *exploded* in the roll-in-the-hay sort of way. Who knows what might have happened if I hadn't hurt my ankle about the same time."

Her new friend cleared away plates and silverware before replying, as if needing time to process such an intimate confession. "Was your injured ankle a godsend or a nasty interruption?"

Janice was turning out to be just as insightful a friend as Celia. Damn! "A bit of both, I guess. I really wanted to go through with it. So did Scott. But it probably would have been a mistake. Even though there was no one around, someone might have shown up and seen us. Plus, office romances aren't the smartest thing."

"My advice? Whether it's an office romance or not, sounds like you need to scratch the itch to find out. But next time? Do it behind closed doors," she added, eyes sparkling.

Would her own mother have counseled such action? The woman's hippie garb wasn't just for effect. Janice's thinking seemed to embody the more independent thinking of the era.

Once she cleared away breakfast things, Janice prepared sandwiches and a salad for the rest of the day. "I should get over to the gallery. I don't like to leave my assistant alone for too long. Call if you need me to come back."

Before she left, Janice made Lacey assure her she would stay on the couch as much as possible and keep off her ankle. Once her friend had left, the hours passed slowly. Too slowly for someone who was accustomed to being constantly in motion.

The ankle continued to bother her despite the painkillers. When she wasn't dwelling on her injury, she was wondering when Scott would call or why he hadn't called yet. Around eleven, when her cell phone chirped, she nearly sprained the other ankle trying to retrieve the phone in time. "Hi," she said somewhat breathlessly.

"Are you speaking to me yet, after our dreadful cards session the other night?" Brian asked.

"Oh, hi." She tried to keep the disappointment out of her voice.

When she recounted how her flight from the bull had caused her to injure her ankle, he was both furious with Scott and immediately consoling. "Where were his brains? Traipsing around an open field. You'd think he'd grown up in New York City instead of the Midwest."

"Don't come down on him. He's the one who deflected the bull's attention while I ran for cover. I'm just a little rusty climbing over farm fences."

"Guess your injury nullifies my idea," he said, disappointment underlying his tone. "I thought we'd take care of the flowers for Mother's grave this weekend rather than next Wednesday."

"Oh." He hadn't given up on the tradition, even though she'd hinted she wanted to stop. Then she remembered Janice's words about people grieving in different ways. Janice hadn't come right out and said it, but Lacey suspected her friend had meant to add, even though her feelings were somewhere else, she should honor Brian's.

"Tell you what, Bri. I'll call the florist and place the order. Why don't you pick up the arrangement from them tomorrow and go to the cemetery yourself. I'll go next Wednesday."

Silence on the other end of the line. Darn. She'd offended him. Or, at the very least, he didn't like the idea.

"Okay," he finally said. "Remember to tell them pink roses."

He wasn't upset. She breathed a sigh of relief. "Of course."

After his call, she tried reading through her project file and redoing her sketches. Couldn't afford to lose any more work time despite her injury. But her mind wasn't in it, because she kept listening for the phone. Scott did have her cell phone number, didn't he? Of course he did. He'd called last night when she was asleep. Maybe he'd come by instead? She should change clothes. She didn't want him to see her in her frumpy gray sweats.

With great effort, Lacey hobbled to her bedroom and changed into a sheer black nightgown and peignoir. As far as she was concerned, she'd crossed the line of no retreat when she'd given in to him the day before. Sensible or not, she meant to follow through on the feelings she'd been repressing. One look at her in this get-up, and there'd be no question in Scott's mind about her intentions and hopefully no indecision for him about what to do next.

One more trek, this time to the kitchen to put her best, and only, bottle of wine on ice, and then she returned to her nest on the couch to wait.

By eight, the waiting had become unbearable. She'd skipped her latest painkiller, because she thought she'd be imbibing the wine soon and didn't want to mix them.

Maybe his parents were still monopolizing his time. During office hours? Perhaps, if a family emergency had brought them back to town. What kind of problem would keep him from calling her for twenty-four hours, though?

Then she checked her phone. No charge. Good grief. She charged her phone every night. Except last night, when she was in too much pain, too groggy to remember. Somehow it had retained the charge through part of the day, long enough for her to receive calls from Janice and then her brother, but then it went dead. As much focus as she'd placed on hearing from the guy, why hadn't it occurred to her to check the charge?

No point waiting for a call that wasn't going to come. She gave in to taking more of the painkiller.

Around nine, she drifted into a deep sleep until morning.

The next day was pretty much a repeat of the day before, although this time she stayed in her sweats all day. When Janice called to offer her services again, Lacey begged off. Not because she didn't want to see her new friend, she didn't want Janice to discover the tangle of black silk lying on her bedroom floor. She'd been too weak and too disappointed to put it away properly.

Throughout the day, she debated whether she should call Scott. When she finally succumbed to temptation around four, he didn't pick up. "Hi, it's Lacey. Looks like I'll be out of commission the rest of the weekend thanks to this stupid ankle, but all this staying off my feet will give me more time to think about the project. Hope things are going well with your parents." If he was screening his calls, maybe he'd call back.

But instead of a call, she received a text a few hours later. "Urgent I contact Cam. Staying off phone, in case he calls. Sorry about ankle. Hang in there. Rest."

What was so urgent? How was Cam involved? Did it concern their project? What about his parents—what happened to that emergency? Sometimes she hated texts. They raised more questions than they answered. The medium seemed invented for men, so they could abbreviate their communications. But if that's how they were going to play it, she'd respond in kind. "What's with Cam? The project? Injured, but still available by phone."

She didn't have to wait long for a response. "Don't worry. Not project. Personal. REST."

The last part was pretty clear. He didn't need her help nor apparently any more texts. Did he not realize how crappy she was feeling? And bored.

Okay, fine. She'd obviously read too much into their growing relationship, especially what happened after they escaped the bull. Dejected, she succumbed to a fitful sleep the rest of the night.

"Sorry I didn't get here sooner," Celia said, arriving on Sunday morning to check on her. "I didn't hear about your injury until I went into the office on Friday, even though I was with Scott Thursday night."

"You were?" This was news. He'd said he and Celia were quits back in the field, just as they'd been about to get it on. A hot stream of bile filled her throat. She swallowed. "I don't recall our setting up another date for the two of you." Did she sound too proprietary? Surely she wasn't jealous of a fake romance?

"It happened so fast. His parents breezed into town, heard about our so-called relationship from our dear boss and insisted we all go out to dinner."

Who were these people who seemed to be taking over his time? "What are they like?"

Celia angled her head, apparently considering her response.

"They're very nice, in their own overbearing way. They'd already convinced Cam—he's an old friend, I guess—to give Scott a *promotion*."

"Promotion?" She'd be on her own for the rest of the project? The thought sent an Ice Age glacier up her back. As much as the thought of overseeing this huge project appealed to her, she wasn't sure if she was ready. Besides, Scott and his outrageous style were growing on her. "Scott must have been delighted. Word has it he's been waiting to be named principal."

Celia bit a lip. "Actually, he wasn't a happy camper. He sort of blew up. The new job is as Marketing Director, not principal. He planned to talk to Cam right away to get it straightened out, but I haven't heard from or seen either since."

Now she knew why Scott had been so anxious to contact Cam and why he seemed to have gone off the radar. "Scott said something about his parents not being typical. Guess he wasn't kidding."

Celia suddenly noticed Lacey's sweats. "How's your ankle?"

"Not broken. One good thing. But it hurts like the devil, which is keeping me from concentrating on our project."

"Ooh, that's too bad. Good thing you've got Scott as a partner. If anyone can pull something out of the fire, he can."

Right. Scott could pick up part of her share. If he'd just call.

"Can I help? Get you anything?"

"Thanks, no. My ankle just needs time to heal, time I don't have."

Celia winced. "Got time for a friend?"

"You? Always. What's up? Something to do with Brian?"

Celia settled into the easy chair next to the sofa where Lacey reclined. "I shouldn't bother you, not while you're feeling so awful and time is running out on your project. But you're my best friend and the only one I can turn to."

Sounded ominous. But she couldn't have run into Brian when she was out with Scott's parents, or Brian would have mentioned it when he called. Something else must have happened. "What's up?"

Celia prefaced her reply with a huge sigh. Her entire body seemed to deflate. "After Scott and I left Brian's Wednesday night, he made me face a hard fact, throwing our supposed new relationship in Brian's face wasn't working. He suggested I do the opposite, stay out of Brian's orbit. It sounded like a good idea, since our plan wasn't working, but it was a huge risk. I could be making it all the easier for Brian to forget about me."

The same thought had occurred to Lacey. "So you've decided to call off your fake dating?" Scott seemed to think so.

"I considered it. I even went to the cemetery yesterday to seek guidance from your mother."

"The cemetery?"

"Although I never met your mother, I needed to vent. First, I congratulated her for raising two great kids and preparing them to deal with life once she was no longer here, then I questioned why she hadn't prepared Brian better to move on. I think his reticence to make our relationship permanent is related to her."

"To our mother? No, I'm the one who isn't ready to commit. Brian never lost faith in marriage like I did."

"He told me the same thing after he overheard me talking to her grave."

Of course! Brian had delivered the flowers she ordered and run into Celia. "What did he say?"

"He told me he wasn't tied to your mother's apron strings. But I didn't leave it alone. I suggested he'd broken things off between us because I didn't measure up to your mother."

"Are you sure you want to tell me all this? I feel like a voyeur."

"I have to share this with someone, Lacey, because I still don't understand his reasoning. He said he'd never compared me to his mother. I was my own distinct, wonderful person."

"You are! We both love you in our own ways."

Celia's eyes misted. "And I love you. But look at me. I'm crying, just like I did then. Brian stepped out of the shadows where he'd been watching me, approached and swiped away a tear with his finger. 'I can't go through this again,' he said. When I pressed him, he said he was afraid of losing me someday, too."

Tears deluged her face, making her gasp for air.

In tears herself, Lacey hobbled over to her friend and cradled her in her arms, though Celia was half a foot taller. "It's okay," she cooed, comforting as best she could. Then it hit her. "You finally have an answer, Cee. He told you why he doesn't want to get more serious."

Celia pulled away. "Okay, maybe, but now what do I do? He's afraid of losing me someday. How can I get him to stop worrying?"

Lacey shook her head. "Brian needs to learn to trust in love. Unfortunately, I can't help you there. I don't trust in love, either."

CHAPTER 15

Lacey awoke on Monday morning ready to take a bite out of the hide of one Scott Dalton. Or anyone else who got in her way. The color of her bruise had deepened, although the swelling around her ankle had receded somewhat. With a little persistence and grinding of teeth, she was somewhat mobile, although her ankle still ached like someone had hit it with a sledgehammer.

The steady downpour of a spring shower beat at her windows throughout the night. It refused to subside in the morning hours. The thought of negotiating her car through traffic with a bum foot, making her way to the building in the downpour, and hobbling around her office all day sapped what little energy remained. It didn't take much to convince her to stay home another day, especially when she could polish the design concept from there.

She hadn't heard from Scott at all on Sunday. No call, no text, no visit. Nor did she attempt to contact him. Unless she'd come up with a killer design concept, which she hadn't, because she couldn't concentrate while wondering about Scott through a haze of pain, there was no reason for her to get in touch with him. She felt like a fool for putting so much faith in his words, delivered with no intention of following through.

"I shouldn't care," she told the image in the mirror. "I must have imagined or misinterpreted his parting comment on Thursday." He was no more interested in continuing what he started than he was in nurturing the professional friendship she thought they were developing.

He'd seen an opportunity to gain the upper hand, show her she was no different than the other women who panted after him, and he'd seized it.

Hadn't it been his idea to get away for the afternoon? He'd even been the one to suggest a fast food picnic. How hokey could it get? But she'd fallen for it, even to the point of investigating the hillside with him. He probably knew the bull was there and staged the animal's attack to scare her enough to forget her common sense and fall into his arms.

Talk about your cock and bull stories! She'd really been taken in with this one. Sucker!

Lacey smeared the eyeliner she'd been trying to apply. "Dammit! No man is worth the trouble of a committed relationship." Such a thing didn't exist. At least not for her.

She wasn't the one who'd gone back on her word. Who'd fled the scene when her companion needed medical attention. Okay, okay. She'd told him to go see to his parents, then called Janice, even though he offered to take her to the hospital. But his minimal attempts to check on her condition really cut.

She was hurt and humiliated and tired of coping with her sore ankle. Most of all, she was upset with herself for having believed something might be happening with Scott Dalton.

WHAT WAS HAPPENING with Scott was a nightmarish weekend second-guessing his abilities and questioning the direction of his career. Nothing new there. For some time, he'd been concerned about not yet being named principal. But his parents' little bomb of an announcement suggested he was never going to receive the title. Cam was throwing him a bone, because he owed Scott's parents. But Scott had to be sure, and the only way he could do that was to confront Cam, in person, however the man had mysteriously disappeared Friday morning. He wasn't at his home, because Scott had been there ringing the bell, then pounding on the door, more than once. Scott left countless messages on Cam's phone, none of which were returned. Probably avoiding him until the shock wore off, though it still didn't make sense. Cam wasn't one to cave to anyone. Not even Marcia and Gordon Dalton, the infamous steamrollers.

Scott barged into the office Monday morning in a nasty state of mind, daring anyone to cross his path. "I want to see Cameron Mackenzie as soon as possible. Don't take no for an answer," he barked at Jean without preamble or even a "good morning."

Jean snapped to attention. "Yes, Mr. Dalton. First thing."

He slammed the door of his office, threw his briefcase on his desk and sank into his chair to rub his eyes. He'd hardly slept all weekend. He was so wired, his usual morning coffee might not be the best idea today.

Jean entered within two minutes, her expression wary.

"How soon can I see him?"

"He's not here. At least not this morning. His secretary said he didn't come in, and she's being quite cagey about revealing his plans for the day."

"What?" Scott was out of his chair, leaning over the desk.

"I-I'm sorry, Mr. Dalton. I couldn't unearth any more information. Should I set up something for tomorrow?"

Figured. He'd been leaving messages for the guy for three days. Cam had to know by now how much Scott wanted to see him. How long did the boss think he could stall?

"Keep trying."

After Jean left, the only productive thing he could do was pace. Had to calm down. Think this through rationally. Get himself under control. He tried counting to one hundred. Got to twenty-two before he slammed his fist into his desk, the impact barely registering.

God, he hated this, other people controlling his life. Cam was a coward. He'd rolled over to pressure from his parents and now was hiding out because he knew Scott would be furious. Because the guy knew there was no way he could defend such a stupid move.

The door opened and Jean stuck her head in. "I brought your morning coffee, but I also included a pot of hot tea, which you might prefer instead." She came into the room with a tray in hand and set it on his work table.

His chuckle broke the foul mood. As usual, Jean was way ahead of him. He went over to the tray and peeked into the teapot. "I'll bet money it's herbal and decaffeinated."

Her lips quivered but didn't quite form a smile. "I have an idea regarding Mr. Mackenzie's whereabouts. But before I tell you, will you promise to stay here at least fifteen minutes and drink your tea?"

"You know where he is?"

"Nothing so specific. It just occurred to me he probably isn't at home, because if he is avoiding you, it would be too easy for you to find him there."

He looked at her expectantly. "Yeah, so?" She eyed the tray.

"All right. You win." He poured himself a half-cup and took a sip.

Her gaze wandered to the couch.

Obediently, he dragged himself to the object of her attention and flopped. He leaned back but drew the line at reclining. "Satisfied?"

She returned a half smile. "Take a few more sips. Then breathe deeply."

"Don't you trust me?" She didn't answer.

Exasperated, he did as she ordered.

"Perhaps you should consider running off your nervous energy over at the fitness center?"

"What?" He vaulted off the couch in a flash. "Don't play with me, Jean. Why would I want to—" Understanding hit. "You think he's hiding out there?"

"It's a logical possibility."

As he started for the door, she moved into his path, her expression grim. "You promised." She didn't budge until he returned to his seat and picked up his cup. She backed out the door. "I'm right outside, and I'm not above tripping you if you leave too soon."

He gave her eight minutes to play guard while he paced some more, making a mental note to give her an afternoon off soon. Her resourcefulness continued to amaze him. When he could stand it no longer, he slipped out. Jean was nowhere to be seen. He'd apologize later, with the time off.

Her hunch was correct. He found Cam at the fitness center. "Exactly when were you going to tell me about my promotion?" he asked, catching the other man off guard. "Before or after my parents left town?"

Blinking at Scott's sudden appearance, Cam reached for his water bottle before replying. "Scott! How was your visit with your parents?"

"They told me I have you to thank for bringing them up to speed on my social life. Insisted Celia join us for dinner Thursday night. But then, I suspect you know already."

Mackenzie continued to drink his water, avoiding eye contact.

Scott gripped the weight machine on which his boss was seated and leaned in. "They also said it was high time my career went into warp speed, and wasn't it lucky you agreed? So tell me, Cam, what the hell does a *marketing director* do at an architectural and engineering firm?"

Finally turning Scott's direction, Cam scrunched his eyes, then shook his head. "Don't tell me they told you about their crazy idea. Those two don't give up."

"You didn't agree?" He spit out the question.

"Calm down, Scott."

There was more to this than he'd thought. Scott inhaled slowly and attempted to assuage his temper. "Where've you been since last Friday? I've been trying to track you down all weekend."

Cam sighed and shook his head again. "Got called out of town suddenly. Daughter and her college roommate had a falling out. She was frantic to leave her apartment right away, so Marianne and I had to help her find a new place, then move her stuff in." He raised a hand over his shoulder and began to massage the kinks. "I'm not used to so much lifting and carrying. But there was no time to find a moving company."

Scott suspected Cam of overplaying his role in his daughter's relocation, but he was so relieved to hear the guy didn't support the marketing director idea he let it go. "I thought you were avoiding me."

Cam chuckled. "You and everyone else. My daughter kept me so busy finding boxes, hauling trash and vacuuming carpets, there wasn't a spare minute to check messages. I had no idea you needed to talk to me."

"They sounded so convincing with their little *announcement*."

"What's with those two, Scott? They burst into my office determined to pitch this scheme. I probably shouldn't have listened without you there, but they just kept talking."

"I thought you and my parents had some sort of understanding. You know, from the early days, when you were just getting started and needed investors?"

Cam stared at him. "I paid them back years ago. I'm grateful they were willing to take a chance on an unknown like me back then, but I don't owe them anything further."

The guy had probably paid them back big time by hiring him. But Scott didn't want to go there today. It was enough to clear up his parents' latest incursion into his life.

Cam eyed him closely, his eyes narrowed. "Are you interested in marketing? God, I hope not. I need you too much on Project Arabella. Speaking of which ..."

"Is coming right along. A few more tweaks and we should have a draft ready for your review." He kept his voice calm, positive despite the way his stomach roiled every time he thought about the approaching due date.

"Good, good. I'm counting on you. And your parents ..."

"I've already told them I don't want to be a marketing director. Since they sold their business and have taken to traveling the globe, they don't know what to do with themselves. Every so often they appear out of nowhere and rearrange my life."

"Well, keep them out of my life from now on. I don't like being the man in the middle when it comes to family matters."

Scott turned to go, but Cam grabbed his arm. "Marianne and I will have to pass on your dance class tonight." He rubbed his shoulder again. "My body suffered a real beating this weekend. The wife actually took pity on me."

Dance class! It had completely slipped his mind after he'd learned of his so-called promotion. He should be planning tonight's class with Lacey. Lacey! Good grief, he'd forgotten about her, too! He'd talked to her, when—Thursday night? No, she was sleeping. He'd learned about the report from the ER from Janice Collier. Discovering Lacey was okay and sleeping off her injury, he'd been able to go to dinner with Celia and his parents. Then all hell broke loose. He'd been so caught up waiting to hear from Cam, he hadn't dared use his phone to any extent, other than text. He had texted her, hadn't he? He vaguely remembered telling her to take it easy. Something like that, anyhow.

God, was that it? He hadn't really talked to her or even sent flowers? How could he have done such a thing? Simple, he'd been so angry at his parents and worried that Cam had actually gone along with them, he'd forgotten about her. Though Cam's words had dispelled the knot in his stomach, it quickly reappeared when he realized he'd totally forgotten about his partner. Could he be a bigger jerk? He'd spent the whole weekend brooding about his bad luck, forgetting she was the one with the sprained ankle.

He tore out of the fitness center only to find her office empty. Had she been hospitalized after all? Panic seized his gut as he wondered if she'd been hurt worse than they thought. Fortunately, another of the architects on her floor wandered by and told him she was at home resting.

He grabbed for his cell phone. Nah, too impersonal. He had to see her. Assure himself she was okay. Long overdue concern but the best he could muster.

~

"Go away!" Lacey shouted into her security system.

"But Lacey," Scott spoke into the uncaring speaker, "I need to see you."

"You didn't *need to* all weekend. Why's it so imperative now?"

"I have to explain. Please let me come up."

She stared at the intercom, her pulse rate increasing. His arrival had caught her unprepared. She ran a hand through her hair, attempting to fluff up the curls smashed from a weekend spent mostly lying down. She must look a wreck. But she didn't care what he thought at this point.

"Okay. You win. I'll release the lock. But I warn you, I'm not dressed for visitors nor in the mood to entertain."

When she opened her door a few minutes later, she was greeted by a ball of soft brown and black fake fur. "Hello. I'm Ferdinand come to apologize for my pitiful behavior last Thursday."

A small stuffed bull stared up at her from his perch on the largest bouquet of red roses she'd ever seen. "Your pitiful behavior? What about the so-called gentleman who accompanied me?"

"He's sorrier than you realize." Scott moved into her sight from behind the door.

She bit her lower lip so he couldn't see it quiver. "Really? Could have fooled me."

"Yeah, I know. I should've done more than just called and texted. I did call, you know? Last Thursday. You were sleeping at the time."

He sounded sincerely contrite. Looked pathetic with his hair messed, his clothes appearing like they'd been slept in, eyes bloodshot. Even in his rumpled state, he was still eye candy. As angry as she was, she couldn't stop her heart from beating faster. "You and your friend can come in for a minute," she said with hesitation. "But put him down over there on the end table, away from me. Can't shake the memory."

She tottered over to the sofa and settled with great care. He sank into the nearby easy chair.

"How's your ankle? Does it hurt?"

"Guess it's healing, but there's still a lot of pain. I have meds, but they wear off fast. It was too much to go to work today."

He leaned forward to gaze into her eyes, as if trying to read something behind them. "That the only reason?"

Shivering, she huddled back into the sofa. "Why do you ask?"

He picked up a throw and arranged it around her. She really didn't need the blanket. Her temp heated up the minute Scott appeared. "I thought you might have been regretting what almost happened between us last week," he said breathily.

She flung the throw to the side. "What about you? That the real reason you've kept your distance since?"

He lowered his eyes. "I can explain."

"No need. Actions speak louder than words. If you weren't interested, why didn't you just say so?"

"Weren't interested—?"

"You don't need to sugarcoat it for me, Dalton. I'm a big girl. If you found yourself going down a path with no appeal, you could have simply said so rather than make promises you didn't intend to keep."

He crinkled his brow. "Promises?"

She knew it! He hadn't been serious. Didn't even remember what he'd said.

"Look, Lacey, I don't know what you think I said, but my life's been turned upside down since then and ..."

"Oh, right!" she remembered what Celia had told her about his big promotion but wasn't about to break the confidence. "Your parents. Did your reunion go well?"

"They were under the mistaken impression they needed to ramp up my career, so they arranged with Cam for me to be his new marketing director."

"Weren't you aiming for principal?"

"Thanks for remembering. They didn't."

"Why would Cam agree to such a thing?"

"Actually, he didn't. He humored them by listening to their pitch but never intended to go through with it. Told me this morning. Spent my weekend trying to locate him to no avail, he was out of town, which is why I, uh, didn't get back to you."

She took a moment to process what he'd said. Did all parents behave like this? Forget the parents. Their actions didn't excuse his token interest in her condition. "In other words, you got so caught up trying to find Cam you forgot about me?"

He took her hand. "I, uh …"

She withdrew her hand, looked away. "Thursday was just a moment in time. A moment you didn't care to repeat."

He closed his eyes briefly, then shook his head. "You got it wrong. Look, I was an insensitive clod not to call you despite what I was going through. I wouldn't blame you if you kicked me out, but please don't."

She allowed a small trace of a smile to curve her lips. He really did care. Or it could be more of the Dalton charm in action, fearing he'd insulted his work partner. "I can't exactly execute a kick right now."

He chuckled. "You'll give me, us, a second chance?"

Was he talking about their work relationship or otherwise? Jumping to conclusions had not worked in her best interest of late. Better play it safe. "At what?"

He stared at her as if she'd spoken gibberish. "At? Oh, I get it. I left you wondering all weekend what was going on between you and me. You want me to spell it out."

Yes, of course I do, you idiot! But she didn't want to come across as too needy. "Let's table that discussion for another day. Right now, I need to focus on my ankle and you've got your parents to contend with. You are going to tell them to mind their own business, aren't you?"

He didn't say anything. "I know I should," he said finally, shrugging.

He was so tentative. Where was the super ego, the in-charge mentality she knew? "But?"

He paused as if to consider his next words. "I'm not very good at telling my parents what I need. And they're not very good at listening."

"Like how?" With no parents of her own, she had no frame of reference for gauging what was normal. She would have thought nothing could stop Scott from doing what he wanted.

He blinked, apparently surprised by her interest. "They tell, not ask. Quiz them about my friends, my favorite foods, what I read, and they'd be hard-pressed to give you a correct answer. Any answer."

"Describes a lot of parents, from what I've heard. Generation gap, you know."

He rolled his eyes. "There's more to it than that." He averted her gaze, switching his attention to an architectural journal she'd left lying on the floor. He picked up the magazine, placed it on the coffee table.

There was more, but he needed prodding. "What is it, then?"

He stared vacantly at an ad in the magazine. "They seem to see me like I'm some sort of investment they've made."

"Investment?"

"Every so often, they check in to see how I'm doing, decide what to do with me next."

"Sounds so … cold. Surely they show and tell you how much they love you?" He eyed her sharply. Had she overstepped? "Probably too personal. Forget I asked."

He rose and moved over to the table where he'd left the roses and the bull. "They feel a certain warmth toward me, I'm sure. They just never planned to be parents."

"A lot of people don't plan on having families, but when the little ones show up anyhow, they do fine." She didn't plan to have a family, but not for fear she wouldn't know what to do. Her fear was having to do it on her own once the father deserted her.

He rubbed his scalp. "Maybe so. But mine seem to be missing the parent gene." He picked up the bull, bringing the tiny, ferocious face up to his own. "After college, they joined the Peace Corps and went to Africa to save the world. They were convinced they could make a difference but not content to wait for change to occur.

"What happened?"

He paused, still gazing at the bull, as if staring down Ferdinand might help him figure out what had transpired. "My dad contracted malaria, which brought them back to the States to recuperate."

"And you came along soon after?"

"Yeah. I was an accident, one they've spent nearly thirty years trying to fix." He set down the stuffed animal, then turned to her, a wistful expression on his face.

"I didn't realize."

He lowered his head momentarily, then ran a hand around his neck. "So much for Scott's dysfunctional upbringing. I only told you because I wanted you to know how much their visit threw me. My not checking back with you is still inexcusable, but maybe you can sort of understand what was going through my head." He sidled over to the window to glance out on the street below.

She, too, turned away, clueless how to help him. She ached for the hurt little boy who wanted so much for his parents just to love him. "I wish I could say something profound, but I have no experience to fall back on."

"Damn! I'm sorry, Lacey. I forgot about your situation."

The strength of his reaction surprised and pleased her. She rearranged the throw to break the tension. "You didn't offend me, but keep this in mind, no matter how your parents tend to mess up your life, you at least still have them *in* your life. You need to tell them how you feel."

He slammed his fists together. "How I feel? No!"

She shifted farther back into the sofa cushions, regretting her suggestion.

Seeing her reaction, he sighed, his shoulders drooping. "You don't know how many times I've wanted to sit them down and lay it all out for them. But I can't. The one time I tried, when I was in college, I put my dad in the hospital with a heart attack."

"Oh, Scott."

He gave her a half smile. "I don't know if the malaria years before had somehow weakened his constitution or if he'd been working too hard, but my mom freaked. Even though he recovered in record time, from then on, she acted as if he was an invalid and not to be pressured."

"In other words, his decisions weren't to be challenged."

"Mom convinced Dad to step down from the company."

"What do they do now besides make your life miserable?"

He returned to the easy chair where he'd sulked earlier. "Travel. Every so often, they show up in town when they need to touch home base."

"Maybe they're bored with this lifestyle?"

Scott narrowed his eyes, considered her question. "Perhaps. Their destinations seem to get more and more off the beaten track. Why do you ask?"

"You said they didn't have a lot to do with you when you were a kid. So why now?"

He rubbed his head again and gave her a blank look. "Beats me."

"Think about it, Scott. You have what they don't, a job, a place to go every day. Purpose."

An incredulous smile seized his face. "You mean they miss working? That's never occurred to me."

Because you're too busy fighting them.

Scott sprang from the chair and began pacing again, bumping into the end table in the process. His movements made her nervous. He needed an outlet. "Could you find a vase or something for those gorgeous flowers? There should be something in the upper kitchen cabinets."

He went off to locate a container. "What should I do about my parents—find them hobbies?" he called.

"Ask them about it, I guess," she called. "Or start pinpointing when they tend to get involved and figure out how to avoid those times."

"Suppose I could come right out and confront them." He entered the room, carrying the roses like a trophy. He set them on the same table where Ferdinand resided. When he thought she wasn't watching, he snuck a whiff. "But I like the other idea better. Keeping an eye on them."

"You never know what a little attention will do. With some luck and a bit of perception, you may soon have them dancing to your tune."

She thought her words would encourage him. Instead, he stood bolt upright and thumped his forehead. "Oh my God! We've got a class tonight. It slipped my mind when I stopped to pick up the flowers and the bull. Looks like I'm going have to solo, and I have no idea what to teach those people."

She'd also forgotten about the class. The mere idea of putting weight on her ankle made her cringe, but she didn't want to let Scott down.

He took her hand again, his expression earnest. "Are we okay? There's more we should discuss, but I need to head out if I'm going to pull off this class. Still, I don't want to leave you hanging this time."

Her heart zinged at his concern. "What if I act as sideline coach? If you can get me there, I can sit without too much discomfort."

His brow furrowed. "You need your rest."

"I can do that there just as well as here. Besides, I'm bored."

He continued to frown while he rubbed the back of his neck.

She knew he would give in, she'd seen the light flash in his eyes when she made the suggestion. But he needed to go through his chivalry act first.

Eventually, he caved. "But you're not to get up and demonstrate for any reason. Understood?"

He was cute when he tried to bully her! Not like he could, of course. "Okay, if you insist," she replied meekly. "This will give me an opportunity to observe our subjects without raising their suspicions. I'll grab an occasional word with them as they're resting."

He headed for the door. "I'll be back around six. Rest 'til then." He seemed to catch himself and returned to kiss her briefly. "Make friends with Ferdinand. This one's here to protect you."

Once the door closed, she relived the feel of his lips on hers. One kiss and liquid fire pooled in her stomach. She turned to her new companion. "Well? Start doing your job. You need to protect me from myself."

CHAPTER 16

Scott surveyed the Mackenzie and Associates conference room, where the second dance class was about to take place. Despite being unprepared, Lacey's bad ankle, and the incessant rain outside, things seemed to be on track. Of course, it was still five minutes before the class started, but he was beginning to think he might be able to pull this off.

Lacey smiled at him from across the room. God, she looked great despite the trial their trip from her apartment had turned into. He'd literally picked her up and carried her to his car. She'd held his umbrella over them both, so he'd avoided becoming completely drenched. Unfortunately, with his obstructed vision he'd walked into a wall and inadvertently hit Lacey's ankle, resulting in a thump on his head when she lost her grip on the umbrella.

One of the early arrivals approached him. "So what's it going to be tonight, Teach?"

Momentarily, his brain went to gauze. "Our lesson? Tonight we pick up the tempo on what you learned last week." He was still making it up in his head.

The woman nodded as if she knew exactly what he'd been saying, and then wandered off to join Lacey and Janice Collier.

Scott surveyed the room, ticking off the participants in his head. One missing. Jean? The woman was never late. Just then she slinked into the room, edging her way along the outside wall, glancing around nervously for something, or someone, refusing to make eye contact with him.

Couldn't start the class until he knew what was going on with her. He moved over to where she hovered, trying to appear inconspicuous. "The place looks as exotic as last week, Jean."

She glanced up at him, startled, and embarrassed. "Mr. Dalton! I-I'm so mortified. I can't believe I let this happen. I try so hard to be on top of things. I never dreamed—"

"Darling! Why didn't you tell us about this little soiree?" His mother and father sauntered toward Jean and him, faces animated, absolutely unaware of the impact of their presence.

What the devil? How had they found out about this class? Jean? Of course. It explained her mood. But not how they'd found out. Jean's ability to keep her mouth shut would make a mime seem a chatterbox.

"Nor did you tell us you'd picked up a new sideline, son," his father added.

Scott braced himself, forcing a smile across his face. "Just for tonight, Dad. I made the mistake of showing off my moves at Cam's birthday party and attracted a following." How was he going to conduct this class with them here? "What brings the two of you out in the middle of this monsoon? Surely you're not into Salsa?"

His parents exchanged guilty looks.

"We sort of inadvertently learned what you were doing this evening," his father began.

Jean's account of finding them looking through the calendar on her computer screen the previous week flashed through his mind.

"We've seen so little of you lately," his mother added, "we decided to join you tonight. That's okay, isn't it? Cam said he and Marianne wouldn't be able to make it, so we thought we could be their replacements."

They had it all lined up. Bless their organizational hearts. Lacey was right. They needed something more to dig their teeth into than their little globe-hopping junkets.

He glanced across the room at Lacey to get his bearings. Stupid! Obviously she couldn't read his thoughts, but she caught his eye. Smiling, she nodded toward his parents and raised her eyebrows. Maybe she could read his mind.

This one's for you, Lacey. "Mom. Dad. Got a great idea." He switched into enchant-the-client mode. "My partner over there," he indicated Lacey, "sprained her ankle and can't help demonstrate the steps. How 'bout the two of you filling in for her?"

"Us?" Both parents reacted at once.

"I really could use your help," he said as sincerely as he thought he could get away with. He didn't want to lay it on too thick or they'd become suspicious.

"It's been ages since we've danced," his father said.

His mother glanced hesitantly at the assembled group. "I don't know about this. In front of all these people?"

They wanted to be coaxed. No problem. His stock in trade. He touched his mother's arm. "Since when have you two been afraid of an audience? Choose your own steps if you want. Anything you do will be eagerly received."

Once again, his parents exchanged looks.

"I'm game, if you are, Marcia," his father said.

His mother ran a hand through her hair. "I've never been one to ignore a challenge. Let's do it!"

Scott turned to the rest of the group. "Gather round, everyone." He waited while his pupils cut short their conversations and assembled. He explained why Lacey was sitting this one out. "Fortunately, we've got some last-minute substitutes who'll go over the steps for you instead. My parents, Gordon and Marcia Dalton."

His dad seemed to stand taller and his mother glowed. His father took his mother's hand, spun her around, ending by dipping her halfway to the floor. Who were these people? What hams.

"Uh, yeah," he said, attempting to get his thoughts back on track. "Let's start with a recap of last week's lesson." He ticked off all the steps he and Lacey had demonstrated. Then he turned to his parents. "How about it, you two? Care to walk us through our repertoire?"

The older Daltons took their positions and executed the routine. Flawlessly. Even ending with a short flourish.

Scott was impressed. He'd seen them on the dance floor before but had never paid much attention. They were good.

The group erupted in a burst of applause.

"Wow, guys, you were great!" he said without pretense.

"Now we know where Scott gets it," one of the men said.

His mother fanned her face with a hand, appearing somewhat flustered. And delighted. She was eating this up.

His parents went through the paces as if they were meant for ballroom competition. His mother kept her face close to her husband's, her eyes staring directly at him. The effect was quite hypnotic and sensual. Scott was almost embarrassed to be in the same room.

Scott attempted to reclaim his authority. "Great show, you two. But these folks aren't quite ready for such high drama. Let's get back to the previous routine."

"Oh, but we do want to try those moves!" another of the women cried out. "They're proving how hot we baby boomers still are."

"You think we looked hot?" his mother purred.

Pandora's Box had opened for business. Before Scott realized it, his parents took over the class, just like they glommed onto everything else. While his parents continued to show off new steps, Scott made his way to Lacey.

She leaned toward him, a conspiratorial grin on her face. "Well done!"

"I took your advice," he whispered. "I'm not sure it worked."

"What do you mean? They're having the time of their lives and it isn't hurting you at all."

She had a point. "But isn't it sending them the wrong message—they can take over whenever they want?"

"Not if you pick the arena. They've got so much excess energy to burn, they simply needed a place to direct it."

"Better be careful, or I'll direct them toward you and your sprained ankle."

Her eyes widened in alarm. "You wouldn't!" Then she seemed to realize he'd been playing her. "Don't even kid about such things. I have no experience dealing with parental scrutiny."

"You called this one to a tee." About then, he noticed Jean nearby, still trying to avoid his notice. "Jean, you haven't danced yet. Since I seem to be out of a job, how about you and me partnering up?"

Apparently relieved he wasn't blaming her for his parents' arrival, Jean offered Lacey an apologetic look. "Will you be okay?"

"Go. I'll be fine. I couldn't have a better cover for gathering my information. Everyone stops by to see how I'm doing."

"We'll be back to check on you shortly." Scott offered a hand to Jean.

Lacey watched them go, Jean preening and Scott the perfect gentleman. Until they started to dance. Good grief! This was the first time she viewed Scott from behind when he was going through the steps. No wonder all the women hung around him, mouths agape. The man was a walking, well, swiveling, poster child for healthy butt cheeks. World class healthy butt cheeks. The pain in her ankle seemed to disappear.

"Laney, is it?"

"Lacey." She glanced up to find Scott's parents taking stock of her. Or so it seemed.

"Lacey." Scott's mother extended a hand. She wore a broad though tentative smile, as if not quite sure what to make of her. "We're having a great time tonight, especially leading the class."

Though it was light, social chatter, Lacey couldn't get past feeling there were depths to this chitchat even her water witching couldn't detect. *Proceed with caution.* "I'm so glad you could join us, Mrs. Dalton. You rescued our class."

"Call me Marcia. I'm sorry about your ankle, but it gave us the opportunity to do something for Scott for once."

"Oh?"

"He's so independent, we rarely get the chance to act like parents," his father observed. "And I'm Gordon." He offered his hand.

"I'm pleased to meet you both," she said with sincerity. "Scott and I are working on a project together here at the firm involving baby boomers. Your names came up in the course of our research."

"Baby boomers?" Marcia Dalton looked at her husband. "I guess we could be called boomers, couldn't we, Gordon, since we fall into that age bracket? What have you been researching, Lacey? Maybe we could help you there, too."

Uh-oh. How was she going to dig herself out of this one?

"You're very gracious," she began diplomatically, inventing as she went, "but this project is quite hush-hush. The slightest mention to the wrong parties of what we're planning could lose us the business. Of course, you wouldn't say anything," she rushed on to say, "but we have to be very careful."

"We completely understand." Gordon Dalton's dark brown eyes appeared to sweep the room for potential competitors.

"Confidentiality was the order of the day in our own business," his wife added.

Lacey took a deep breath. Thank goodness, they understood. Scott must have exaggerated their meddling natures.

"We're old hands at this, dear," Scott's mother said. "You can trust us to treat whatever you tell us with the utmost discretion."

"What?" Lacey looked around the room frantically. Where was Scott? She needed reinforcements. She forced a smile. "Uh, I'm sure I could, but actually I thought perhaps you could tell me something."

They returned her smile with bland ones of their own.

"We're hoping to expand our market share where boomers are concerned." She desperately hoped she wasn't giving away too much.

Scott's father nodded. "Makes sense. Baby boomers hold a lot of purchasing power."

His wife appeared to be stumped. "I'm not sure we can tell you much. We're not really typical. We're just two people who went after one goal in life only to find more than once we had to change course because life intervened."

Changed course more than once. Life intervened. Lacey froze, replaying the woman's words in her head. Marcia Dalton had just delivered gold.

No wonder it had been so difficult getting a read on boomers! True, they were heterogeneous, but in addition, according to Scott's mother, every baby boomer was a study in life changes. What was the saying? "Change is the only constant."

"Lacey? Are you all right?"

Lacey came back to earth to find the Daltons staring at her with concerned expressions. They had no idea they'd given her the final piece of the puzzle. Wouldn't Scott cringe when he learned his parents' interference was the crowning touch to their design concept?

"Oh, sorry. What you just said triggered an idea. I can't go into it right now, but one of these days I'd like to take you to lunch and explain." Both visibly relaxed.

"We'd very much like to, wouldn't we, Marcia?"

For a moment, Lacey was afraid Scott's mother wasn't ready to drop the subject. But Marcia Dalton surprised her, taking Lacey's hand. "What a wonderful idea, dear. We'll look forward to it. Perhaps we could treat you to lunch at our club? They make the most fantastic lemon chicken. And peach cobbler. I'll have to introduce you to—"

Gordon Dalton put a fond arm around his wife's shoulders. "Yes, Marcia, she gets the idea."

"I'll look forward to it," Lacey told them.

"Look forward to what?" Scott finally came to her rescue, just a trace of trepidation in his voice. "I see you've met my dance partner."

"We were making lunch plans with Lacey," his mother said. "She wants to thank us for—"

"For salvaging our class tonight," Lacey cut in, not yet ready to enlighten Scott about his parents' help with their project.

Though Scott's expression suggested he'd downed sour milk, he managed a lopsided smile. "Lacey's right. You really did save our skins."

They continued to trade thank yous until another couple joined the group and reminded Scott's parents they were taking them out for drinks to celebrate. The four left in a flurry of excited chatter.

Scott's smile melded into a concerned frown. "What was really going on before I got here?"

"What took you so long?" Lacey asked.

He grabbed the undersides of his shirt collar and tugged. "Despite my parents' overwhelming debut as dance instructors, I still seem to have my own following."

"All female, I presume."

"Yes, well, the ladies wanted to tell me how much they'd enjoyed the classes."

"And watching your tail end go into high gear on the dance floor."

He lifted a brow. "Are you speaking from personal experience?"

She parted with a knowing smile. "You do look pretty good from behind."

"I do my best."

"How many asked for your phone number?"

"Lacey! You're not jealous?"

She widened her eyes. "I already have your number, Scott Dalton."

He pulled a trigger finger, as if to say, "Touché! Ms. Rogers, our job here is done. Ready to head out?"

She hadn't thought about her ankle for some time. Plus, she couldn't wait to get home to work on the design concept, thanks to Marcia Dalton's unintentional help. She'd worry about how to bring Scott up to speed later.

CHAPTER 17

"You told them about Project Arabella?"

Lacey and Scott made it as far as his car before she broke down and confessed. She gulped air and steeled herself for the rest of his reaction. "I had to say something. You were right about the way they home in on you and apply the pressure until they know all."

"Ah, no!"

"They were so effusive," she hurried to say, "thanking me for letting them teach the class, and seemed so proud of how they'd done, I felt I had to say something. I told them we were using the class as a way to learn about baby boomers."

"Uh-huh. And they immediately surmised that meant Project Arabella?"

"Not exactly."

"Enlighten me. How did they make the leap?

How to explain? One minute she'd been on top of the situation, confident she could handle their questions, and the next, it was like they bored their way through her resolve like a woodpecker on a hollow tree. "I'm not sure. I didn't mean to tell them anything, but they kept smiling and looking concerned and asking increasingly less innocuous questions."

He reached over and covered her hand with his. "Say no more. Been there. More times than I care to remember."

The contact did not reassure her, although it kicked her body temp up a couple degrees. "You understand?"

"Perfectly. Doesn't mean I like it."

Despite her body's growing awareness of him, she drew a relieved breath and chuckled. "Now I understand what you meant when you said they *swoop* in and take over."

"I should've been there sooner. They can pull their routine on me, but you're a stranger."

"Thanks." That made her feel so much better. Not.

He reached for her hand again and this time held it. "You know what I meant."

She nodded, his touch leaving her momentarily bereft of speech. Then she remembered. "Actually, their prying gave me an idea. It was just what I needed to salt away the design concept."

He took his eyes off the road long enough to shoot her a questioning glance. "You didn't tell them, did you? We'll never hear the end of this, if you did."

"I told them their comments had caused me to think of something I needed to investigate further."

"And?"

"I diverted their attention with the luncheon invitation. Then you showed up."

"They dropped the inquisition?" His tone held more than a little skepticism.

She was losing patience with this discussion. "Can we let this go? I've confessed, apologized and assured you all is well."

Scott remained silent.

"Besides," she added, "what I really want to tell you about was the idea they gave me." She explained his mother's comment about boomers' changing lifestyles.

He still didn't react.

"Don't you see? We combine the idea of boomers constantly changing and reinventing themselves with what Janice told me about boomers needing to stay active and involved. Change plus Purpose. Don't you love it? Two simple themes pull the whole design concept together. We're going to finish this project on time, after all."

Scott stared ahead at the roadway. The rain had discouraged traffic this evening, but the occasional oncoming vehicle spattered water across his windshield. The interior of the car remained silent except for those *whooshes* of spray. "Change plus Purpose?" He repeated the phrase a few more times.

Surely he understood? Of course, he did. He was sharp. But did he like it? Or worse, did he see problems she'd overlooked? She had to know. "What do you think?"

"Patience. You gave me all of three words to consider. I need time to absorb them."

He was bluffing. He didn't understand one thing about it. Then he surprised her. "Change suggests we lay out the entire community to accommodate modifications as they're needed. Modifications to individual home sites, to segments of the community and to the community itself. Not unlike typical planning efforts, only more would be added." Now he was pontificating.

She let out a drawn-out breath. Should have known. Not only had his creative genius absorbed her nebulous thoughts, it was already busy embellishing them.

She squeezed his hand. "Very good."

He smiled at the acknowledgement. "Purpose is a little more difficult to grasp." He angled his head, considering. "They want to continue to live active lives. So at least one room in each house should be for hobbies or other activities."

"Right! Only 'hobbies' is a dated term. We have to come up with something else. I've been playing around with new language since I talked to Janice. You saw some of it in the draft outline I showed you. Things like lifelong learning, amenity centers and recreational enrichment."

"Which are only now starting to make sense. Your suggestions were interesting, but they seemed to be more a treatise on the lifestyles of baby boomers than specific design ideas."

"Enter the genius of Scott Dalton. You're a better designer than me."

"Well, what do you know? You're actually admitting as much?"

"You've had a few more years than me to develop your talent. I'm more the conceptualist right now. My design skills will come, with time."

"Some admission. Our partnership seems to have advanced a notch."

As he pulled into the parking lot of her apartment complex, the tires sloshed through several inches of water on the pavement. "Looks like you've got yourself a personal taxi to your door, Ms. Rogers. I'm not letting you stumble around in a mini-lake."

Secretly delighted, Lacey debated whether to protest, but the thought of being back in his arms again was too tempting. "Can you stay a while?" she asked, then quickly added, "We can continue this conversation while the idea's still fresh."

Scott turned off the ignition and relaxed into the seat. "Sure you're not going to take advantage of my weakened state?"

"Weakened?" she laughed. "I'm the one with the bum ankle."

"After I carry you all the way to your apartment, it may take a while to catch my breath."

"I take your breath away?" She couldn't resist the pun. "Wow."

He seemed to stiffen. "You sure did last week. I don't know what came over me at the site. Maybe the country air."

"Or maybe the adrenaline rush from escaping the bull?"

"If Jean hadn't called, panicked by the arrival of my parents ..."

" ...who knows what our friendly bull might have witnessed?"

"Yeah. Earlier, we started to talk about what might've happened, then I remembered the Salsa class." He left his statement hanging, as if waiting for her to take the lead. "Should I apologize?" he went on to say when she remained silent.

"For what? For starting something out in that field or for not finishing it?" She kept her tone somewhere between teasing and testing, realizing this was like a lovers' game of chicken, a question of who blinked first. Each of them wanted to know what the other would've done and neither wanted to be the first to say.

The rain beat steadily on the car roof while one stream of water after another sluiced down the windshield. The semi-darkness inside the car separated them from the world outside. They were alone, just the two of them. Lacey had called the question. Would one of them answer?

The air around them sizzled with more electricity than the lightning outside.

"I was out of my mind to come on to you, right there in the open. But I was also out of my mind from repressing the urge."

"I was just as busy ripping off your clothes as you were mine," she said in a softer voice.

"How do we get past the, uh, incident?"

"Do you want to get past it?"

He hesitated, as if searching for just the right response. "God, Lacey. Don't do this to me. Don't tempt me to finish what we started. Or—"

"Or what?" Her voice had gone husky, almost catching on those two words.

"Or this." He pulled her into his arms and claimed her lips. Nothing else seemed to matter, other than giving in to the swell of desire growing since their entrapment underneath the tree trunk.

This was not the kind of kiss she gave him after she returned from interviewing Janice Collier. Nor was it spawned from the relief of having outrun a bull. This kiss was fueled by pure passion. The ferocity with which his lips pressed hers nearly melted her bones, while his arms encased her as if sentencing her to life imprisonment. Outside, the heavens burst, accompanied by the low boom of approaching thunder and rapidly increased flickers of lightning.

Her lips returned his kiss with equal enthusiasm as she laced her fingers behind his neck, straining to get even closer. The rich smell of man, a man who'd recently expended much energy dancing, hit her nostrils, unleashing her own long dormant pheromones.

The sounds of heavy breathing and whimpered moans competed with Nature's fury outside. The strain from days and nights of suppressing their mutual attraction broke like the storm raging around them.

Hands greedy for familiarity roamed over shoulders, backs, thighs; touching, rubbing, gripping. Scott's were the first to move under clothing as his fingers slid up Lacey's spine and unhooked her bra. His splayed palm massaged the area between her shoulder blades, curved down and around to the front to slip under the bottom of her bra and cup a breast.

She didn't realize until then how much she'd been anticipating his touch. There.

He pulled his lips away from hers. "You feel so good."

The rubbing and squeezing continued, escalated. She pushed into him, willing him to claim more of her flesh.

But Scott seemed in no mood to linger. He sought her mouth again, crushing his lips against hers with even more force than before, thrusting his tongue between hers, flicking, probing, demanding. His kiss was urgent, determined. Though aware she could hold her own against his insistence, somewhere in the back of her mind, she knew doing so meant crossing some as yet undefined line. Little remained of better sense, only the knowledge she was about to jump into the abyss, willingly releasing herself to his spell.

One steely arm pulled her deeper into his embrace while the other left her breast and skimmed down her leg, then under the hem of her skirt, burning its way up the inside of her thigh.

Someone moaned. Her. She had no idea the whimper would slip out until it materialized in a coaxing, pleading tone. As his hand wandered further up her leg, she could no longer remain still. She arched her back, sensing her body grow wet with arousal as his hand found her most intimate region.

He leaned toward the door and locked it. He took his lips away from hers again. "You okay with this?" he muttered. His voice had grown as dusky as a whiskey-throated cabaret singer.

"Yes, God yes! There's no turning back now." She fumbled for his zipper. Finding it, she let her hand explore the territory. Hard. Rock hard. *Oh. My.* Intrigued, impressed, she gave in to the urgency of the moment and pulled the zipper down.

"I'll take it from here." He retrieved a small packet from one of his pockets. He freed the bulge in his pants and stuck on the condom. His speed and agility surprised and titillated her as he pulled down her panties and entered her. Each thrust went deeper and faster, sending her on a wave of euphoria beyond her experience.

This wasn't lovemaking. She knew and accepted the realization. She didn't want love or commitment. But she did want to find out what sex with Scott would be like, and now she was. Not far off, a bright bolt of lightning zapped the ground, followed shortly by a heavy explosion of thunder. Neither could compete with the earth-shaking impact of their coupling.

Spent, he finally moved away, laid his head back against the seat.

While she tried to resume normal breathing, Lacey attempted to gauge his reaction. Would this be one of those "wham, bam, thank you, ma'am" scenes? She'd experienced a few of those in the past, but she hadn't really cared. She herself wasn't above collecting men for her own sexual gratification. But she wanted something more from Scott. No undying declaration of love, of course, but something. The sex had been so spectacular, he was so different, their relationship deserved more.

"You should supply a guy with oxygen for afterwards," he said finally in what sounded like a gasping breath.

"I need some myself."

He turned to face her, the low-beam parking lot lights illuminating a portion of his face. "That was unreal."

"I haven't made out in a car since high school," she said.

"I never have. True confession. But seeing you over there, looking so luscious despite your ankle, I couldn't resist."

His words were kind of sweet. Especially for Scott.

"I like your thinking."

"I don't normally—"

"No need to explain. It was what it was. Highly enjoyable," she said.

He cocked his head, studying her. "You, uh, don't want to talk about it?"

"You want a review? Or a rating?" she chuckled.

"Well, no, but ..."

"I already crossed my personal no-relationships with-coworkers line with you, Scott. No looking back, no regrets. I don't expect anything more."

He hesitated momentarily. "Why'd you cross it?"

She considered her answer. She'd already put herself out there. Should she go further? Oh, hell. "Hold on to your ego, but you intrigue me. I had to find out what it would be like to, uh, do it with you."

"And?"

"C'mon, Scott. I just told you plenty. More than enough for now."

"Still more to learn?"

Though the shadows hid his expression, she was sure he'd raised an eyebrow. "Maybe. How 'bout you?"

"God, Lacey. After that, I could go to bed with you for a week and only come up occasionally for air. But we've got a project to finish."

"Right. You want the title of principal and I want to make a name for myself. We shouldn't risk damaging either by continuing."

He reached for a strand of her hair, curved it behind an ear. "Even touching you makes my blood boil. You have to be the strong one."

How could she be sentry, when his fingers had just reawakened every one of her nerve endings? One time hadn't been enough. She wasn't sure she could ever get enough of Scott Dalton. "Okay." *Fool!*

They called it a night after Scott carried her upstairs. No further talk about what it all meant. No discussion of Scott staying the night. Whether they were both a little shy about testing the waters, exhausted or worried about the project, they agreed to work apart the next day. Scott would revisit the site. Since she couldn't very well tramp around the countryside with an injured ankle, she would remain at her apartment and begin turning that rough outline into the concept piece, thanks to his mother's contribution.

As Lacey showered, her mind kept replaying the scene in the car. None of her fantasizing about having sex with Scott had ever included a scene in the middle of a rainstorm, on the front seat of a car, sitting up, no less, and fully clothed. It happened quickly, because they were both anxious to get to the end game. She'd never experienced such furious physical interaction, and yet there'd been a certain gentleness to it. No tearing off clothing, no acrobatics, no biting, scratching or pinching. Been there too many times before. Not her thing.

As she toweled off, she remembered the feel of his hands on her. Experienced hands, rubbing and kneading without hurting, rough enough to remind her this was a man enjoying, exploring her. In a word, masterful. Though she'd been sated, the wonderful wash and rumble of orgasm overtaking her more than once, a tiny bubble of sadness caught in her chest. Why?

No time to ponder whatever was clouding her complete enjoyment of their time together. She had work to do. At least another hour or two at the laptop before calling it a night.

EARLY THE NEXT EVENING, having just returned from the site, Scott waited impatiently for Lacey to open the door. After he'd carried her to the apartment the previous night, he'd gotten out of there as fast as he could for fear of what he might do if he stayed longer. His attraction to the woman was making him do and think things he knew he should avoid. He couldn't seem to stop himself. He'd even stood outside her building a few minutes letting the storm's remaining drizzle soak him, like the water would wash away the weird vibes he'd been feeling ever since he'd emptied himself into her.

No denying, it had been great sex. A physical rush like none he'd felt before had urged him to feel her up through her clothing, even sliding a hand up her skirt to make himself at home. Lacey had given as good as she got. She'd not only been receptive to his moves, she'd initiated a few of her own. She hadn't tried to pin him down trying to define what had happened. She'd merely accepted what they'd done, apparently enjoying it.

So why the letdown? Why did he feel like he'd left something undone? Maybe it was the stress of the project hanging over them. Whatever, he'd needed a fast, cold shower, after which he'd dropped into bed and cleared his brain of everything.

Now, almost a day later, he couldn't wait to see her again. He'd stopped at a fast food place and picked up dinner for them, anticipating a full evening comparing notes. "Hi." Could he sound more like a teenage boy on his first date?

"Hi, yourself. Come in."

"Your text said you'd completed the first draft of the concept piece." He followed her into her small living room.

She beamed at him. "Once I had that last part, thanks to your mother, it went together like it was always meant to be."

He made himself comfortable on the couch, anxious to tell her about his discovery. "Before we get into that, I've got to tell you what I found when I went back to the property."

"What?"

"I followed the creek farther into the woods. It branches. More than once, actually. The specs show the main juncture but not the others."

"Good news or bad?"

He leaned back and patted the space next to him in invitation. "Good, I hope. It certainly adds to the site's attractiveness, and it will allow more homeowners direct access to the water. But the hydraulics will be a little more challenging."

She made her way slowly to the couch, but she walked without a limp.

"You're doing better."

"Can't run yet, but getting around is easier."

He held up the bags. "Hope you don't mind burgers and fries. I'm a real food junkie when I'm under the gun to produce."

They ate while Scott went through the notes he'd taken as he'd traipsed around the property. Engineering experts would plan the actual infrastructure once the client approved the overall concept, but he'd already identified some potential streets and open areas they should consider.

She set her soft drink on the coffee table and chuckled. "Sounds like you were a lot more serious in your assessment of the site today than the first time you were there."

"Place is growing on me. Bull and all, who was nowhere to be seen today."

"Too bad," she joked. "You could've made friends with him."

He liked the way her blues sparkled when she laughed. If possible, the hue became even bluer. Without realizing he was going to do it, he strummed his fingers across her cheek. "Couldn't resist. You don't laugh enough," he said when he saw the look of surprise in her eyes.

"Chalk it up to the strain of this project. I'm usually pretty care-free," she replied.

"Carefree? Wouldn't have pegged you as such. Good to know."

"I'll be all smiles when this project is done and the client raves about it."

They finished their burgers, topped off with a bowl of strawberries from Lacey's fridge, and then set about reviewing and debating the draft document Lacey had prepared the rest of the evening. At first she took notes, but when more of the writing pad started going into confetti she would fling at him every time she disagreed with one of his suggestions, he took over.

At one point, he didn't speak or look at her for several minutes. Just kept working on the pad. "What are you doing over there? It couldn't possibly take so much time to write down what I said," she blurted out, apparently unable to hold her curiosity in check no longer.

He acted as if he hadn't heard her and went on doodling.

"Scott!"

He let his gaze reflect the same pleasure as someone who'd just scratched off a winning combination on a lottery ticket. "That was fun. The first real fun, other than hassling you, I've had on this project."

"Show me."

He covered the pad with his chest. "It's pretty rough. It may be difficult for you to picture what I have in mind."

"Scott Dalton, if you don't show me this minute—"

"You'll what." He let his expression grow mischievous.

"I'll … I'll call your parents and tell them you'd like to have break-fast with them."

"You wouldn't."

"Don't push me. I'll hint you need their help picking out a new car." She jutted out her chin to underline her threat.

"Lacey!"

She sat back and relaxed her chin. "Okay, forget it. Shouldn't jest about your parents. But it was too tempting."

At length, he swiveled the pad around so she could see what he'd been up to. "Remember the hill we climbed?"

She stuck out her injured ankle. "Like I'd forget?"

"I played with our themes of Purpose and Change. We could leave a parcel of land community-held and for a while, undeveloped. Over time, we'd see what would happen when our residents decide to give it a purpose."

"Uh-huh. I understand what you're getting at, but if we apply your philosophy to everything, the place will remain amorphous."

He snatched the pad away from her and surveyed his drawing again. "This was just an example. A quick shot at testing your theory. Tomorrow I'll inventory today's finds and get down to some concrete ideas. I'm burned out tonight."

She checked her watch. "I guess so. It's after ten."

"I should be going." He made it sound like a question. He took her hand, loving the skin so soft and smooth to the touch. Hard to believe those same fingers could hold a drafting pen and create masterpieces as well as stroke him like she had the night before. He leaned in and nuzzled her neck, taking in her wonderful scent once again. "Ummm! Can't get enough of that smell." He ran a hand through her golden curls. "I've missed you."

"We've been together all evening."

He let his voice grow husky. "You know what I mean."

"I wasn't sure. After last night? We'd no sooner, uh, finished in the car, and you were rushing me home."

"Thought I might've scared you, making it with you in the car and all."

"It was exciting, especially coupled with last week's tumble in the field. Got an encore in mind?"

What an invitation. One he couldn't pass up, especially since his dick was already coming to life just being this near her. Truth be told, this was the real reason he'd come to her place tonight. He couldn't get enough of her.

In one swift movement, he picked her up and laid her on the couch, settling in next to her. He crushed his lips to hers while his hands traveled all over her body, enjoying every hill and valley. He marveled how she could be so soft and pliable in some places and taut and firm in others. The woman was definitely fit, but also sexy and voluptuous despite her petite frame. Her willingness to share herself with him made her all the more desirable.

She kissed back with the same intensity as she had the night before, her hands wandering up and down his back. At length, she broke away briefly. "You can't begin to know what you're doing to me."

He breathed into her hair. "If it's anything like what I'm feeling, we're in for quite a night." He held her even tighter, fanning one hand slowly up and down her back, soaking in the warmth of her even as his own body nearly burst into flames. Lacey clung to him, the gentle undulation of her pelvis willing him to grow bolder, her hands pulling him directly on top of her. All he could think of was blanketing the incredible playground waiting to be consumed. But the couch wouldn't accommodate his frame.

"Too confining," she whispered. "Let's go to my bedroom."

Yet another invitation he didn't have to think twice about. In her bedroom, he placed her gently on the bed, flicking on the radio on her nightstand before joining her. The slow, sensuous strains of a rhumba surrounded them, suggesting he ignore the insistent bulge in his pants and take his time as well. God, he'd give it a try. Last night was for him. Tonight, he was hers. He plucked each of her fingertips, one by one, and softly kissed each, lingering before proceeding to the next. His eyes never left hers.

"I like this field better. Much more private," she murmured. "Just you and me."

"Not so urgent. More time to explore." He brought one of the hands he'd been kissing to his lips, letting his warm breath play across her knuckles.

Her moan, a low hum, tantalized whatever self-control still remained. The need to see her, all of her, fought with his resolve to apply the brakes to his need.

Didn't stop him, though, from unbuttoning her shirt, spreading it to cast his eyes on the treasure beneath. Good God, she was delectable, in a sheer black bra leaving little to the imagination when it came to mounded flesh and encased nubbins pleading to escape, his solemn duty was to set them free.

Before he could follow through, though, she reached for his shirt and pulled it from his pants. Mission accomplished. She began undoing his buttons. "Time to show your stuff, buddy."

God, she was assertive. Made her all the more desirable, urging him to keep pace. He obliged, removing all her clothes, and then his, within a minute.

"Oh, my!" she said, admiring. "I didn't mean for you to take me literally, but since you did, wow!"

"Wow back at you," he added as he cupped her breasts. Then the gentle kidding stopped. "You are absolutely perfect," he uttered, his voice huskier than the moment before. "I can't get enough of you."

SHE GASPED for breath as Scott's mouth found a nipple, gently tonguing it. His hand fondled the other breast briefly, then wandered downward, seeming to know exactly where to go, what to touch. His touch was gentle and strong at the same time. Every nerve ending in her body tingled. No, pulsated with unspent energy about to erupt. She writhed in anticipation, willing him to speed up.

But he took his time, sampling each breast at his leisure, his tongue making wider and wider circles. This man was practiced. All the office scuttlebutt about his sexual prowess had been true. His tongue, fingers and breath alone had her perched on the tip of her own personal volcano.

She nearly came when he began to suck. The man's mouth assumed a life of its own, claiming her, leaving her awash with his mark. She arched her back, pushed her chest forward, begging for more sweet agony. The night before had been frantic, animal-like in its urgency. This was … could she even frame a thought to describe it? This was … absolute pleasure realized. Enjoyment beyond belief.

But he didn't stop there. Nor did she want him to. He straddled her hips, his magnificent torso towering above her, his engorged penis ready to take them both even higher in the gratification of their needs.

Her hands scrubbed his thighs, feeling the power of the taut muscles and prickly growth of hair as they moved upward until his own hands grasped hers and imprisoned them over her head. The maneuver brought his body over hers, his mouth free to roam and play.

Every inch of her burned and ached from his touch by the time he entered her. Every movement intensified the craving for more. She grabbed fistfuls of the bedding, grasping to hold on, to ride the wave, to experience every heart-pounding moment.

When they'd both climaxed, he continued to hold her close, whispering gentle nothings in her ear, running his hand through her hair.

She opened her eyes once to find he, too, had closed his as well. A contented smile had seized his face, and he hummed softly.

Explosions of emotion tore at her insides. She felt spent and adored and … and … loved? No, she didn't dare go there. She fell asleep in his arms shortly thereafter still wondering. Hoping.

CHAPTER 18

s Lacey tentatively opened one eye the next morning, a freshly-showered and clothed Scott greeted her. "Good morning, beautiful. I helped myself to a shower. Hope you don't mind." He rubbed his jaw. "Gotta dash back to my place for a shave and clean clothes. Want me to make coffee first?"

She blinked several times before her eyes stayed open. "How can you be so chipper? We were up half the night." Even in her semi-stupor, she couldn't help note how sexy he looked, his face covered with dark stubble, his hair still wet with tiny water droplets.

He leered at her. "Up, down, in, out. Didn't know I had it in me, so to speak."

"What time is it?" Had she been drinking? She felt totally disoriented. Or something.

"Six forty-five. Wednesday. Hump day." He pronounced those last two words with familiarity. "Was I that good? Made you forget what day it is?'

"You're good, Scott. But not that good." She felt more lethargy than even the sex of the previous night should have produced and she wasn't sure why. She wasn't sick. She was exhausted without a single bone or muscle in her body aching, except for a hollow feeling around her chest. Then she remembered. "Today would've been my mother's fifty-fifth birthday."

His eyes went to hers, as if checking her mood, wondering what to say.

"Brian still insists on taking flowers to her grave every year on this day so we don't forget her. With my ankle, I begged off this time, so he went alone Saturday. But—"

"Now you're having second thoughts?"

"It's not like I have to do this to honor her memory." Which was true, although she'd told Brian she'd go today. Now, for another reason entirely, one she didn't want to share with Scott, she reaffirmed her decision.

"I can work on my own for a bit, if you want to go. Unless you want company?"

"Thanks, but I'll be fine. I should be able to drive now. I won't be there long."

A little more than an hour later, she stood before her mother's grave. The display of pink roses Brian placed there the weekend before, now turning brown, still rested against the headstone. Should have thought to bring a fresh bouquet.

"Happy Birthday, Mom. I used you as an excuse to get away from someone. Hope you don't mind, because I really do need your advice, however you can send it to me."

She bent and flicked away a few stray leaves from the grave. Must've landed since Saturday. Brian would never have left them behind. "There's a new man in my life. The sex has been great. I've never felt so desirable. Sorry, don't mean to shock you, just wanted you to know how it started out. I've never lacked for men. Just didn't keep them around long. This one doesn't seem to mind my no-commitments philosophy, although I'm starting to question it myself."

That's what had been nagging her when she awoke this morning after spending the whole night in bed with Scott. Until she actually spoke the words out loud just now, it had simply been an amorphous uneasiness cheating her of fully enjoying their time together. Now she could put a name to it. Something was happening between them. The idea floored her. Scared her. This wasn't supposed to happen. It couldn't happen. Not without getting her heart broken again.

"I don't know what to do, Mom. My better judgment tells me to end this now, before things get complicated." A gentle breeze caressed her hair. "Oh, Hell—sorry, Mom—it already is complicated."

"Lacey?" a male voice called from several feet away.

She caught sight of Scott making his way toward her, gingerly side-stepping graves along the way. "Wasn't sure where to find you," he said, pulling up to her. "I asked Celia for directions."

Had he heard her talking? She desperately hoped he hadn't. It was enough dealing with these feelings by herself. She didn't need Scott questioning her as well.

"What are you doing here? Did something come up at the office?"

"The office? Uh, no. I just didn't like the way we left things earlier. You looked worried. Thought you might like some company. But if I'm intruding?"

"You didn't have to come, but I, uh, appreciate the gesture." Was his arrival a sign from her mother? Her mother's way of telling her to share her concerns with Scott.

He read from the headstone, "Rachel Elizabeth Rogers. Your mother?"

"Yes. I was fourteen when she passed away. Pancreatic cancer. Her illness made her terribly weak, and in the last few months, filled her with pain. Brian was twenty, a sophomore in college. He transferred to Iowa State to be closer to Mom and me, and once Mom was no longer with us, became my surrogate parent."

Scott blew out a breath of air. "No wonder he seems so—"

"Protective? Stiff? He was already on the path to being, shall we say, conservative, but taking on parental duties, especially with a rebellious teenager, probably pushed him over the line."

"Rebellious?"

"Fourteen-year-olds notoriously question anything their parents say. I was no different, except how was I supposed to challenge someone who could barely sit up? I took out my frustrations on Brian. He got me through some pretty grim times."

Good start to what she wanted to tell him. The rest wouldn't be as easy. She focused on a nearby monument, not daring to face him directly. "Clinically, my mom died from the cancer, but I really suspect it was a broken heart that made her susceptible to the disease, because my father deserted us when I was six. I blamed myself. Thought I'd done something bad to make him go."

"You never saw him again?"

"Not in person. But a few years ago we learned of his death. Apparently he'd left us after he'd been exposed to radiation poisoning, deciding it would be better for all three of us if we thought he'd deserted us rather than watched him deteriorate with the disease. He'd changed his name and gone to stay with some monks the rest of his life, which ironically, lasted longer than my mother's."

Scott placed a hand on her arm. "I'm sorry, Lacey. I had no idea you'd gone through so much tragedy."

"His grave is on the other side of Mom's. We figured she would have wanted him there, even though we didn't."

He glanced briefly at her father's grave. "Sounds like your mom never gave up on him. You did the right thing, placing him there."

And therein lay the rub. "Let's walk. There's something more I need to tell you."

He returned a quizzical expression but stuck his hand under her elbow and helped her negotiate the path.

She dove in immediately, before she lost her nerve. "I don't trust my feelings where you're concerned, Scott. I'm all for having a good time, but my instincts are telling me whatever this is between us could go deeper. At least for me, which would not be a good idea"

He held up a hand. "Whoa! That was a mouthful. Let me catch up. You're okay with the physical part?"

She couldn't hold back a smile. "Sex. Yes, the sex has been great."

"But you think more is happening?"

"Starting to. For me, anyhow."

"And that would be bad because—?"

One way or another, she had to put it out there, though she knew things would change. She stopped before a stone bench overlooking a small hillside. They both sat. "Look what happened to my mother. She gave her heart to a seemingly loving man. And he left her, no notice, no reason, no contact the rest of her life."

"You said there was a good reason for his leaving you all behind."

"Maybe. But we didn't know about it until after his death. My mother never knew, yet she believed in him anyhow, forgave him. Once I stopped blaming myself for his desertion, I shifted my disdain to my father for doing this to our family, especially my mother. My father gave me my first and most convincing life lesson about the hazards of trusting men."

"But you grew out of that stage, right?"

"Yes. By the time I got to college. Talk about 'out of the frying pan, into the fire.'" She snorted at her own foolishness.

"Brian took my guardianship seriously, which made me crazy. Even though he was probably the only man I could put my faith in, I tested him at every turn, which included getting engaged when I was a sophomore because I wanted my independence. A month before my wedding, my fiancé dumped me for another woman. His rejection shredded my self-esteem. I even dropped out of school for a while." She stopped. Gathered her thoughts. Retelling the story required so much energy.

Scott waited for her to continue.

"Actually, my fiancé's betrayal was the best thing that could have happened, because he was a self-involved jerk who would've made my life miserable. But I didn't see his true colors then. All I knew was pain and heartache."

His hand slipped over hers, squeezed it.

"I don't ever want to experience such despair again, so I haven't allowed things to get serious with anyone since."

He didn't reply for a bit.

Well, of course not. She'd totally thrown him by getting so serious. *Was this really what you intended me to do, Mom?* "I'm sorry, Scott. You didn't expect me to lay all this on you after you'd been so kind to join me here."

"No, I suppose I didn't. But I'm glad you felt you could tell me."

"The last two nights with you have been incredible. No man has ever made me feel so much a woman and alive." Her head bowed slightly. "But each time, I had this feeling something was missing. That's why I came to my mother's grave today. To ask her to help me figure it out."

He didn't laugh or scoff at her admission. "What did she tell you?"

She took his hand and gazed at him. "You showed up, didn't you?"

"You think she came to me in a dream or whispered in my ear to find you?"

"No. Of course, not. But I do believe she's telling me you're the kind of person who cares enough about others to check on them when you think something may be wrong."

"Probably more credit than I deserve, but thanks." He moved his gaze away from her, apparently processing her words.

"I'm moving into new territory with you, Scott. I need to be able to trust you. Not just as my work partner. As my partner in bed. I'm not planning on your staying in my life forever, but don't just up and leave. I don't think I could get through that again."

THE AIR around Scott seemed to have rarified. Other women had attempted to take him on a different trek, toward permanency, and he'd resisted, fought them off. Those affairs made him feel like he was stuck in quicksand, sinking into oblivion until he made a hasty escape. This woman was giving him license to enjoy their time together, no strings attached.

The incredible thing? He was almost offended. Though he hadn't been so foolish as to buy a ring, the possibility of someday considering the purchase had crossed his mind once or twice since he'd worked with Lacey, especially when his parents hinted, declared it was time for him to settle down.

He trailed his fingers across her cheek. "It's not enough for me to swear you can trust me. You have to feel and know it for yourself."

She gave him a half-smile. "I'm getting there. I trusted you enough to tell you about my father and my fiancé. How about you? Do you trust me?"

His brain's early warning system kicked into gear. This sharing stuff could rear its head and bite a guy in the butt. "I've already given you the lowdown on my parents."

"True," she agreed, though the hesitation in her tone suggested she'd like to hear more.

"And told you about my principalship frustrations."

"Yes, although anyone in the know at Mackenzie and Associates is also privy to such information."

Good point. Since she'd shared her concern about being abandoned by the two most important men in her life, maybe he should reveal a little of his soft side. Just a little. "I had a brief fling with another architect at the firm. She played me for a fool. Stayed overnight at my place a few times. Must've gone through my things during one of her visits. Some of my best ideas wound up in plans she claimed as her own. Got her on the fast track at Mackenzie, followed up by an offer with a prestigious San Francisco firm."

She stared at him as if seeing him for the first time. "You didn't want to work with me because you feared history would repeat itself?"

Trust Lacey to cut to the chase. "Yeah. But I was also insulted to have been stuck with a partner again."

"Stuck?" Her voice rose, causing a nearby squirrel to scamper off.

"You have to admit, our being teamed up didn't get off to the best start. You refused to back off and go find Cam when I slid under that tree."

"There wasn't time."

"When you insisted on *rescuing* me yourself, you wound up in the same place for all your efforts."

She shrugged. "I'm not much of a super hero."

He grabbed her by her upper arms. "Do you know what hell you put me through? Mud and rotting leaves all around me and all I could breathe in was your scent, lilacs. All I could feel was your body pressed up against mine. All I wanted to do was draw you even closer."

His lips were within an inch of hers, ready to kiss her right there in the cemetery. She pulled back at the last second. "My body went on alert also." She placed a hand on his chest. "Tell me more about the other architect."

"I told you everything pertinent. Except her name. Jorja. You don't know her. She'd come and gone before you joined the firm."

She shook her head. "I've not seen your home. Apartment, condo, house? I have no idea. But—Jorja, you said?—apparently had the run of the place. Was it serious?"

"Serious? Hell, no! It was casual, occasional, whenever one or the other of us got horny. I've, uh, never had a serious relationship. Wouldn't know one if it bit me in the rear."

"We're quite the pair."

He took her hands in his. "We are, aren't we?"

"Sounds like as long as you don't walk away without notice and I don't steal your ideas, we're okay," she said.

"Want to shake on it?"

She fluttered her eyes like a Southern belle. "Another way occurs to me."

The visit to the cemetery came to an abrupt end. Needless to say, although it was Wednesday, cards night, Brian had to find his own group of players. Celia, obviously, would no longer play. And Lacey and Scott found another form of recreation.

CHAPTER 19

"Lacey Rogers, Scott Dalton, I'd like you to meet our client, Jake Bonneville," Cam said as Lacey and Scott entered the inner sanctum also known as the executive conference room. Almost a week had passed since Lacey and Scott talked in the cemetery. A week packed with days finalizing the design concept and selling it to Cam and nights filled with heated passion. Now it was show time.

Scott forced the million-dollar smile he'd gone in with to stay in place as his brain fought to make sense of the scene before them. Jake Bonneville? The mega-entertainer? Why would he be interested in a retirement community? He was barely in his thirties.

The superstar rose from the chair at the far end of the conference table and offered his hand, first to Lacey, then to Scott. "Ms. Rogers. Mr. Dalton. I'm pleased to meet you."

Scott forced himself to relax. He'd been under the impression their client had yet to arrive. Now he had to launch immediately into presentation mode. He studied their client/guest. The guy was a little shorter than him but not much. His light brown hair was close-cropped on the sides, the top a little longer, jagged cut, the kind of refined scruffy look guys paid at least two-hundred dollars to achieve.

Bonneville offered a confident, friendly enough handshake, but there was something in his expression that gave Scott pause. The guy's eyes didn't quite meet Scott's when their hands came in contact. "The pleasure is all ours, Mr. Bonneville," Scott said. "Caught your act in Vegas last year. Never would've guessed that same big-time entertainer was our client."

Bonneville gazed at Scott, his mouth a straight line. "Entertainers make investments, too, Mr. Dalton. Especially in their home towns."

"That's right. You've been away so long, I'd forgotten you grew up here," Lacey cut in, attempting to smooth over Scott's sudden stiffness. "Please, call us Lacey and Scott."

"Lacey, Scott." Bonneville didn't return the offer.

Introductions made, Cam suggested they be seated at the large mahogany conference table where the portfolios they'd assembled for their boss and client awaited.

Bonneville followed but remained standing.

"I've been telling Jake here even though you're two of my most creative people, I'm still marveling at how you've put something so spectacular together in record time."

"Yes, well—" Bonneville said.

"Why don't we let them get right to it?" Cam interrupted, apparently not wanting to give the man any chance to delay. "Scott, Lacey, enlighten Mr. Bonneville about baby boomers, change, and—"

"Their presentation won't be necessary," Bonneville cut in. "I've been trying to tell you, Mackenzie, my plans have changed. I'm no longer interested in developing the property we discussed."

The sound level in the room dipped to nothing as Lacey, Scott and Cam absorbed the shock.

"I beg your pardon?" Cam finally said, dropping his portfolio. "Surely I didn't hear you correctly? You're still interested in building a retirement community for baby boomers, aren't you?"

Bonneville removed the hand he'd been resting on one of the spread portfolios, as if to demonstrate his decision to disassociate himself with the project. "Yes. Yes, I do still want to build. But not like we discussed. Not outside town. Nor as a collection of individual home sites."

"But, but—" Though obviously at a loss, Cam attempted to counter Bonneville's announcement.

Scott knew his boss well enough to anticipate a major eruption once the surprise wore off. Cam had been had. People didn't undercut their boss.

Eyes narrowed, jaw taut, Cam marshaled his dignity. "Why didn't you tell me you changed your mind before my staff committed so much time to this project?"

Bonneville sat a little higher. "I fully intended to go through with the plans I discussed with you until I ran into an accountant friend of mine several days ago. Though I kept our plans in confidence, I shared the general idea with him. He convinced me it would be a waste of money. I'd get more return on my investment if it were in a high-rise here in town."

"A high-rise?" Scott bolted from his chair. "Have you checked out that theory, Bonneville? It may be more cost-effective, but research shows the people who live in such structures really don't feel a sense of community. Especially baby boomers." Had he really said that? Jean's research and Lacey's theories had fully permeated his brain.

"I'm well acquainted with baby boomers, Dalton. At least my mother, and she's the only one I care about. That's why I'm pursuing this development. To get her out of the rundown neighborhood she lives in and keep her safe while I'm on the road."

"But—" Lacey attempted to add.

Bonneville turned to Lacey and Scott. "I'm sorry I wasted your time." He shot a gaze at Cam. "Of course I'll pay you for your firm's efforts to date. Sorry this didn't work out, Mackenzie. No hard feelings."

He headed for the door. "Dalton. Ms. Rogers," he said as he passed Lacey and Scott. Raising his eyebrows, he turned back to Lacey. "Rogers? You wouldn't be related to Brian Rogers, would you?"

"He's my brother," Lacey said flatly. "Why do you ask?"

Bonneville paused. "I suppose there's no harm telling you now.

Brian Rogers is the accountant who advised me to switch to the high-rise."

He exited the room, leaving three mouths gaping behind him.

CAM WAS the first to speak, his initial bewilderment replaced with denial. "He can't do this to me!" He started for the door. He turned back to them, grim-faced. "I'm going after him. See if I can't talk him out of this absurd idea. You two stay here. If I can't save this deal, we've got to figure out our next steps."

"Next steps?" Scott spit out the words as soon as the door closed behind their boss. "Aside from finding a new client, nothing's going to salvage this project. Geez, Jake Bonneville is an—"

"Perhaps," Lacey interrupted, sparing Scott from saying the word. She'd gone to the sideboard to find a glass of water, hoping a few sips would help her process what just happened. "It sounds like the real culprit might have been my own brother. But that can't be. Bonneville had to be wrong about the accountant's name. Brian would never interfere in my business."

Scott's eyes sought hers. "You really think so?"

She swallowed more of the liquid before answering. "Brian hasn't said anything about this, especially knowing this big-time entertainer. But then, I haven't seen much of him lately, since we've gone underground to finish the concept piece."

Scott moved to her and placed a hand on her arm. "Bonneville must've been mistaken. Brian's not exactly my favorite person, but I can't believe he'd deliberately set out to sabotage us. At least you. He's a pretty honorable guy. He definitely wouldn't hurt his own sister. Why don't you sit down? You look like you've been hit by a truck."

They returned to the conference table and settled in to wait for Cam. Neither said much for the next several minutes. "What are you thinking?" Scott asked eventually.

Lacey had been flipping idly through her copy of the proposal but set it back on the table to answer. "Nothing coherent. I can't get my mind around this setback."

"I know what you mean. The only lucid thought I've had has been to realize I've just made the acquaintance of a mega-entertainer in a business suit."

She couldn't resist a slight smile. "Always the Beau Brummel, aren't you?"

"Made you smile."

Bless his heart. The world was collapsing around them, and he was trying to keep her laughing.

If Cam couldn't convince Jake Bonneville to change his mind, or find a new taker for the project, this really was the end of Project Arabella. She analyzed the situation philosophically. She'd put so much of herself into it, into her research on boomers. She'd probably get past the disappointment after a bout of soul searching, several times around the walking track and a pint of maple nut ice cream. Then she'd wait for the next project to come along with which to make her name. But she doubted she could say the same for Scott. "Wish I could return the favor," she told him. "Make you smile. I know this project meant a lot to your career."

He curled his lips in a rueful version of a smile. "If this is a wash, something else will turn up, though I may be waiting longer than ever for the word *principal* to follow my name."

"Surely Cam won't hold Bonneville's defection against you?" How could what appeared to be such a bright future for both of them just minutes ago have turned so totally against them? If Brian had anything to do with this, her relationship with him was in for hard times, only surviving relative or not.

He squeezed her hands. "Too late to be concerned now. We have to focus on recouping our losses."

Lacey glanced at the door. "Do you think Cam will be able to change Bonneville's mind?"

"Maybe, but don't count on it. Bonneville was pretty clear the deal was off. Cam's gonna be hot if he can't turn this around, so let me do the talking. He'll say things he won't remember when he cools off. Don't take anything personally."

She started to protest, to tell him she could defend herself, when Cam burst into the room. "Pack up your books, boys and girls. Bonneville's a no-go." He went to the sideboard, rummaged through the cabinet underneath. "Where's the whiskey? There's nothing here but gourmet coffee." He pitched a vacuum-packed bag into a nearby wastebasket.

"He wouldn't reconsider?" Scott asked.

"Show people! You'd think all they'd care about are their audiences or going platinum with their latest CD. Who'd have thought they paid much attention to business. The guy even knew what return on investment meant!"

"Did you make a pitch for our doing the high-rise?" Scott asked.

Cam snorted. "Think I'd miss the chance to pick up some of the pieces? He said we could bid on it, but he was starting over and it would be months before he'd be ready to proceed."

Scott's shoulders caved inward as the futility of the situation sank in. "Sorry, Cam. I know how much you were counting on this project. We all were."

Cam hung his head and rubbed his neck. "Go home, you two. There's nothing more you can do here." His voice had gone quiet, full of disappointment and regret.

Lacey had never seen her boss like this. He seemed so defeated and lost. She wanted to reach out to him. "Wouldn't you rather we stay here with you, Cam?"

"You! How dare you try to comfort me when it was your own brother who cut us off at the knees?"

"We don't know that for sure." She could barely get the words out through her cotton mouth, but until she talked to Brian, she wasn't ready to condemn him.

"Really? Bonneville said the guy he talked to was Brian Rogers. Your brother's name is Brian Rogers. The guy was a local accountant. Your brother's a bean counter here in town, yes?"

"Well, yes." She couldn't deny those points, but they didn't necessarily add up to her Brian.

"Bonneville described him as the epitome of buttoned-down conservatism, even though the guy was in his early thirties."

She sucked in her breath. "Okay. That does sound like my brother. But I can't believe he'd deliberately undermine our business. There must be another side to this."

"Then you find it, because I'm fresh out of angles." Cam collapsed in one of the conference chairs and jerked his necktie loose.

Scott motioned for her to accompany him out of the room. In the hallway, his face screwed up in a frown. "I thought you were going to let me do the talking?"

"I had to defend my brother. Do you think Cam will fire me if it turns out my Brian was Bonneville's Brian?" The thought hadn't occurred to her until then, because she'd been so caught up in the drama.

"Probably not. But I'd keep a low profile for a few days, if I were you."

Not what she wanted to hear. She'd hoped he'd reassure her, tell her no, her job was safe.

She had to get to the bottom of this business. If she was to keep her distance from Cameron Mackenzie, she might as well use her time tracking down the facts. "I'm taking off for a few hours. I've got to talk to my brother and get his side of the story."

Brian barely made it inside the door of her apartment before Lacey confronted him. "Since when have you become an architectural consultant?"

He dropped his briefcase on a side chair, then settled on the living room couch. "Got any tea?"

"No."

"No? You always have hot water going when you're home."

"I do. I'm just not offering any. Now answer my question."

"What question?" His expression remained bland.

Lacey glared back at him.

"You mean your offhand comment about architectural consulting?"

He shrugged. "I have no idea what you're talking about. I leave building design to you."

Lacey continued to stand. She took several deep breaths, attempting to slow her rapid pulse before proceeding with her interrogation. "Scott and I presented our design concept to the client this morning. You know, the hush-hush one we've been working on night and day?"

Brian nodded but remained quiet.

She planted herself in front of him. "Imagine our surprise when we learned our client had changed his mind. He no longer wants to proceed with the project because he's been advised he could do it much cheaper as a high-rise."

He blinked. He did know something!

"Said he received this advice from an accountant friend he'd run into recently. None other than one Brian Rogers."

Brian was off the couch in a flash, nearly knocking her over, a look of guilt clearly reflected in his eyes. "That was your project?"

She tapped her foot. "I'm waiting."

He scrunched his forehead, apparently connecting the dots. "Your mysterious client turned out to be Jake Bonneville, the singer?"

She didn't say anything.

"I ran into him in a bar a week or so ago."

Her stomach clenched as the truth of the situation became crystal clear. How was she going to explain this to Scott and Cam? She felt like she'd personally let them down.

"I was at loose ends, so I didn't go right home. I found myself downtown at this bar and grille, and who should sit next to me but Bonneville."

"This superstar entertainer shows up in town and seeks out your company?"

Brian shook his head. "No, of course not. I don't know why he was there. Never said. He was in my class at Roosevelt, although we didn't run in the same circles. He had a band, I was in math club, but he actually recognized me from back then. He didn't strike it big time until you were away at college or in Europe."

"So he said, 'Why, hello, Brian Rogers. What's your opinion of my building a retirement community outside town?'"

"Not immediately. He asked what I was doing these days, so I told him. Then I asked what brought him to town. He hedged at first, instead started asking me about real estate investments around town. I shared some of my views. Eventually, he got around to residential developments. "Told me he was considering putting one up outside of town."

"Uh-huh." So far, his recollection seemed innocent enough though still difficult to take in.

"He described his plans in broad terms. Asked if I thought they sounded like a wise investment. How was I supposed to know it was your project? He never mentioned your firm."

She could think of a dozen red flags he should have seen, but she remained silent.

"So I gave him my opinion."

"Which was?"

"I was flattered to be asked. I probably laid it on a bit thick."

She knew all about Brian's tendency to expound when it came to finance. "A *bit* thick?"

"I suppose I spoke with more expertise than I actually possessed. You know how I feel about urban sprawl, especially digging up the countryside, wasting good farmland. I couldn't resist the opportunity to make a pitch for responsible urban development. Building up rather than out."

She was well aware of his opinions about responsible expansion. They'd argued more than once about her role gentrifying previously undeveloped properties. She'd countered by spelling out how many green features she incorporated into her single-family designs.

"He said he agreed with me. Something about the land he planned to develop having been in the family for years and a promise he made to his grandfather to be a wise steward. He questioned whether developing the property would be in keeping with his commitment."

She'd heard enough. One bar conversation and more than a little exposition from Brian and their project and futures went down the tube. "How could you?" she charged, grabbing his forearm. "You're not an expert in those areas. That was pure proselytizing."

He pursed his lips. "I had no idea he'd take me seriously. We had dinner together. Well, shared a couple burgers at the bar. For as much as I knew, he was simply passing time before he could get back to the Coast and all his high-priced consultants."

"Your *passing time* with him caused Mackenzie and Associates to lose the account! Probably our biggest project ever."

He swiped at a few stray beads of perspiration dotting his forehead. "Gosh, Lace. I'm sorry. I never realized."

Though he sounded contrite, his apology wasn't enough. The disappointment was still too new and too raw. "My boss and Scott know you're the one responsible, which makes me look bad." She held back from sharing her fear of losing her job.

"Look, sis—"

"How could you do this to me, Brian? I've spent several weeks trying to help you get your life back in order, and now you've turned mine upside down."

He cocked his head, squinted. "Helping me? Get my life back in order?"

Damn! She hadn't meant to get into the business with Celia, but now she had no choice. "I couldn't bear to see you so miserable without Celia, so I fixed things so you could get her back."

He retreated a step, his expression incredulous. "You what?"

"I thought you'd come running back to her if you saw her with someone else."

At first, Brian simply stared, like he didn't comprehend what she'd said. Then a pinkish tinge inched its way up his neck to his ears. She'd witnessed a similar reaction several times in her rebellious teen years but had rarely seen it since. "You played matchmaker with her and Dalton?"

Her heart caught in her chest. Although her plan hadn't worked, she never meant for him to find out.

Her brother drew himself up to his full six-foot stature. "Since when did you become an authority on love? You've chased away every guy who ever showed the slightest interest!"

Ouch! Though he was correct, their situations were completely different. She wasn't about to capitulate, because she'd acted in his best interest. "You were so tight-lipped about why you broke things off with her, I thought all it would take to get you back together was for you to see her with someone else and realize what you'd done."

His eyes flashed. "Does Celia know about this?"

"I, uh, worked it all out with Scott, but Celia agreed."

"Dalton's in on this?"

"Uh, yes. They sort of broke things off after the Euchre night at your apartment."

"Why didn't she say anything when I ran into her at the cemetery?"

This was getting complicated. "Obviously, she didn't want you to know. Guess she was embarrassed."

"How could you accuse me of sabotaging your life when you've been so busy making me look like a fool?" Brian nudged past her, retrieved his briefcase and made for the door. "I've looked out for you ever since our dad disappeared. This is how you repay me?"

Before she could answer, she was staring at the door as the harsh sound of it being slammed penetrated her ears.

He'd turned the tables on her. For Pete's sake, she was the injured party.

Lacey debated whether to go after him. She couldn't bear to be at odds with Brian for long. He was her only living relative and the person she trusted most, despite her developing relationship with Scott. Brian's part in all this was unintentional, although he certainly hadn't helped. But before she went after him, she needed to bring Scott up to speed.

Scott spent the rest of the day holed up in his office, unsuccessfully attempting not to dwell on the demise of Project Arabella. He idly considered how they could convert some of their ideas to a high-rise environment and heaved a big sigh as he cast a look at the pile of rejects. The old Scott, the guy who could charm almost any client with his wit and ability to convince them they liked his designs, seemed to have disappeared. This new Scott, one half of the team of Dalton and Rogers, was having trouble putting two and two together.

He didn't blame Lacey for her brother's indiscretion. The guy was a self-important know-it-all.

Even Lacey had conceded as much. But it sure did beat all, his being the one who undercut their project. Had Lacey inadvertently revealed too many details to the guy? Nah, she'd been just as surprised by Bonneville's mention of her brother as the rest of them. At least, she appeared to be. What could she possibly gain from their losing the project? It wasn't like she planned to go after the high-rise on her own.

The sounds of a commotion coming from the hall punctured his self-recrimination. Jean's raised voice called out to someone. Within an instant, he got the rest of the picture as Brian Rogers burst through the door.

His unexpected visitor was not smiling. "You and I have some issues to settle, Dalton."

"I'm so sorry, Mr. Dalton. I couldn't stop him," Jean said from behind the intruder.

"That's okay, Jean. I have a few things to say to Mr. Rogers as well."

Once Jean hesitantly retreated from her post, Scott motioned to one of his visitor chairs. Brian continued to stand, so Scott rose as well.

"Celia Fairchild is very dear to me. I don't care to see other men take advantage of her vulnerability."

"What?" Scott had anticipated hearing something about the Bonneville fiasco, since he was sure Lacey had by now found her brother and raked him over the coals. The subject of his dating Celia came as a surprise.

"I didn't like it when you started seeing her. Your reputation as a ladies' man reached beyond your firm. But she seemed to see something in you, so I kept my peace."

What a self-righteous prick. "Like you did at Mackenzie's birthday party?" Scott couldn't help inserting.

Rogers sniffed. "I'm still very fond of her. Now I hear you were only dating her to make me jealous."

Foiled. How'd he find out? "Look, I don't know what Celia told you, but ..."

"My sister told me."

"Lacey?" He'd made Celia promise not to tell Lacey.

Rogers straightened. Pulled at his collar. "While my sister was busy chewing me out for advising your client to drop your project, which I knew nothing about, she let it slip how she'd arranged with you to make it look like you and Celia were an item. Talk about the pot calling the kettle black."

What a cliché, but then, the guy was the cliché type. "You rejected a really special woman, who for reasons I still don't understand wanted you back, so I agreed to be her fake boyfriend. But you've got things wrong. It wasn't Lacey who arranged this. It was Celia."

"Celia? No, Lacey told me she talked you into it."

Why would Lacey tell him such a thing? To protect Celia? "Maybe you should check with Celia."

Lacey's brother stomped toward the door. "We'll just see who told who what."

After Rogers departed, Scott realized they never once discussed the guy's role in their losing Project Arabella. Damn!

Then he recalled the part about Lacey setting him up with Celia. Could it be true? If it was, no wonder Celia agreed not to tell Lacey. She already knew.

Had it really been Lacey who pulled the strings behind his so-called courtship of Celia? Made more sense than sweet, straightforward Celia orchestrating things. Why hadn't he seen it before? Because he'd just started working with Lacey when Celia approached him and wasn't yet aware of his partner's facile brain. She definitely was capable of putting such a plan together.

Even though he'd asked Celia not to tell Lacey, why hadn't Lacey confided her part in the scheme once they got closer? It didn't make sense. She'd made such a big deal about them sharing, being able to trust each other. If she hadn't told him about something as innocuous as her role in his fake courtship, what else hadn't she told him?

His copy of the portfolio lay on the desk, abandoned, forgotten. It couldn't be more than three-quarters of an inch thick, and yet within it, he thought he'd seen his future. No longer. Its only future now was the wastebasket.

He studied the other name on the cover sheet. Then it came to him. "The project!" She made no secret about wanting to jump-start her career. With Janice's help, she'd put together a great concept. But he'd been the one to deliver on the design segments, his forte, which she'd readily admitted. Had she invited him into her bed just to assure the success of the project? Used him, just like Jorja had years before?

She was beautiful with a fabulous body. An inspired lover. Helped him deal with his parents when they invaded his space. He'd liked her enthusiasm and dedication from the start, but he'd also come to like her as a friend.

Doubt fought with his growing belief in his partner. Had she duped him? He'd learned of Jorja's betrayal too late to confront her. But Lacey was still around. Only one way to find out. He moved over to where the portfolio landed, retrieved it, smoothed the cover and set it gently back on his desk. Then he exploded from the room.

"Scott! I was just about to come see you," Lacey said.

He couldn't bring himself to sit once he'd entered her apartment. He concentrated on framing the right question. Ah hell! Just spit it out. "Are you the brains behind my squiring Celia around town?"

"I … why do you ask?"

"Not that it matters, but I heard it from your brother. He just left my office after telling me what a low-life I was. Seems you told him my pretending to be the new man in Celia's life was your idea."

"Brian came to see you?"

He nodded. "I'm surprised my head is still attached to my body because he sure wanted to chop it off. Didn't even touch on how we'd lost Bonneville as a client thanks to him."

Her eyes took in everything in the room except him. "I'm sorry he came to see you."

"Sorry because it wasn't the most pleasant experience or sorry because he gave you away?"

"Sorry because I let my own personal fears interfere in others' lives, including yours."

Unexpected response. "Huh?"

"I haven't had a traditional two-parent family since I was six, like I told you, so having my own family has become a driving force in my life. The irony is, thanks to my father's desertion and my fiancé jilting me, I don't trust any man to stay with me long enough to make my dream happen. Brian's the only man capable of that kind of loyalty, so I was counting on him to give me my family through my nieces and nephews."

Her words slammed into his chest. All the pieces, all the clues had been there just waiting to merge into the simple truth she'd just revealed.

She continued. "When Brian broke things off with Celia after almost two years, I panicked. If he couldn't make himself commit to someone as perfect for him as Cee, he was never going to find someone. Which meant I was never going to get my family. Since Celia was as devastated as I was, well, you know the rest."

"Well, yeah, but why me? When he let me have it earlier, your brother pointed out how he'd worried from the start I'd hurt her because we traveled in such different circles. Why not someone who would've been a more believable suitor?"

She wandered across the room and picked up her stuffed bull. "Because you were too great a temptation for me." She raised her eyes and gazed directly at him.

"Temptation? We hardly knew each other when I agreed to Celia's scheme."

"When we were trapped under that tree trunk, I knew instinctively you were going to be trouble."

Trouble? He'd caused havoc in a lot of lives over the years, but what had he done to Lacey? "I didn't cause that accident. You're the one who insisted on rescuing me, to your own detriment."

"Emotional trouble. Something happened when I was stuck there so close to you. And I'm not talking about the hard-on you stuck in my back," she stopped to smile, "although it was the first warning sign."

Was she going where he thought she was with this? When they talked about trust in the cemetery, she'd mentioned sensing something was happening between them. She hadn't explained what she meant, nor had she brought it up again since, as they'd simply enjoyed being with each other. Did he really want her to go on? If she said too much, he'd have to disappoint her, because he wasn't ready for something more. Was he?

"I hoped your squiring Celia around town would act as a buffer between us, keep me from doing something I knew would not be good for my emotional stability. And if you thought I believed the story about you and Celia, it would prevent you from crossing the line with me, which is why I didn't want you to know my role in Celia's plan."

It all made a crazy kind of sense. Sort of. "Why didn't you tell me once we, uh, got together anyhow?"

"Why didn't you tell me?" she countered.

"I asked first."

She handed him the bull. "I guess once you and Celia *broke up* and you and I made love, it no longer mattered."

Made love? He'd never heard her use that expression to describe the sex they shared. Significant? Should he be concerned? Then he knew. She was being completely open and honest. No matter where things went from here, she trusted him, a huge step for her. He also realized he trusted her. Cared for her. More than he'd been willing to admit to himself until now.

"But your explanation does matter now, because it explains so much."

She lowered her eyes. "I guess it does. Funny. We've just lost the biggest opportunity either of us may ever have to send our careers soaring and rather than gear up to go after the consolation prize

Bonneville held out to us, we're talking about withholding information which is no longer important."

He took her hands, gazed into her beautiful blues. "The information we withheld from each other may no longer matter, but why we both held back does. Truth be told, I didn't want to be tempted by you any more than you tried to avoid me."

She blinked, apparently surprised by his admission. "We're okay? You were pretty angry when you arrived."

"I thought you'd duped me. Although this thing with Celia was no big deal, I worried it meant you could withhold other information. Worse yet, be working against me."

"Like Jorja."

"Yeah. I was wrong. This trust thing we've been striving for wasn't quite there yet, until you explained why you'd gotten so involved in your brother's life."

"And now?" Her tone held a tentative note.

"As you pointed out, we both held back. From here on, trust is no longer an issue. It's just there."

She slipped her hands around his neck and pulled him toward her. He happily obliged, picking her up and heading toward her bedroom. He laid her gently across the mattress and began unbuttoning the silk blouse she wore under her new pant suit. God, he'd come to anticipate these times when he'd strip her of clothing to reveal her fantastic body. His cock was clearly ahead of his fingers.

She raised already darkening eyes to his. "Jake Bonneville isn't going to defeat us, Scott. You're still my superstar, in the bedroom, the office and everywhere."

Though his body was already primed to take hers, her words permeated the blur of sexual arousal. Superstar, she'd said. He was, God dammit! He never should've let Cam go after the entertainer. Their boss was a great leader and organizer, but he didn't have Scott's gift for selling an idea.

He jerked his head up, removed his hands from her front. Maybe there was still time to regain Bonneville's buy-in.

"Scott? What's the matter?"

He gave her a quick but firm kiss. "You reminded me who I am. I'd almost forgotten."

He rose and readjusted his clothing, tucked the boys into place and hoped his dick would understand postponed coitus. "I've gotta find Bonneville before he leaves town. Stay here. Keep the home fires warm."

"What are you going to do? You don't even know where he is, do you?"

"Good point. But your brother might. I need his number."

She followed him to the living room, reached in her purse and took out her cell. "I'm transferring it to you now. Be nice. He may have chewed you out, but it was his way of covering his embarrassment from ruining our project."

He followed her advice, kept his tone noncommittal when Brian picked up. "I ran into him at Morgan's Pub downtown," Brian said. "But I doubt he'd go back there again. It was just close to the place where he'd given a lecture. The night I talked to him, he was catching a late flight back west. Private jet. Apparently he's got a friend who's a pilot. You might check the airport."

Fortunately, a former client of Scott's owned one of the town's few private air services. Scott called him and pulled a few strings to get his info. Yes, Bonneville was known to occasionally fly in and out of town on a private jet piloted by a friend. The aircraft varied, because the friend borrowed them from his friends, so the former client couldn't confirm whether Bonneville was still in town. But there was an executive jet still on the tarmac, so it was possible. All the incentive Scott needed. He ran for his car and headed to the airport.

The former client met him at the gate to let him in. Scott couldn't go beyond Security, but if Bonneville was on the way, he'd have to come through the unsecured area first. Scott remembered to pull out one of the high-end bottles of scotch he carried in his trunk for special customers to thank the former client.

They didn't have long to wait. A town car pulled up and Bonneville and a sandy-haired guy emerged to walk briskly through the small lobby. "Bonneville." Scott slid in front of the megastar.

"Yes?" Bonneville responded, pulling up. "You're from Mackenzie's firm, aren't you, Dalton, right?"

"Yes, Scott Dalton. I know you're in a hurry to get going, but I'd appreciate you giving me a minute or two."

"Your boss doesn't give up, does he? I haven't changed my mind since this morning and I don't intend to."

"Cam sometimes gets overexcited when he's explaining a concept to clients. I thought perhaps I could clarify any points he might have missed."

Bonneville gave him a you've-got-to-be-kidding expression. "Not necessary. My mind's made up. Your trip out here was pointless." He shifted to the side and began to pass him.

"Wait! If you're absolutely set on a high-rise, let's talk about transferring to it some of the features of the plan we presented. My partner and I conducted quite an in-depth study of the wants and needs of baby boomers. You read the 'Change plus Purpose' part of our design concept, right?"

Bonneville took a deep breath, as if seeking the patience to deal with Scott's continuing presence. "Look, I appreciate the time you and the Rogers woman put in working on this project. Like I told Mackenzie, I'll reimburse your firm well for your efforts. I just don't want to go that direction any more. Now, I've got a plane waiting for me. I don't want to discuss this further." He shoved past Scott, making his intent crystal clear.

Scott stood there for what seemed like hours, only a minute or two in actuality, trying to get his head around the guy's attitude. He'd been so smooth with his arguments, but Bonneville still didn't want to listen. Clients rarely turned him down outright. They might find their resources couldn't support the projects he proposed, but they always loved to hear his ideas. What had happened to the superstar architect? Had he really lost his touch, as he'd considered just a few weeks ago when he'd first been teamed with Lacey?

Noticing his former client eyeing him from across the room, Scott straightened, threw out his shoulders, and forced a smile. No need to telegraph his failure to this guy. Shaking his head, as if Bonneville was the loser and not him, he steered toward the door like he owned the place.

Once back in his car, though, everything collapsed, his ego and spirit most of all. He'd made things worse. Bonneville probably wouldn't even consider their pitch to do a high-rise now. Damn! He really thought he could charm the guy into reconsidering.

Though he didn't want to, he called Cam from the car. The boss needed to know even his golden boy couldn't retrieve this one.

"You did what?" Cam screamed once Scott briefed him.

Scott repeated his report.

"Of all the stupid things to do. What gave you the idea you could do this without first consulting me?"

This wasn't the response he was expecting. He thought Cam would be disappointed instead of angry. On the other hand, the guy probably needed something/someone to blame for his frustration. "You've never questioned my going directly to the client in the past."

"We've never had a multimillion-dollar deal slip through our hands before. God, Scott, you've been so close to earning the title of principal, but this decision showed absolutely no good judgment."

Panic seized his gut. Cam finally said the word "principal" out loud, only he'd made it sound like a near miss, a chance already come and gone. Scott fought to keep his tone even. "Bonneville was leaving town. I caught up with him on his way out to a private jet. There was no time to call you, Cam, either to get you here or get your permission. My way with clients has always stood me in good stead before. I saw no reason why it wouldn't work this time."

"But it didn't, did it?" Cam was no longer screaming, but his tone had turned belligerent. "Maybe your charm has finally run its course."

"What do you want me to do now, Cam?" Could he sound more pathetic?

"You and your partner had better start cranking out a scheme for landing his high-rise. Better yet, maybe I should turn this project over to some of the senior architects who know what they're doing." With that, Cam clicked off.

Had he finished off a carton of sour milk, Scott couldn't feel more queasy. The boss' temper was notorious, but he'd never gotten quite so personal and vindictive. Scott had really misjudged this one. That old ego mistakenly assumed it could bring anything back from the brink. Not only had he lost Bonneville's support, he'd lost the boss' approval. Kiss being named principal good-bye. His silver tongue was gone as well.

What would he tell Lacey? When he left her, he'd acted like the super hero who could save the world. Now he'd not only jeopardized his future, if Cam really did bring in someone else in the firm to pick up the pieces, he'd cut off her chances of showing her stuff as well.

Time to cut his losses. At the very least, give himself space to reevaluate his abilities. Lacey didn't deserve to be linked with the loser he'd become.

CHAPTER 20

Lacey no longer had any secrets from Scott. Well, just one, her realization she was in love with him was too new to share yet. She hardly believed it herself. Besides, he'd run off before she even considered telling him after something she'd said convinced him he could save the project. "Come back soon, Scott. More happened today than losing our client."

Meanwhile, she needed to warn Celia that, thanks to her, Brian now knew they'd set him up. She rebuttoned her blouse and within minutes, found herself at Celia's apartment, not quite sure what she was going to say, but determined to forge ahead.

"I'm so sorry your project fell through," Celia said. "Talk of Jake Bonneville as our almost-client went viral in the office this afternoon."

Lacey collapsed into one of Celia's easy chairs. "I imagine it provided quite a conversational morsel."

Celia shrugged. "You know how office gossip is."

"Did you also hear why Mr. Bonneville changed his mind about the project? Brian counseled him to go with a high-rise?"

Celia gasped. "Brian? How? Why?"

"First, you need to be aware Brian knows your fling with Scott wasn't real and I'm the one who set it up."

"How did he find out?" Her tone was guarded as she took the chair next to Lacey.

"I was so angry with him for the Bonneville thing, I just blurted it out."

"Uh-huh."

"Thinking Scott and I had set you up, he went to confront Scott to protect your honor. Scott told him you knew all about it being a made-up arrangement and you were the one who suggested it to him."

"Brian was worried about me?"

"At least until Scott told him about your part in all this. I came to warn you before either Brian or Scott showed up at your door."

Celia crushed a throw pillow to her chest. "We've made quite a mess of things, haven't we?"

"You're not angry with me? My brother was."

"I went along with your plan, friend. I'm the one who pitched the idea to Scott and didn't feel the least bit of remorse by agreeing not to tell you because I knew you already knew." She stopped, shoved the pillow aside. "What a recitation. That sounded absolutely ludicrous. If I'd repeated it out loud before, I would have known this was a bad idea. Brian isn't like other men. He can't be programmed to change his mind."

"He is unique."

"Which is why I love him."

Lacey took her friend's hand. "I'm so glad you're not angry with me."

"You told me everything, right?"

Oh, boy. She'd been so absorbed with finishing the project the last several days, she hadn't taken time to bring Celia up to date about her changed situation with Scott. "No," she said in a tiny voice. "I slept with Scott."

Celia's eyes widened. "What? You said you wanted to keep your distance from him. You didn't trust your feelings. That's why we selected him as my new beau, to relieve the pressure on you."

Lacey nodded, at a loss how to defend her actions. "You'd already decided your fake dating wasn't working. We hooked up just prior to the second dance class, when it seemed our plan to make Brian jealous had fallen through. He came to my apartment to check on my ankle and—"

"I get the picture. Is this more than one of your usual flings? Are you in love with him?"

She wasn't ready to talk about her feelings for Scott with even her best friend until she became a little more familiar with them herself. "I've grown to like him a lot, which is saying something, considering how egotistical he came across at first."

Heavy pounding at the door interrupted whatever Celia was about to respond.

"Celia! Cee? I need to talk to you right away," Brian called through the door.

The two women exchanged conspiratorial looks. "Brian. Does he know you're here?" Celia asked.

"Probably saw my car on the street, unless he parked out back."

Celia rose, tugged at the hem of her blouse and went to the door.

Brian hurtled into the room, nearly knocking over a floor lamp. Then he saw his sister. "Lacey? What are you doing here? Blaming Celia, too, for losing your client?"

"Calm down, Brian. Lacey's had a tough day," Celia said before Lacey could reply.

Brian's gaze moved from Lacey to Celia. "Did she tell you how she lit into me earlier? Like I deliberately set out to harm her project."

"The project she's worked so hard on was cancelled because of you, even though you're no expert in real estate."

Brian slowly released his breath. "I told her and I'll tell you, I had no idea Bonneville would take me seriously. I certainly didn't know he had any connection to her project. But that's not why I'm here." To Celia, "I came to verify something Dalton told me."

"I heard how you no sooner left my place than you tracked down Scott. You just couldn't wait to confront him," Lacey spit out.

"Good thing I did, too, or I wouldn't have learned about your part in this little melodrama, Celia. I would have come over here right away, but I was too angry to think straight. I can't believe you'd stoop to playacting just to get me to marry you."

"Now wait just a second, buster," Celia answered in a louder tone than usual, sticking her index finger in his chest. "If you'd told me or even Lacey of your concerns about our relationship before you took such precipitate action, maybe we would have better understood your decision."

Lacey stepped off to the side. This was between her brother and her best friend. She was done playing the middleman.

"I wanted you back," Celia continued. "Enough to make me agree to this crazy scheme when Lacey suggested it. But we've both realized all we were doing was incensing you. Scott and I stopped seeing each other a couple weeks ago."

"You actually thought you could get me to change my mind about us by seeing you with another man?" Brian asked, still processing.

Celia offered a rueful smile. "I was desperate. You think I liked turning to some crazy scheme reminiscent of 'I Love Lucy' to get you to reconsider?"

Brian released a heavy sigh. "I'm sorry, Cee. I never meant for you to resort to such tactics," he said, his voice much calmer.

"Until we talked at your mother's gravesite, I had no idea why you'd broken things off."

"In the cemetery, it all came rushing back to me. The loss, the regret. I relaxed my guard and told you I could never go through such an experience again."

Though she already knew this from Celia, it was Lacey's turn to address her brother directly. "You're afraid to lose another loved one?"

Brian sucked in his lips and stared into space. "I've always known the risk was there with you, Lace. I had to accept and live with it. But I couldn't widen my circle of concern further, even with someone as wonderful as you, Celia."

"I can't promise I'll never die," Celia said in a much softer tone. "No one can. If you can't accept that fact of life, then you've sentenced yourself to a very lonely existence."

Brian's shoulders collapsed, nearly breaking Lacey's heart. He looked like an animal enmeshed in a trap, frightened, hurt and miserable. "She's right, Brian," she added. "You can shut yourself away from those who love you to protect your heart, but in the long run, your heart will dry up from lack of use."

"I can't deal with this now." He retreated. "I need to think." At the door, he stopped. "Don't give up on me, Cee."

When he'd left, Lacey turned to Celia. "Hold onto what he said. He'll come around."

Celia's eyes sparkled with unshed tears. "I hope so. I don't know what I'd do without him in my life."

"He's never shared these feelings with either of us. He just needs to absorb what we told him and come to believe life with you is worth someday, perhaps, having to let you go."

"I can wait, now I know there's hope." Celia straightened the lampshade Brian's near collision had set askew. "What are you going to do about Bonneville?"

"Do? About losing him?"

Celia faced her, a tolerant look pasted across her face, like one dealing with a child. "That's not an absolute yet. I thought he offered you a chance to bid on his new plan, the high-rise?"

Lacey stared at the other woman, amazed. "You've certainly caught up fast."

Celia chuckled. "You and Scott may have run off, but Cam stayed behind in the executive break room and brought anyone who'd listen up to date, except for the part about Brian."

"I feel so humiliated. My chance to make a name for myself in the firm is gone." Would she even be able to show her face at work the next day?

"Why? The guy threw you all a curve. From what I heard, you and Scott put together a really excellent concept piece. Cam raved about it, even *after* Bonneville dumped you."

Lacey seized upon Celia's comments like a drowning person clutching at a life preserver. Earlier, when they met with the entertainer, she'd been so devastated by his news, she'd dismissed this option. Now? Maybe they could adapt some of their conceptual framework to a high-rise.

She smiled for the first time in hours. "Thanks for the idea. It's worth a try." She said a hasty good-bye, hugged her friend, and ran out to her car. Her heart pounded in her chest at the thought of recapturing their project, but for the first time in hours, the horrible, wrenching sensation in her stomach subsided.

The next morning, Lacey swished by Jean's desk, caught up in her positive mood. "Good morning, Jean. Is Mr. Dalton in yet?" She hadn't heard from him since he'd dashed out of her apartment the day before, charged up by some new way to save the project, which he didn't take time to share. While she waited to hear from him, she worked through the night on a new design concept. Charged with anticipation, she was anxious to tell him how she thought they could salvage the project.

Jean lurched from her chair and reached the door to Scott's office before Lacey, looking more serious than ever. "Mr. Dalton's not in there."

Lacey finger-combed her hair, still damp from her hasty shower. "That's okay. I'll wait."

Jean inserted herself between the door and Lacey, but the tight set of her mouth loosened slightly. "You must not know yet. Mr. Dalton, Scott, resigned. He cleared out his desk last night."

Lacey backed up a step, the news slicing through her like a dagger. "He's gone? What happened?" Was this why he hadn't called?

"He was very close-mouthed about his reasons."

"But the last time I saw him, he seemed to think he could rescue our project."

As she started for the stairwell, Jean grabbed her arm. "I didn't see his letter to Mr. Mackenzie. I found it on my desk, sealed, when I arrived a short while ago. I've seen him lose sure-bet clients before. Not often, but on occasion. He took those setbacks in stride. There's more to this, but I don't know what. I thought perhaps you knew something." She gave her a hopeful smile.

Surprised and touched by the other woman's rare demonstration of camaraderie, Lacey had no idea what was going on. "I, no … I had no idea he was leaving." Mumbling thanks for Jean's information, she fled down the stairs to her own office and sanctuary.

Once there, however, she wasn't very productive. Jean's words kept running through her head. "There's more to this, but I don't know what it is."

Gone. After how many years with Mackenzie and Associates? Five? Six? Scott had so wanted to become the firm's principal architect. Now, he'd simply walked away. To where? To what?

"Lacey?" Cam stuck his head through her door, then made a beeline for her visitor chair. "At least you stuck around. You've heard about Dalton deserting us? Can't believe the guy would leave us in the middle of this Bonneville fiasco."

"I just heard the news. What happened? The last I knew, Scott thought he could get Bonneville to reconsider."

"Fool! Thought he could change Bonneville's mind, even though I'd already talked my head off with the guy. Scott buttonholed Bonneville at the airport as he was about to board his private jet."

That explained where Scott had shot off to but not his quitting the firm. "Why would he resign just for failing to do what we'd all been unable to do earlier?" Her boss mumbled something, but she couldn't make out the words. "Excuse me? I didn't catch what you said."

He released what sounded like an infuriated harrumph. "I chewed him out."

"You fired him?" Mackenzie terminated his golden boy?

"Of course not! Granted, I was outraged he'd gone off on his own, thinking he could save the world. Might've suggested he was losing his touch, not principal material, but he knew I was just blowing off steam. Hell's bells, I've lit into him more than enough times in the past. Just part of the game."

He'd suggested Scott might not be named principal? Did he not know how sensitive Scott was when it came to receiving the title? Of course not. Cameron Mackenzie was on top of the game when it came to drumming up business but not where human relations were concerned. "Have you, uh, talked to him since?" she asked.

"Tried. He's not taking calls. At least from me. Didn't he call you?"

"No." He hadn't returned her voice messages either. Or texts. Why? Had she done something to trigger his leaving? "I didn't learn of his resignation until a little while ago. I went to his office to tell him ..." Was she ready to let Cam in on her alternate plan?

Cam hunched forward. "Tell him what?"

She didn't have much choice. "I thought about Bonneville's suggestion we bid on the high-rise and worked out some ideas at home last night. It may not result in as big a fee, but I think we could do quite well."

"Really?" Cam leaned in further, a gleam entering his eyes.

Except she'd planned on Scott doing the design work. *Scott, where are you?* He'd abandoned her just like her father. She'd let down her guard and trusted the guy, the very thing she'd avoided all these years. Look where it had gotten her. Back to Square One, where she'd found herself at age six. Deserted once again.

"Lacey? Are you okay?" Cam asked, cutting into her thoughts.

"Yes. Yes, Cam." She kept her voice even and stared him directly in the eyes, though her brain was skittering all over the place.

"With Scott gone, you'll be in charge. You'll need to put together something spectacular overnight. You up for the challenge?"

A month ago, even three weeks back, when she first encountered Project Arabella, she would have been flabbergasted at the opportunity. This was her big chance, even bigger than being teamed with Scott, because now she was head honcho. She should be excited, thrilled at the prospect. Instead, she felt like all the air had been siphoned from her.

Without Scott, the project was no longer fun, but solo lead would have to suffice as the most meaningful thing in her life. With what remaining energy she could still muster, she offered her boss her most enthusiastic fake smile. "I'm definitely up for the challenge. I appreciate your confidence. I'll have something for you in a week. Soon enough?"

"It'll have to be. I'm counting on you. We all are." He shook her hand and departed.

They were all counting on her. Her heart was broken, her spirit trampled and she'd just agreed to produce the design concept of her career in seven days. No pressure.

She stared at the notes she'd made the night before. They weren't computing. The words blurred. Good thing she was seated, because her rubber legs would no longer support her. Any minute, she could lose her breakfast thanks to the roiling caldron in her stomach.

When she and Scott had talked about trust, they'd had to get past their fears about what the other might do to them, and they had. Or so she thought. Hadn't she made it clear she didn't expect a lifetime commitment from him? At least, she hadn't then. Since? Maybe she was moving a different direction, but it was too soon, too scary to give it a name. Had Scott picked up on the change in her feelings and run off before he had to deal with it?

No. Don't go there, Lacey. Scott was not her father or Alex, her former fiancé. Without realizing, she and Scott had crossed some invisible line in the last few weeks, and the trust they'd talked about in theory had materialized in fact. Wherever Scott had gone or whatever had made him go, it was for a good reason. She had to trust him to let her know why in his own time.

As if on cue, her cell dinged with an email from Scott.

Things didn't go well with Bonneville. Lost my edge. Big time. Don't know why. Have to find out. Can't saddle you with a loser. You deserve much more. Please trust me. Us.

Trust him. She'd just come to that decision herself, but oh, it was so difficult with so many questions unanswered. She reached for the edge of her desk to hold on. Her world was spinning. *You can do this, Lacey. Just keep hanging on, for both you and Scott.*

The phone rang. Scott! She raced to answer.

"Lacey?" Janice. "Thought I'd check in to see how your presentation went yesterday."

Her innocent, well-meant question was all it took to open the floodgates. "Oh, Janice! I don't know … (gulp) … if … (gulp) … I can talk right now."

"You sound like you've lost your best friend, but I'm still here. What's wrong?"

"Our client decided to go a different route and wouldn't even consider our plan," she managed to get out. "Scott went after him but struck out. Now Scott's gone. Resigned. Apparently blames himself for the project falling through."

Lacey finished her tale of woe.

"Repeat the part about the client reneging on the deal," Janice said, her tone changed.

"Our client turned out to be the megastar, Jake Bonneville. He didn't even give us a chance to go over our plans. Just thanked us for our time and said he'd changed his mind."

Janice didn't reply at first. "We need to talk," she said finally. "I'll be at your office in fifteen minutes."

Lacey hung up, relieved and only slightly curious about the change in her friend's manner. So she'd lose precious minutes to rethink the design concept. She needed a break. If Janice could help get past the excruciating ache in her chest, she'd willingly trade in some creative time for a little relief.

When Janice arrived, she made a big show of closing the door and scooting her chair close to Lacey's desk. "This is your boomer project, right?"

Lacey nodded.

"And you say Jake Bonneville was the client who wanted to build this retirement community?"

"Right. He said he was building the development for his mother because she refused to relocate to California."

Janice's eyes darted around the room as she digested Lacey's words.

"Janice? What's going on?"

Her friend hesitated slightly. "I am Jake Bonneville's mother."

The words didn't register at first. Janice and Jake Bonneville? Didn't make sense.

Janice must have sensed her confusion. "His real name is Ned Collier. Nathaniel, actually, which he hates. Jake Bonneville is his stage name, my father's first name and favorite car. Ned thought they sounded more glitzy for a budding superstar."

"He's the one who travels?" It fit, but it was still a huge mental leap.

"I'm not surprised you were unaware of the connection. Most people around town have come to accept the fact I'm related to a celebrity and leave me in peace. They know I'm not comfortable with the lifestyle he's had to adopt."

Lacey's head pounded as it had the day before. So much had happened, and not happened, in the last twenty-four hours. So much to process. Janice, their client's mother. Why, she was the inspiration for this whole project!

"It's sinking in, isn't it?"

"It's a lot to absorb." Like a thunderbolt, another thought struck. "Did you know about this?"

Her friend closed her eyes briefly and clasped her hands. "Of course not! I'm just as surprised as you. Ned calls every so often, but he's never even hinted about having business back here in Iowa, let alone spearheading a building project that involves me."

Lacey rubbed her forehead, then pushed a hand through her hair. "I'm sorry. So many things I thought were one way two days ago have been turned upside down."

"This is a shock for both of us."

They sat back in their chairs, both attempting to absorb the news. Janice finally spoke. "Tell me again how I figure in this. What Ned—Jake—said about me."

Lacey replayed the scene from the day before. "This retirement development was a way of giving you something you'd accept. That's why it had to be tailored to baby boomers, not typical retirees."

Janice rubbed the bridge of her nose. "Sounds like Ned. He's always giving me things. Checking up on me. Ever since his father died, he's taken me on as his responsibility." She chuckled. "I'm barely fifty-five, and he treats me like I should be ready for the home."

"You're the same age my mother would be, if she'd lived," Lacey said, marveling how the comparison had eluded her in all their discussions of baby boomers.

"Really?" Janice smiled. "Maybe that accounts for our compatibility? I like the coincidence."

"Me, too." Lacey held out a hand, which Janice readily squeezed.

"I can't believe I caused all this," Janice said in a hoarse voice.

"What do you mean? You said you just learned about your son's plans."

"Maybe so, but if he hadn't been trying to take care of me, he never would've come up with this idea." She rose, went to gaze out the same window Scott had the day of their impromptu picnic, which now seemed like years before. "Where did you say this project was to be located?"

Lacey told her about the property west of town.

"I should have asked that question when you first interviewed me. Maybe I could have warned you or done something to prevent this disappointment. That's my father's farmland. He left it to Ned before Jake Bonneville entered the picture."

"Oh. I didn't know. There was only a dummy corporation name on the title."

Janice turned, offered a weak smile. "That's Ned. Jake Bonneville has become big business."

"He's the business my firm wants. And now I'm charged with getting it back by revising our plan to fit a high-rise."

Janice lifted an eyebrow. "High-rise? I hate heights."

"You do?" The man was so out of touch with the very person he was trying to help. "Would you even consider living in the place he builds?"

"I'm touched he wanted to do this for me, but not if it's to be in this tower in the sky. I like the original idea. That's where I grew up."

"Well, I'll be!"

Janice grinned. "I just handed you the project on a silver platter, didn't I?"

"Are you sure you want to do this?" The thought was dizzying, but she didn't dare latch onto it until she knew for sure Janice wasn't doing it just for her.

Janice rose. "Depends."

"On what?" What kind of bargain would she have to make?

Janice moved around her chair, resting her hands on the backrest. "I want the team of Rogers and Dalton to do it."

CHAPTER 21

Lacey pulled her car up to the curb of the nondescript ranch style home in Clive and rechecked the address Jean had provided. Yes, this was it, though she never would have guessed this to be the home of Marcia and Gordon Dalton. It was a nice enough neighborhood, and the place appeared to be in good shape, but it certainly wasn't what she would have imagined for the domicile of the two jetsetters.

Even after she shut off the ignition, she remained in her car debating if she really wanted to do this. Whether she even should be doing this. Scott would certainly not approve of her getting involved with his parents any more than she already had, but he hadn't left her much choice. Three days of phone calls and two trips to his apartment had failed to locate him, let alone talk to him. His parents either knew where he was or could contact him for her.

"Lacey!" Marcia Dalton exclaimed when she came to the door. "We didn't miss our lunch date, did we?"

"No, Marcia. I need your help getting Scott back to work."

Marcia's forehead folded into several wrinkles, but she motioned for Lacey to enter.

The interior belied the rather unexceptional outside of the house.

Rather than several small rooms, Lacey found herself in a very au courant great room. The walls, a light dove gray, were framed by several comfortable-looking aubergine and charcoal gray sofas and easy chairs. Though exotic souvenirs from their many trips abroad flanked the room, a large photograph of Scott held the place of honor.

Once they were seated, Marcia Dalton raised inquisitive but slightly wary eyes. "What's this about getting Scott back to work? Where is he?"

Might as well get to the point. "Through no fault of his own, we lost the big project we've been working on. The one I told you about at the dance class. When Scott failed to get the client back, he assumed responsibility for the loss and resigned."

Marcia Dalton clutched her chest, shock written across her face. "Scott resigned?"

Lacey's stomach dropped. If his mother was unaware he was no longer at Mackenzie and Associates, she probably didn't know where he was either. Time was running out. If necessary, Lacey could put together the new design concept on her own, but she much preferred getting her partner back. She needed his flair, his ability to plow through the research data and imagine a finished product. "Do you know where he is? He won't return my calls. I thought maybe he'd talk to you."

"He called a few days ago, saying he was taking off on a business trip. He didn't say anything about quitting his job."

"Who's quitting his job?" Gordon Dalton entered carrying a stack of file folders. "Oh, hello, Lacey. I didn't know you were here."

"Hello, Gordon. I stopped by to see if you knew where Scott was. I didn't know you were unaware he'd left the firm."

"What?" He set the folders on a nearby end table and collapsed onto a divan. "When? It wasn't because he didn't get the marketing job, was it? He told us it didn't appeal to him in very clear terms."

"No, no." She repeated her story about losing Bonneville's business.

"Scott's lost clients before, hasn't he? Why would he give up now?"

Scott's mother tilted her head, and a strand of jet black hair fell forward until she pushed it back behind her ear with her fingers.

So reminiscent of Scott, it was like a dagger filleting Lacey's insides. She wanted to peel through the door, leaving all these reminders behind, but she couldn't be rude to these people when it was obvious how much they cared for him. She gulped air. She didn't want to reveal too much, but it was time they knew a few things about their son. "Scott's been under a lot of pressure lately. He's been anxious to be named principal, partly to please you, but also because it's overdue, given his track record."

Both sets of eyes gazed back at her. She went on. "Scott is an incredible architect. I only hope my designs mature to his caliber someday. He's also been great with the clients, coaxing their deepest wants from them and convincing them that's the way to go. But when the title of principal didn't come as soon as he hoped, he started questioning his abilities. Second-guessing yourself can be like a cancer; once it starts, it's difficult to stop it from spreading."

"I had no idea he was struggling so," his mother replied.

"Nor I," his father added. "What can we do to help?"

"He needs reassurance," Lacey said. "I need to help him through this period, but he's staying away from me because he doesn't want to taint me with his so-called slide. I was hoping you could maybe talk to him, encourage him to go back to his job, perhaps even tell him how much you believe in him."

Scott's mother rose and retrieved her purse from a nearby table. "I'll call him right now."

"Get him to come over here, Marcia," Gordon Dalton said. He turned to Lacey. "Please stay. He doesn't always care about our opinion."

Lacey backed away. "Oh, no. He'll be very unhappy to learn I've involved you. I wouldn't have done so, except I didn't know how else to get in touch with him."

"He's not our biggest fan when it comes to career advice," Marcia Dalton said as she pulled her phone from her purse. "But he will come over, if we ask him."

Lacey considered their offer. Scott needed to get back to work, more for his own sake than hers. If it meant appearing to ally with his parents, so be it. She would take the risk,

Within minutes, Marcia Dalton had her son on the line and was arranging for him to come to their home. She returned to Lacey. "I know you said you need Scott's help with your project, but I sense there's something more behind your actions. Are you and Scott, uh—"

"We're getting there." Lacey tried not to promise too much. "Neither of us has been very much into commitments in the past. But I care for him. A lot."

"I can see that," his mother replied. "His father and I are probably partly responsible for his disinterest in commitments. We've pushed too hard for him to settle down."

Interesting. These two were much savvier about their son than Scott realized.

"Right now, I'm just here to get Scott back to work."

"Understood," Gordon Dalton said. "Right, Marcia?" Scott's mother gave them both a nod of resignation. "Yes. But once you convince him to return to your project, we really do have to have lunch."

Despite her qualms about dealing with Scott in the next few minutes, Lacey had to chuckle. If this woman became a part of her life, she really had to be on alert. "Sure."

Gordon showed her to a small office at the back of the house, where she could wait until Scott arrived. Two desks, each equipped with top-of-the-line personal computers, faced each other. Along the walls, pictures of Scott at various ages provided the main ornamentation.

By the time Scott arrived thirty minutes later, Lacey had developed new insights about his parents. Somewhere along the way, Scott had decided he didn't amount to much in their estimation. If the pictures displayed throughout their house were any evidence, he was very mistaken. At some future point, maybe she could share what she'd learned about his parents with him but not today. Her immediate task was getting him back on the job.

She heard low voices in the great room, but she couldn't make out what they were saying. After a minute or so, Gordon entered.

"He's all yours. We haven't said you were here, so he'll be surprised when you walk in. We'll fade away as soon as you appear."

"I still don't understand why I had to drop everything and dash over here," Scott was saying as she approached.

Summoning her courage, she entered the room. "Because I asked them to call you."

Scott jerked her direction. "Lacey? What are you doing here?"

"You haven't been returning her calls. Lacey needs to talk to you, so give her your attention." Marcia backed out of the room. "Your father and I are taking our leave, so you can discuss things in private."

Lacey watched her go, smiling a silent thanks as the woman passed. Then she turned all her attention to Scott. "I got your email. I know you didn't leave because of me, but I wish you would have talked to me first before you made such a rash decision."

Scott stared at something over her shoulder. "Coward's way out. I agree. But I didn't want you or anyone else trying to change my mind, which is why you're here now, I'm guessing."

"I, we, need you back. To finish Project Arabella."

He widened his eyes in surprise. "That's still on?"

"I've told you so in the many messages I've left you."

He shifted his attention to several magazines arranged on the table before them, ran his fingers over the covers. "Thought they were a ruse."

"Scott! I'd never do such a thing."

When he lifted an eyebrow, she got the message. "Okay, yes, I engineered Celia's fake romance with you. We already established that. Let's get past it."

"You got my parents to lure me here."

"You wouldn't return my calls. I get that you need time to figure out what's going on with your career and you don't want to blemish my professional reputation by association, but I need your help. Cam's put me in charge of the revised design concept."

He started to say something but held back. "Congratulations. What you've been waiting for."

"It's a hollow victory without you."

"You don't need me weighing you down. Just like my parents can do fine without me."

"Have you ever looked around this house? It's almost a shrine to their one and only child."

He had the grace to take in the room. "Props, for their friends. A false front."

"Oh, really? What about the façade you put up? You don't tell them what you want, what you believe in, what makes you smile, what makes you cringe. You just humor them and keep a low profile. Yes, they interfere in your life. They have time on their hands. But you shut them out. *Interfering*, as you call it, may be the only way they can get you to open up."

"Enough, Lacey. I'm their trophy, the footnote on their list of accomplishments. But do you think they even realize how good I am at what I do or believe in my talents? They bought my job for me!"

His words so shocked her, she dropped his hand. Utter misery and defeat filled his eyes.

"Wherever did you get such an idea?" Gordon stood just inside the doorway, his arm around his wife. Both appeared to have been struck in the face.

Surprised, Scott took a step back. Then he resumed his previous position, chin tilted upward. "You invested in the firm in return for Cam hiring me."

Holding each other's hands, his parents advanced toward him. "Cam told you this?" Gordon asked.

"No. I've never discussed this with him. About a year after I joined the firm, I overheard the two of you talking. You were congratulating yourselves on your investment and how it had worked out so well for my career."

"I don't know what you think you heard us saying, Scott," Marcia said in a soft, strained tone, "but we never bought your way into the firm."

Still holding his wife's hand, Gordon gazed at his son with troubled eyes. "Don't you know how proud we are of you? Not just your accomplishments as an architect. You're a terrific person."

Scott stared at them, eyes glazed over. He attempted to say something but couldn't.

"We couldn't help overhearing what you told Lacey," his mother added. "You have to know you're the most important thing in our lives. We love you more than anything else."

Lacey became increasingly more uncomfortable with this turn of events. She hadn't meant to bring his parents into this encounter. "Maybe I should go?" she said.

"No, Lacey, please stay," Marcia said. "We didn't intend to interrupt until we heard you refer to us. Scott seems to be under several misconceptions about us. This discussion has apparently been a long time coming." She eyed her son. "We need to know what has been troubling you all this time, Scott."

Gordon offered Lacey a misty-eyed look of thanks. "We've suspected things were not as they should be between our son and us. But we've never faced it head on, as you've made us do."

Lacey checked Scott's reaction. His lips formed a tight line around his mouth, but his eyes seemed to have softened somewhat. "Let me get this straight. You never made a deal with Cam to invest in the firm if he hired me in return?"

His father put his fingertips to his temple, apparently trying to recall anything he might have said which Scott could have misconstrued. "We did invest with Cam about the time you started there. But he'd already offered you the job."

"You were so set on doing everything yourself, you wouldn't let us call in any favors or do anything to help you," his mother continued. "When you decided to take a job here in town, we wanted to do whatever we could to protect the firm, keep it running."

Scott turned to his father. "I heard you say to Mom, 'Scott should do well there, after all the money we've put into it.'"

His father winced as if he'd been sucker-punched. He shot his wife a glance. "Did we ever say anything like that?"

Marcia Dalton narrowed her eyes, as if trying to remember some far-off moment in the past. "If your father said those words, they weren't meant the way you think."

"What else could they have meant, Mother?" Scott wasn't being argumentative. He was simply attempting to make sense of a buried memory.

His parents exchanged glances once again. "About six months after you joined the firm, after Cam hired you completely on your own merits, we learned through the grapevine he was about to go under," his father said.

"You were working on your first major project," Marcia added. "You were so excited about it. We didn't see much of you, but when we did get together, you talked of nothing else."

"I didn't think you paid attention." Scott's voice had grown quiet.

Surprise took hold of both parents' expressions. "Of course, we did!" his father said, his own voice rising. "We wanted so much for you to succeed, on your terms, we thought we could help behind the scenes. So we invested enough in the firm for Cam to get his head above water."

"He paid us back within a year," his mother filled in. "No conditions, no expectations. A simple business deal. If we purchased anything for you, it was enough time for Cam to get his affairs in order while you proved yourself."

SCOTT DREW A LONG BREATH. He wasn't thrilled to have been shanghaied into this discussion, especially by Lacey, but painful though it was proving to be, his parents were shedding new light on the hurt he'd carried for years. "What you said to Mom kept running through my head all this time. I didn't think you believed in my ability to make it on my own."

His mother cut the distance between them, grabbing his hands. "You didn't think we … You think we believe you're a failure?" She buried her head in his chest.

His father joined them, placing an arm around his son's shoulders. "How could you think such a thing, Son? Have we been so uncaring, unsupportive all these years?"

His throat constricted and his tongue felt as if it had tripled in size.

The three of them huddled, crying quietly, holding each other.

Finally, his father broke away. "Why, why didn't you ask us about this years ago, when you first overheard me?"

Scott hesitated. "I didn't think you were up to a heated discussion."

"Why?"

"Because the last time I came clean with you, back in college, I caused your heart attack." Scott's voice broke.

"You? Caused my heart attack? Where did you get such an idea?"

"I was there when you started having chest pains," Scott said.

"Scott, Scott," Gordon cried, "I'd been having chest pains for days and I ignored them. They finally caught up with me. Coincidentally, you and I just happened to be having a discussion. Okay, argument."

"But … but—" Scott said.

His mother took his arm, tears streaming down her face. "I know I overreacted trying to protect your father from further episodes. I hope I didn't give you the impression I blamed you."

He hadn't planned to tell his parents any of this. *Damn Lacey!* She may have meant well, but she couldn't leave well enough alone.

He'd never run from a challenge, until this project came along and he'd begun to work with Lacey Rogers. His life hadn't been the same since. Now she'd set this scene in motion. Maybe tomorrow or the next day he'd be able to understand everything said between himself and his parents, but for now, his insides were so tangled and raw, he could barely remain standing.

"This is too much to grasp at once," he said, his voice raspy. He turned to Lacey. "Thanks for believing in me, us. But I can't deal with the job or us right now."

He backed up a few steps and then ran out. Lacey raced after him. "Scott! Please don't go. Your parents need you. The firm needs you. I need you." The last three words were barely audible.

Halfway down the walk leading to the curb and his car, he swung around, letting the emotion flash in his eyes. "I need more time."

He turned to go, but she caught hold of his shirtsleeve. "There's something you don't know. It's important."

She gazed at him, her eyes red and teary. He ached to comfort her, to hold her in his arms and whisper everything would be all right. But he held back. He loved her, dammit. Must've snuck in under the radar. This was all too much to deal with.

He glanced down at her hand resting on his sleeve and gave her an expectant look. She pulled back. He pivoted and headed again to his car. He kept walking, but he heard her soft footfalls behind him. Before he opened the driver's door, she threw herself in front of him, blocking his entrance. "Jake Bonneville is really Ned Collier, Janice Collier's son."

That stopped him. "What?"

She took a deep breath, as if collecting her thoughts. "That's what I've been trying to tell you the last few days. But not in a voicemail."

"How? When?" Her statement was so ludicrous, he couldn't form a full question.

She told him how the overage hippie had come to comfort her the morning he'd walked out and, when she learned the identity of their client, revealed their client was her son.

"She didn't know anything about his project?"

Lacey shook her head. "Remember what Bonneville, uh, Collier, said in Cam's office? This project was supposed to be a surprise gift to his mother."

Information overload. His head hurt, but through the blurry maze, a tiny thought increased in size. "Does that mean ..."

She nodded. "Janice wants our design concept, not a high-rise. How long do you need to get your head together before we can get this project back on track?"

"What about Cam?"

"You mean his yelling at you for going after Bonneville on your own?"

"Uh, yeah."

"You know our boss better than I, but haven't we both learned he blows hot then turns into a puppy dog? He didn't mean it when he threatened your future with the company."

He glanced over his shoulder toward his parents' house. They were standing in the front door, watching, waiting. First things first. "It's time I talked with them before I do anything else."

"Take whatever time you need. Call me tonight? We need to move on this tomorrow."

Since when had she assumed the upper hand? Since she'd realized he needed her as much as she needed him. She truly had become his partner in every way.

CHAPTER 22

"It's barely three o'clock," Lacey said to Scott from her side of his car. "I thought you needed time to decompress as well as talk further with your parents."

"There wasn't much more to say after that exchange you witnessed. All three of us were exhausted. My mom fixed a quiet lunch on the patio after which I did something I rarely do, took a nap. Never realized how much of a beating the body takes when the brain is confused."

"You're feeling better now?" As happy as she was he was still willing to see her, Lacey wondered at how readily Scott had shaken off all the bad vibes of late.

He seemed to consider her question before responding. "Yeah, I do. For the most part. It's going to take a while for my parents and me to get things straightened out entirely, but we're going to work at it. Can't ask for more right now."

She reached over and patted his hand. "I'm glad to hear that." Realizing he might not be ready for physical contact, she quickly removed her hand.

He glanced down, returned a shy smile.

As they headed west on the freeway, they passed the turnoff to their office building. "Where are we going? I thought you wanted to talk to Cam."

"Not yet. You and I need to talk first. Thought we should do it back where this all started," he told her.

Bonneville's property. She hadn't been there since that infamous day when they crossed paths with the bull and she wound up with a badly sprained ankle.

"Thought maybe you'd like to survey the property when it's dry and there's no bull camping out on a nearby hill." He pulled his car up to the fence she remembered so well.

She glanced down at her slacks and loafers, wishing she'd worn sneakers, but her current footwear should hold up. "Okay. Are you sure our *friend* isn't around?"

He shrugged, as if dismissing the possibility of history repeating itself. "Didn't see him that day I came back. C'mon, we should be okay."

Unlike their first visit, he maintained a pace she could keep up with as they navigated the field and ascended the hill they'd checked out the day they saw the bull.

Since he'd been the one to bring her here, she expected him to start their discussion. When he didn't say anything immediately, she blurted out, "Did you work things out with your parents?"

"Not completely. But we made a start."

"I'm glad. They really do care about you."

"Guess I have you to thank for my reconciliation with them." He kicked a clump of dirt at his feet. A few stray branches lay scattered on the ground, remnants of the storm a few weeks before. The same storm as the night of their session in his car. He grabbed a forked bough, flicked it back and forth a few times. "Did you ever get back here to check out the water tables?"

"No. First I couldn't walk, then I completely immersed myself in the design concept."

He examined the switch in his hand. "Why not try it now?"

"Now?"

"Humor me. Show me how to witch water."

She scrunched her eyes as if trying to read his mood, then shaking her head in apparent resignation, accepted the limb and began her routine. She counted five steps, then pivoted ninety degrees and moved off.

Scott remained where he was, watching with growing interest. "How do you know when to turn?"

"I just do."

"Do you take the same number of steps each direction?"

"Depends."

"On what?"

She stopped, appearing baffled. "I don't know. I never thought about it before."

"It's pointing down, like it did the last time." His tone carried a growing excitement.

"Bring me one of the straighter branches." When he complied, she held it in front of her, just like she had the forked branch. Within seconds, it started to bob. "Help me count."

"I got forty," he said when it finally stopped bobbing.

"That's what I got too."

"Meaning?"

"There's a vein of water about forty feet below the surface," she replied. She turned to him. "Not bad. Another aquifer we didn't know about."

"How sure are you it's really there?"

"The water? Pretty sure. Or my witching ability? It's always been there. There's no call to question it now."

He stared at his shoes. "I used to feel the same way about designing buildings."

She dropped the branch. "Used to feel? I don't follow."

"Every time I summoned ideas for a project, they came. Swiftly, without hesitation. Lately, it's been a struggle."

His words weren't computing. "You have talent coming out your ears. Why would you think such a thing?"

He booted away another clump of dirt. "Several reasons."

"Such as?"

"Believing my parents didn't appreciate my work."

"Which you now know was a mistaken impression."

"Thinking I was hired as a favor to my parents."

"Even if that had been true, there was no reason you couldn't take it from there and establish your own fabulous career. And you did," she said.

"So I thought. But I hadn't been named principal yet. When Bonneville pulled the rug out from under us, I blamed myself. I've made my career by reading people. Call it my way of witching water. But I missed this one completely."

"You're beating yourself up for nothing. You couldn't have known."

He shook off her hand. "At one point I even blamed you. Thought it was Cam's way of telling me my star had fallen and the best I could do from here on was mentor new stars, like you."

"I want to hear what you have to say, Scott, but base it on reality."

"That is my reality!" he said, his voice rising. Then it fell again. "Or at least it was. Once I got past my initial jealousy of your enthusiasm and your approach to designing, it's been a real trip."

She stared at him.

"All that chasing around to study boomers. I felt the same kind of thrill a private eye must feel when he discovers a clue."

"But—"

He took her hand. "I must've known from the day we were trapped under the tree trunk I was going to fall in love with you. Which is probably why I fought working with you so much in the beginning. I put down your ideas, until they turned out to be such gems. I mocked your approach to work. I scoffed at your naiveté. And then, when my defenses were down, bam! I fell big time."

She didn't reply, but her eyes had grown large and misty.

"When Project Arabella imploded, I blamed myself for letting my mind get scrambled thinking about you. For a nanosecond before I came to my senses, I suspected you for orchestrating this Bonneville fiasco."

"Like Jorja?" she asked.

"Yeah, but even before I confronted you about the deal with Celia, I knew I'd jumped to the wrong conclusion. When you conspired with my parents to get me to see you, you let them take center stage. Jorja wouldn't have been so generous."

She released her breath. "You realized you trusted me?"

"That I did. But what about you? How did you feel when I didn't return your calls?" he asked.

"Scared. For a second, I worried I'd misjudged you. At the same time, I was worried for you, because you wouldn't have skipped out without having a very strong reason. I had a decision to make. I could either believe in you or not. After all we've been through, I chose to believe."

"Even after I left you holding the ball?"

"I wasn't exactly elated by your running out, but my theory is you've got so much talent, you got bored. So you've been coasting for a while. You put your talent on automatic pilot and let your personality take over. When this project came along, you had to wake up, and it took time for you to get your bearings."

His gaze caressed her face, her eyes. "Your faith in me is important."

"But not as important as your faith in yourself."

"Good point," he returned.

"Does that mean you'll come back to the firm?"

HE TOOK A DEEP BREATH. The last few weeks had been such a rollercoaster. Stay. Wonder if the word *principal* was still in his future. Leave. Now return. Was he ready? Well, hell! Could he be any more picky? This woman had never given up on him, even though he'd given up on himself. It was time to let down his defenses.

He reached down and placed a stray lock of hair behind her ear. "Okay, partner. You've made your case."

"Terrific! We're going to make this project work, Scott. I just know it, now you're back!"

He pulled her into his arms and kissed her like a soldier returning to his woman after surviving a hard-fought battle. Though passionate, the kiss was also a promise, sealing not just a pact between co-workers but also recognizing their commitment to each other outside the office, wherever that might take them.

When she stepped out of his embrace moments later, he gazed down at her, feeling complete for the first time. "Thanks for not giving up on me."

Off in the distance, safely behind the sturdy fence of the adjoining field, the bull pawed the ground and snorted. Anyone witnessing the animal's behavior might have blinked and wondered if they'd really seen what they thought they saw, something resembling a smile laying claim to the bull's mouth.

Meanwhile, Scott and Lacey returned to his car and set off for the office of Cameron Mackenzie.

Scott knocked and then walked in unannounced, avoiding any chance of being rebuffed, at least until he'd had his say. "I want to come back."

Cam glanced up, crossed his hands in front of him and sat back. "Well, well."

Now actually here, urged on by Lacey, who waited outside, he wasn't sure the words would come. She'd advised, "Speak from the heart. Tell him what's been troubling you and then remind him how much he needs you. Because he does. And so do I."

"I'm sorry I walked out on you without warning. I needed time to clear my head after the Bonneville thing. Thought I'd lost my edge."

He waited for a response. Cam tilted his head, arched a brow. "And? Since you're here now, I assume the *edge* has been *found?*"

"Thanks to my parents and Lacey, I discovered I'd never lost it. I'd let myself get so caught up in my quest to become the principal to impress my parents, I forgot how much I enjoyed just being an architect."

"About being named principal …"

"Haven't forgotten about it. It's just no longer essential to defining who I am. I'm good at what I do. I know that now and I think you do, too."

Cam stared at his clasped hands. "Probably went a little too far when I questioned your leadership abilities. But if you come back, I need to know you'll stick it out when times get tough. I expect you to use your best judgment with clients but keep me informed."

"Then all is forgiven?" Scott tamped down his concern Mackenzie wouldn't want him, attempted to keep his tone flat.

"Didn't hear you agree to my terms."

Fair enough. "Yes, Cam, I agree."

His boss sprang from his chair and walked around his desk to shake hands. "Welcome back, Mr. Principal."

"Principal?"

"If you'd answered your phone or read my texts the last few days, you'd know I wanted you back here, too. Like you so clearly pointed out, I need you. Not just that charming manner with the clients but also your unique design ideas."

Scott continued shaking hands. "Thanks. You have no idea what this means to me."

"Even though we've lost Bonneville, at least until we win the high-rise contract, this experience with the megastar has encouraged me to go after even bigger fish for future projects. We've got the talent to handle them."

Could there be a better segue? "Uh, about that. There's something else you need to know. I wanted to tell you right off, but Lacey convinced me I needed to be welcomed back on my own accord first." He went to the door and opened it to Lacey, who waited right outside.

Her eyes sought his in a silent question as she entered. He nodded and watched the glow come into them. He turned back to Cam. "Actually, this is Lacey's story to tell. You might want to take your seat again, although I don't know how long you'll stay there."

"Hi, Cam. I hope you've welcomed back my partner here, because the original Project Arabella is on again." She explained how she learned her friend Janice Collier was actually their client's mother.

"Incredible!" was all Cam could say when she finished.

"It is a bit to take in, but not so strange when you consider her son is from town. None of us remembered that Jake Bonneville was hometown boy Ned Collier, except maybe my brother, and we didn't know his part in this until just recently."

"The best part is Janice doesn't want anything to do with a high-rise," Scott added.

"But she's on board with the development in the country?" Cam asked.

"More or less," Lacey said. "She doesn't really want a new house at all. She's happy with her place here in town, but apparently her son worries about her security in that part of town. Since Bonneville inherited the property from her father, she's okay with moving back to where she grew up. What with the city's westward expansion in recent years, she won't be all that far from town."

They hadn't revealed one significant detail yet, a detail he and Lacey had debated at length earlier. Rather than bring it up on his own, he waited for it to occur to Cam. It didn't take long.

"Bonneville was fine with going back to the first plan?"

This was Lacey's territory. He'd let her handle it. "He will be," Lacey said. "As soon as his mother tells him he is."

TWO DAYS LATER, surrounded by stacks of canvas and picture frames and other art paraphernalia, Lacey, Scott, Cam and Janice met in a small conference room at Janice's gallery. A somewhat recalcitrant but apologetic Brian had agreed to join them. Janice offered coffee, which Lacey and Scott refused, too nervous about the meeting about to go down. Brian begged off as well. Only Cam obliged their hostess.

"Thank goodness one of you wants coffee," Janice said. "I need something to keep myself busy until Ned arrives."

"Still sounds strange to hear our former client referred to as Ned," Cam said.

"How did you get him back to town so soon?" Lacey asked, attempting to help her friend relax.

"I wondered about that, too," Scott put in.

Janice pursed her lips. "I'm afraid I had to augment the truth a bit. I told him I was considering buying a condo in West Des Moines and wanted him to see it before I signed the contract."

Lacey slapped a hand to her mouth. "No! That's almost …"

"Diabolical?" Janice asked.

"Uh, okay. Your word, not mine," Lacey said.

"Speed was of the essence, right?" Janice said. "So we could keep him from talking to other firms about a high-rise. He could have easily been meeting with someone in L.A. as well."

Brian finally spoke up. "Look, Mrs. Collier, I'm sorry about my high-rise comments. I had no idea Ned would take me seriously." He glanced at Lacey. "I'm only here at my sister's, uh, *request*, to tell him as much."

Janice lifted a speculative brow. "So you're Lacey's brother? She's told me a little about your situation."

Lacey cringed inwardly. *Please, Janice, don't make things worse between Brian and me.*

"All about my love life, I'm guessing."

"Actually, I was referring to your being the one true anchor in her life after your mother passed."

"Oh, I thought you were referring to my sister and Dalton's scheme to get me back with my girlfriend, Celia Fairchild."

"Celia's your girlfriend?" Cam asked. "I thought …"

"Celia was seeing me?" Scott interrupted. "No, Cam, Celia and I weren't really a thing. He reached for Lacey's hand and held it up. "I'm seeing Lacey. We've gotten pretty well acquainted working on this project."

"Scott went along with Celia's and my scheme to make Brian jealous by thinking she was seeing Scott," Lacey explained. "It didn't work. My brother isn't ready for a commitment."

"Actually, the situation has changed since you last saw me, Sis. Celia and I have gotten back together."

Back together? Celia hadn't updated her. But then, her thoughts had been so focused on the project and Scott of late, her friend probably didn't want to complicate things further. She went to Brian and gave him a quick hug. "That's wonderful news."

"Don't go planning weddings yet," he warned. "Well, maybe a few months from now. Right now, we're getting reacquainted."

"Cee's a good friend of mine," Scott told him, in a mock stern voice. "Don't break her heart. Again."

Brian returned a knowing look at Scott but offered him a hand.

"Okay, boys and girls, now that we've all made friends again, what's with Bonneville, uh, Collier? He's not here yet."

"I'll go wait up front," Janice said. "I'll tell him my realtor is waiting back here in this conference room."

Once she left, the other four sat in strained silence. Lacey was relieved Cam now knew about her and Scott, and her brother and best friend were once again together. Brian and Scott had even shaken hands, although it was clear they still had a way to go before either totally accepted the other. *Too bad, guys. Looks like your futures are linked whether you like it or not.*

Fortunately, they didn't have long to wait. "I don't know why you're in such a hurry, Mom," they heard out in the corridor.

The door opened and Jake Bonneville burst into the room, his mouth set in a grim expression, ready to pounce on the poor realtor. He pulled up when he saw who was there instead. "Mackenzie, what are you doing here? How many times do I have to say no?"

Before Cam could reply, Lacey interrupted. "You didn't have all the facts at our last meeting."

Bonneville turned to his mother. "There's no condo deal for me to worry about?"

Janice led him to a chair. "No, dear, I'm not considering a condo. Actually, I wasn't considering relocating at all until I inadvertently learned about your project."

Bonneville shot a steely gaze at Lacey. "You sought out my mother? Behind my back?"

"Behind your back, Ned?" Janice's voice had gone to ice. "What would you call what you've been up to?"

"Me? I, uh …" He leaned into Janice. "This isn't the place to discuss family matters, Mom. Not in front of all these strangers."

Janice stood her ground. "Strangers? How is it all these *strangers* know more about the retirement home you're building for me than I do?"

"No need to shout," Ned said. "And it's not a retirement home. It's a home for your retirement. Big difference."

"At least we agree there," she said, somewhat mollified.

"It was supposed to be a surprise."

"Then you certainly achieved your goal. I couldn't have been more surprised when I learned you were Lacey and Scott's mysterious client."

"That's not what I … Wait a minute." Bonneville surveyed the group gathered around them, then returned his attention to his mother. "Just how did you find out about it? These people were sworn to secrecy."

"Not after you canceled on them. How could you, Ned? My friends here outdid themselves getting your plan together."

"But … I didn't … I talked to …" His eyes lighted on Brian. "Rogers? What are you doing here? Never mind. Explain to everyone why I changed my mind. Why it makes better economic sense."

"Sorry, Bonneville. I'm here to set things right with my sister. I had no idea when you and I had dinner you'd use a few of my idle comments as the basis of a major business decision."

Bonneville glanced from Brian to Lacey. "Then you are related?"

"Let's get back to the main reason we're here," Cam said, attempting to gain control.

"Which is?" Bonneville asked.

"Project Arabella, of course," his mother said. "Were you aware, Ned, that I've already been working with Lacey and Scott on this project?"

Ned looked even more lost.

"It's a long story. Let's just say their plans are based on my ideas."

"Your—" Now Bonneville appeared totally confused.

Janice seemed to enjoy being the center of this discussion. "Don't you think you should table your high-rise idea and reconsider this location?"

"This, this is what you want? You'll give up your rattletrap of a house if I build you one at Sullivan's Creek?"

"I rather like my old *rattletrap*. Our family enjoyed some good times there."

"But, Mom."

"Hear me out. I'm ready for a change. Time to move on to a new stage of my life."

"There?"

"Yes. That's where I grew up. Grandpa Jake will finally get what he always wanted, having me back on his land." She paused. "But there's one provision."

Her son cringed visibly, as if expecting her to extract a pound of flesh. "Which is?"

Janice gazed at Lacey. "We get rid of this ridiculous idea of a retirement community for boomers and focus on making the place intergenerational instead."

Bonneville breathed a deep sigh of relief. "Sure. I just want you to be happy and well taken care of."

Janice touched his arm. "I am happy, dear, but I'd be even happier if you stopped by more frequently," she said, playing the card she'd been holding in abeyance.

"Okay."

Janice paused, as if gathering her courage. "I was thinking you might want to join our community. Build your own place for when you visit Iowa." She said it evenly, but Lacey knew what a great effort it was for her to make it sound offhand.

At first, Bonneville wore the expression of a doomed man, but he seemed to be thinking through his mother's proposal. After a moment, a slight smile crept onto his lips. "Here I was worried you were losing your touch. You always were a much better negotiator than I."

"So?" she asked, failing to keep the apprehension out of her tone.

Bonneville raised his hands in surrender. "Yes, I'll build a house there, too."

Janice rested her attention on Cam. "There you are, Mr. Mackenzie. Two lots subscribed already."

"Well, Mackenzie," Ned said at last, "looks like we're back to talking about a residential development out in the country again. An intergenerational development." He nodded toward his mother. "Take whatever time you need to revise the previous design concept. I'm sure my mother will be happy to assist."

Janice winked at Lacey. "I'd love to, although I have every confidence in Lacey and Scott."

"Now that my mother knows all about this, get rid of that ridiculous name, Project Arabella," Bonneville added. "I want it named after my grandfather, Jake Sullivan. How about Sullivan's Creek?"

Janice clapped her hands together. "Perfect. Dad would be so happy."

"Gramps hated to see the population expansion heading for his property, but he knew someday it was inevitable. So his bequest came with certain environmental stipulations. Those will have to go into the design concept as well."

"No problem," Cam replied. "Right, Lacey? Scott?"

"We'll make this development a showplace for environmental preservation," Scott promised.

Lacey could only smile. The old, glib Scott Dalton was back. Correction, the newly improved Scott Dalton had returned, thanks to the research she and Jean would soon be undertaking, since she'd bet money her partner had no idea what *environmental preservation* entailed.

Cam just happened to have brought along a contract sealing the deal, which, after a short perusal, Bonneville signed, his mother looking on. "You won't regret this, Bonneville," Cam assured.

"As long as my mother's happy with the result, I'll have no regrets. And although I signed using my business name, call me Ned from here on," Collier slung an arm around his parent.

"Well, Ned, how 'bout we all go out for dinner and celebrate. My treat." He shifted his gaze to Brian, who'd remained quiet since his comment to Bonneville. "That includes you, too, Rogers. I want to hear your thoughts on urban sprawl, so I'm ready the next time that concern threatens a project."

Cam and their new client as well as Janice and Brian filed out, discussing places to eat. Scott put a hand on Lacey's forearm, indicating he wanted her to remain behind.

"You two coming?" Cam called.

"Shortly," Scott said, never taking his eyes from Lacey.

Once they were alone, he pulled out the tentative diagram of potential lots they'd put together and pointed to one lot in particular. "This spot halfway up the hill and overlooking the creek strikes me as the prime spot on the entire property. What do you think?"

"Isn't that about where you had me witching for water a few days ago?"

He lifted a brow. "I believe you're right."

"Depends on who'd be building there, I guess. Janice likes the spot nearer the entrance. Who knows which one Ned will select."

"Guess I was asking which one you'd pick, if you were going to build there."

Where was he going with this? "I'd land on the same one you did, then, although I'm not sure if it's the architect in me choosing it or the sentimentalist, since that's where you agreed to come back to the firm."

He took her hand. "I was hoping you'd agree. I think I'm going to buy that particular lot, but I need your help designing it. After all, you're the expert on single-family homes."

Scott had changed his mind about Sullivan's Creek so much he now planned to live there himself? "Okay, I'd be happy to help. But I don't understand. Janice wants this development to be intergenerational, but I doubt that includes bachelor pads."

He brought her hand to his lips, kissed it. "Good point. We should do something about that."

His eyes were looking directly into hers, a glint of determination sparkling back at her. Was he going where it sounded he was going?

"I can only promise to stay with you for our lifetime, Lacey, if you'll marry me. Is that enough of a commitment for you?"

He *was* going there! Dear God, how was she supposed to answer?

Of course, she knew what to say. She'd somehow known it would come to this since the very first day she wandered onto that field, and her fear had denied it until now. "I don't think I'll find a better Salsa partner. Guess I should take you up on the offer."

"I do more than dance," he said, his voice thick. He pulled her into his arms and kissed her as if for the first time, tentatively at first, but within seconds deepening the intensity.

You certainly do, she thought, preparing herself for the ride of a lifetime. This was the man who would give her a two-story, four-bedroom home, complete with a family of her own.

AFTERWORD

Dear Reader,

Thank you for reading this book. If you liked it, won't you please take a minute to leave a review?

To learn more about the eleven contemporary romances and two novellas I've written, sign up for my newsletter at https://www.subscribepage.com/BBContempRom

I've also written two cozy mystery series, the Mah Jongg Mysteries and Nailed It Home Reno Mysteries. You can learn more about them on my website, www.barbarabarrettbooks.com.

Follow me on Facebook: https://bit.ly/2aXZvG9
Follow me on Twitter: https://twitter.com/bbarrettbooks

SNEAK PEEK
TOUGH ENOUGH TO TANGO

Read an excerpt from the next book
in the Sullivan's Creek series, *Tough Enough to Tango.*

"You? You know about sports cars?"

"Not exactly. But I do know pick-ups and my own SUV. Let's see how closely the engines resemble each other."

"Don't bother. You'll get your hands dirty. I'll call the place where I rented this ton of junk."

"Getting a little dirt on my hands is in my job description. Let me play around here a few minutes, and if I can't figure it out by then, you can make your call."

She was just being helpful. What could he say? His macho pride could take it. Yeah, right. But what was she going to do that he hadn't already tried?

Two minutes later, she signaled him to turn the key again. Why not humor her? She actually thought she'd been helping. He gave it a twist, and to his surprised mortification, the engine kicked in and purred like the softest kitten.

When she appeared at his window, she beamed, two thumbs up, almost beside herself with glee.

Reluctantly, he turned one thumb up in congratulations. Beginner's luck. Or else he'd primed it for her. That was it.

She must have sensed his lack of enthusiasm, because her smile died and she rounded the front of the car and got in her side again. "The end clamp on the battery terminal wasn't secure enough to start the car, so I took the rubber ends off a few hairpins and stuck them between the clamp and the battery post. That's all the car needed to start. I just wanted to get out of here before the storm breaks."

The trip back to town was spent in silence. He wanted that contract. They'd been so close to making it happen. But now he wouldn't be negotiating from a position of strength, thanks to his talent at car repair.

It wouldn't be so bad if, when she wasn't studying the sky, she'd cover her mouth with her hand, as if trying not to smirk.

Okay. He'd use this to his advantage. Should he ever again be tempted to pull her into his arms and plant another one on her, he'd remember that smirk. No self-respecting Lothario, horny or not, kissed a smirk.

Learn more at BarbaraBarrettBooks.com

ACKNOWLEDGMENTS

Thank you to The Wild Rose Press, who initially published this book in 2014.

In order for this book to take on new life now that I'm publishing it myself, it needed a brand-new, intriguing cover. My grateful thanks to my cover artist, Chris Kridler of Sky Diary Productions, for taking the few snippets of ideas I fed her about this story and bringing this catchy cover to life. I also have her to thank for the formatting.

Thank you, Sharleen Newton, for proofing the re-edited version of this manuscript. Although many pairs of eyes have reviewed the book over its lifetime, the updates required one more look.

Thanks always to my husband, Veryl, for his continuing support of my writing career. He has seen me through more typewriters, tabletop computers and laptops than I can recall.

BOOKS BY BARBARA BARRETT

A LITTLE ABOUT
BARBARA BARRETT

Barbara Barrett skipped a midlife crisis by writing romance novels at night when she wasn't at her day job as human resources analyst for Iowa State Government. Her first book was published in 2012. She has now published eleven full-length contemporary romance novels and two novellas. More recently, she has published nine cozy mysteries in her Mah Jongg Mystery series and seven in her Nailed It Home Reno Mysteries series. This book is the first of the Sullivan's Creek series.

Barbara is married to the man she met her senior year at college. They have two grown children, eight grandchildren and two great grandchildren.

Now retired, she spends her time in Florida, Iowa and Minnesota. She earned her B.A. degree in History from the University of Iowa and her Master's Degree in History from Drake University.

When not in front of her laptop creating her next story, she plays Mah Jongg, is learning to paint with acrylics and enjoys lunches with friends.